*"Wait," says the woman next to me.
"I do know you. You're married to Ted Dayton!"*

She is holding up the page with the picture of me, waving it in front of my face like a matador with a red cape. As if it's not bad enough that I'm curled up in a window seat in coach—just close enough to first class that I can smell the filet mignon— now I have to suffer *US Weekly,* too.

"I don't know what you're talking about," I lie.

"I guess you had to expect him to cheat," she says, shaking her head.

I put on my sunglasses and try to look like a celebrity who can't be bothered, which is very hard to do in the cramped rows of coach. I realize the sunglasses and distant expression would be far more effective in first class.

"I mean, how are men supposed to resist that kind of temptation? Melanie Slate, I mean—really."

I wish suddenly that I were a Scientologist. Aside from not caring if other people think you're crazy, I read that they believe if they work at it long enough, they can move and control objects with their minds. I concentrate on the head of the woman next to me, willing it to explode.

"You don't look half as bad in person as you do in this picture," she says, undaunted.

"I don't know what you're talking about," I say. "That's not me."

Pink Slip Party

"Readers . . . will be delighted by the character-driven zaniness. . . . Snappy repartee and hot sex scenes keep the story moving along nicely."

—*Boston Herald*

"This amusing chick lit tale pokes fun at the economic recovery. . . . Fans will say 'I do' to Cara Lockwood's latest comical contemporary caper."

—All Readers

Dixieland Sushi

"A warm and friendly writing style."

—*Library Journal*

"[An] hilarious relationship novel. . . . Readers who enjoy chick lit will savor *Dixieland Sushi* because, like its main character, it offers a different take on the standard fare."

—Curled Up With a Good Book

Also by Cara Lockwood

I Do (But I Don't)
Pink Slip Party
Dixieland Sushi
In One Year and Out the Other (anthology)

I Did
(But I Wouldn't Now)

Cara Lockwood

Have a great summer! Never change! All best, Cara Lockwood

New York London Toronto Sydney

An *Original* Publication of POCKET BOOKS

 DOWNTOWN PRESS, published by Pocket Books
1230 Avenue of the Americas
New York, NY 10020

ISBN-13: 978-0-7434-9943-9
ISBN-10:   0-7434-9943-3

This Downtown Press trade paperback edition May 2006

10   9   8   7   6   5   4   3   2   1

DOWNTOWN PRESS and colophon are
trademarks of Simon & Schuster, Inc.

Manufactured in the United States of America

For information regarding special discounts for bulk purchases,
please contact Simon & Schuster Special Sales at 1-800-456-6798 or
business@simonandschuster.com.

Acknowledgments

Ladies and gentlemen, let's have a nice round of applause for the band. On guitar, with more blues riffs than The Edge, my husband, Daren, who plays a mean rendition of "Stairway to Heaven." On drums, my agent without peer, Deidre Knight. And on bass, the famed Lauren McKenna, my editor without equal. Take a bow, Lauren! On special percussion, there's my indomitable brother, Matt, because you can never have enough cow bell.

And last but not least, on backup vocals—the Lockwoodettes, who make me sound better than I am—Elizabeth Kinsella, Shannon Whitehead, Kate Kinsella, Carroll Jordan, Kate Miller, Linda Newman, Jane Ricordati, Christina Swartz, Stacey Cohen, and Kelly Ballarini. A special thanks to crooner Diane Nale, who's recently returned from a solo act in London.

And, of course, I'd like to give a shout out to my producers—Mom and Dad. The tour wouldn't be possible without them. Thanks, guys!

You've been a wonderful audience. Good night and God bless!

For my husband, Daren, a rock star in his own right.

A girl must marry for love and keep on marrying until she finds it.

Zsa Zsa Gabor

I Did
(But I Wouldn't Now)

One

He's got thousands of groupies. And they're all skinnier than you are.

ere's a word of advice: Never marry a rock star.

Sure, date them. Fool around with them. But never fall in love with one. And God forbid, don't, whatever you do, marry one.

You'll end up like me, fleeing your homeland in a coach seat on a one-way trip to London, because only an ocean between you and your ex seems like enough space for comfort, and because you swear if you hear his hit single "Don't Call Me" one more time on the radio/TV/grocery store speakers/iPod commercial you will simply lose it.

Some of my friends have guessed that being married to a rock star would mean that I'd have a life with an endless supply of designer clothing, a minor acting career if I wanted it, and the possibility of living in a castle, throwing dinner parties with celebrity friends like Sting and Trudy. The reality is more like sitting by the phone and trying to get the band's manager to drag Ted (as in Ted Dayton of the Dayton Five) out of whatever is keeping him from answering his own mobile phone. His distractions have a number of names, like "sound check" or "meeting with the label execs," but all I ever hear is "group sex with nubile adolescent groupies." Rock star, after all, is the only profession where a man can come home to his wife with a number of pairs of strange women's underwear and say it's simply a hazard of the office.

I suppose I should have taken it as a sign when Elvis's pants split shortly after he pronounced us man and wife in the Little White Wedding Chapel in Las Vegas two years ago. Our Elvis minister did a leg-spread split after the ceremony in a show of jubilation that ended in him destroying his tight-fitting, white, sequined jumpsuit. I think, under any zodiac forecast, that's a bad omen for a marriage.

Other omens I should have heeded:

1. Three of his four band mates snickering through the entire processional
2. Ted doing tequila shots before staggering into the church
3. The two-to-one odds laid down by the band's manager that our marriage wouldn't last a year
4. The only nonband witnesses to our union were two groupies named Gwen and Liz, who wore leather miniskirts and fishnet stockings and cried the entire length of the ceremony. Between showing off their

cleavage and glaring daggers at me, I'm pretty sure one or both had slept with my husband, even though he did his best to convince me that neither one was his physical type. I would later learn that if you're even remotely attractive, you're Ted's physical type.

Now I realize I've brought this on myself. You don't elope with a narcissist and expect everything to work out. I guess I was blinded by love and by Ted's really well-groomed goatee.

You know him as the slick lead singer Ted Dayton of the Dayton Five—MTV's darlings, winners of an MTV Video Music Award and two Grammys. I know him as the guy who promised to love me forever, but couldn't quite manage sixteen months.

"I'm sorry, I don't usually do this, but do I know you?" the woman in the seat next to me asks. She's got the latest copy of *US Weekly* magazine open on her lap. The one that I've been trying so hard to avoid. The one with Ted on the cover, straddling a surfboard and locking lips with Melanie Slate, actor/model and *People*'s reigning number three every year in their list of the 50 Most Beautiful People. Under their surfboards the headline reads: "WE'RE IN LOVE!" in big blocky letters.

"I don't think you know me," I say. Even though I know, in that very magazine, on page twenty-seven, under the headline of "Ted Dayton and Melanie's Sizzling Romantic Getaway," there's a small square-inch head shot of me. The one that they always use, the photo snapped outside the Iron Cactus, where

I've got a cigarette in my mouth and my mascara is smudged. I look like a lunatic, but only because Ted brings that out in me.

"I could've sworn I've met you somewhere," the woman continues. Absently, she flips a page of her magazine, and there, staring up at me, is Ted hocking Pepsi. He's holding a skateboard and a Pepsi can and has two scantily clad babes in bikinis on either side of him. Since when does Ted skateboard? He's practically allergic to exercise. He once sat and watched four hours of C-SPAN because the remote was across the living room and he was too lazy to get up and get it.

I notice, as usual, that there's no sign of his band mates. I'm sure they're livid. This will only fuel more speculation that Dayton is going solo.

I turn my attention back to my tarot cards. They were a gift from my old neighbor (herself a proud telephone psychic). I don't believe they have any real power, but given my very bad decision making so far, I figure that turning my life over to tarot cards will be an improvement.

Face-up on my tray table is the Ten of Swords, where a dead body has ten swords plunged into it. I'm assuming that represents me.

Before I left Austin, my New Age neighbor told me my third chakra is blocked. Apparently, this is where love and forgiveness lives. My love and forgiveness is stopped up like the tub drain after Ted shaves his chest hair.

I close my eyes and try to focus on my chakras. I'm not sure if I'm feeling them, or if it's just a case of the airplane food not agreeing with me.

I try to visualize my inner self, the one that's supposed to help me get to the "astral plane," but when I try to focus on my inner self meditating, I keep seeing my inner self waling on Ted's outer self. Apparently, my inner self is a bitter single girl with a lot of anger issues.

"Wait," says the woman next to me. "I do know you. You're married to Ted Dayton!"

The woman is holding up the page with the picture of me, waving it in front of my face like a matador with a red cape. As if it's not bad enough that I'm curled up in a window seat in coach just close enough to first class so that I can smell the filet mignon, now I have to suffer *US Weekly,* too.

"I don't know what you're talking about," I lie.

I'll be honest with you. I may, quite possibly, be a bad person. I've done a number of bad things. I may have, although I'll admit nothing in a court of law, publicized Ted's cell and home phone numbers on a billboard on the Sunset Strip, which meant he had to change both after getting a logjam of calls from more than five-thousand fans after the billboard went public on *Entertainment Tonight.* I also may have charged up to $40,000 on Ted's credit cards at the Four Seasons in Austin, where I stayed after leaving his house.

But honestly. You try having your most embarrassing breakup ever publicized to the two million subscribers of *People* and *US Weekly* and see how well you handle it.

So it's no surprise that the last time I saw Ted my knee may have accidentally come into contact with his groin. Actually, I don't think I regret that part all that much. Watching him curled up on the ground, turning purple, gives me a certain satisfaction, I'll admit. Even if he did have me arrested for it.

This brings me back to the part where I'm a bad person.

But it's not every day that you discover your husband shoving his tongue down an actress's throat, right in the open, in an Austin bar where everyone can see. It's not every day that he tells you to go home, that he'll explain later, that it's not what it looks like, even though he has his hand down the back of her pants and she has her hand down the front of his.

I just sort of lost it. The groin kicking that followed (Ted's attorney called it an "assault") was recorded for posterity by a *Star* photographer, who then turned around and sold his film to every major magazine and tabloid in the nation. Believe me, you don't know embarrassment until your second-grade teacher calls your parents and tells them she saw your picture in a magazine, and that it's obvious that even after all these years you still haven't learned to share.

After my Falling Down Moment, Ted got a restraining order, and my sister, Lauren, pointed out that the only things separating me from being a deranged stalker were really bad hair and a criminal record. I told my sister I wouldn't try to ever *kill* Ted. First of all, I don't know where to find silver-tipped bullets.

My recent plan of marrying and then divorcing a rock star in the course of a year and a half is what my mom would call a Lilyism, the general term in my family used at my expense for bad decision making. I am not like my sister, who plans out everything in advance (no wonder she is a wedding planner). I don't see the point in making lists or in using Palm Pilots. What's the point of living if you have to plan out everything in advance? Where's the fun in that?

Still, I wonder if my sixteen-month marriage will rank high enough in my ex's life to make his VH-1's episode of *Behind the Music*. I have a very sudden and strong empathy for all those grainy photos of the premodel first wives in those stories. I have now joined the leagues of the Cynthia Powell Lennons of the world. And I'm only twenty-six.

I feel that old familiar friend Self-Pity making an appearance, and she's got with her a bag of Oreos and a pint of Ben & Jerry's. I tell her she's not welcome because I've already gained five pounds since the divorce, and being a cow is in no way going to help me in my quest to make Ted one day grovel for forgiveness. I want to be slim and svelte when he comes begging to have me back, so my knee will be nice and bony when I give him another kick.

"I guess you had to expect him to cheat," the woman next to me is saying, shaking her head. She is ignoring the fact that I am staring intently at my Ten of Swords card. I put on my sunglasses and try to look like a celebrity who can't be bothered, which is very hard to do in the cramped rows of coach. I realize the sunglasses and distant expression would be far more effective in first class.

"I mean, how are men supposed to resist that kind of temptation? Melanie Slate, I mean—really."

I wish suddenly that I were a Scientologist. Aside from not caring if other people think you're crazy, I read that they believe if they work at it long enough, they can move and control objects with their minds. I concentrate on the head of the woman next to me, willing it to explode.

"You don't look half as bad in person as you do in this picture," the woman says, undaunted.

"I don't know what you're talking about," I say. "That's not me."

The woman's head is definitely not exploding. I guess if Scientology really worked, then John Travolta would just will the entire world to go see all of his movies, even *Be Cool* and *Battlefield Earth*.

"Oh, I'm quite sure it's you. Look, you've got the same dark rings under your eyes. See?"

I give up on willing her head to explode, and simply nudge the half-full can of Diet Coke off my tray with my elbow. It falls onto the woman's lap, soaking most of the magazine and a bit of her gray sweatpants.

"I am so sorry!" I say, when I'm actually not sorry at all. You see? I told you I'm a bad person.

Ted said as much when I filed for divorce and asked for half of everything he owned.

Two

REASON #2 TO DIVORCE A ROCK STAR:

He looks better in leather pants than you do.

I don't need tarot cards or a woman on a plane to tell me that I am not in the same universe of attractiveness as Melanie Slate. She's objectively gorgeous. Even I can admit that. Fortunately for me, she also has the brain power of a hamster, so I can feel superior about that at least. She's not the sort of woman you'd want to grow old with. She'll never be able to help you with a crossword puzzle or be able to guess the next clue on *Wheel of Fortune.* When she gets wrinkled and saggy, she'll just be an old woman who keeps asking the clerk at the grocery store if Chicken of the Sea is chicken or tuna.

The irony is that Ted used to joke about her, about how when he met her for the first time she didn't seem to be able to distinguish between her right and left. They'd met at the MTV Movie Awards, and she'd been his copresenter. She couldn't figure out which side she was supposed to stand on. Melanie Slate is one of those celebrities who giggles a lot, and wiggles a lot, and somewhere in between the giggling and wiggling, she gets $10 million a movie.

When the rumors started that they were an item, I didn't believe it. I knew Ted loves publicity, and I knew he spent some time on the set of her movie *Lone Star Love,* which was filmed in Austin, but he told me it was to help the Dayton Five get on the soundtrack. I never imagined he'd seriously go for a giggly/wiggly girl. After all, he married me. I'm a thrift-store/yoga kind of girl. At least I was until Ted got famous and designers started handing me free clothes.

My ex-boyfriend Carter says that guys don't always pick mates based on logic. If they did, then all the smart and stable women would always have committed boyfriends and all the hot, yet totally psychotic, models would be dateless on Saturday nights. Carter is also the one who opened my eyes to the idea of "the list." Most guys, he claims, have a list of the type and number of women they want to sleep with. Before getting married, some (Carter insists most) guys have in their head a number of sexual fantasies (salsa dancer, black police officer, Asian flight attendant, Russian tennis player, whatever) and that they are far less likely to cheat if they've checked off most of that mental fantasy list by indulging in those sexual fantasies before walking down the aisle.

When I asked Ted if he had a list, he denied ever having one. This made him suspect from the start in Carter's opinion.

"A guy who doesn't admit to a list means he wants to sleep with every woman he meets," Carter said at the time. "It means he isn't selective."

It pains me to think that I should have listened to Carter.

Carter and I dated for a couple of months when I was eighteen and he was twenty.

Some basic facts about Carter: He spends more on hair gel than I do on makeup; he is the only ex-boyfriend I'm on speaking terms with and, not coincidentally, is the only one who isn't either in jail or working on getting there. I am also the only ex-girlfriend Carter speaks to, because, typically, his modus operandi for ending a relationship is to stop calling and pretend never to have known you in the first place. Carter is a coward, and I've told him so many times.

He can afford to treat women badly because, karmicly speaking, Carter helps people. He is a doctor (orthopedic surgeon) and is in the middle of finishing up some fellowship or another in London. So, in addition to saving lives and/or setting bones, he will one day move back to the States, open up an expensive private practice, and make loads of cash.

Carter and I were bound from the start never to work out. He's far too obsessed with his hair, for one thing, and for another, he can't commit to an order at a restaurant much less a long-term relationship. He once changed his order four times before settling on the first thing he asked for. When I told Carter flat out I'd rather be friends, he looked immensely relieved and hugged me like I was a governor who just granted him a pardon from lethal injection. It was one of those rare venom-free breakups, like the Demi Moore and Bruce Willis divorce.

We've been the best of friends ever since.

In my (drunker) moments, I realize this is because I *might* be carrying a bit of a torch for Carter. I've always been attracted to the wrong sort of guy, and Carter is definitely the wrong sort of guy. He's funny, smart, charming, and completely toxic. But Carter is my best friend. He understands me, or if he doesn't understand me, then at the least he doesn't lecture me, which is more than I can say of the rest of my family.

Carter is the first one I called after I got married to Ted. He is also the first one I called when we split up.

When he suggested that I visit him in London, I got on the next plane.

Three

REASON #3 TO DIVORCE A ROCK STAR:
You didn't sign a prenup.

I learned to read tarot cards from my one-time upstairs neighbor, Fran Holman. Her telephone psychic name, though, was Sheba, after her cat's favorite food. Fran thought it sounded "exotic" (as in "Queen of"), and I guess it worked better than her cat's other food choice, Fancy Feast.

I never knew how Fran made a living as a telephone psychic. She has a deep, gravelly voice crafted from thirty years of pack-a-day smoking. She's what I have to look forward to if I keep up my habit. She also has more wrinkles than a Shar-pei.

Fran would read my tarot cards for just twenty dollars. But if I gave her thirty, the forecast would always be good. "I see you getting married," she told me shortly after I met Ted. "I see you wearing very good clothes."

I dream that I'm back in Ted's giant, six-bedroom house overlooking Lake Travis, the one with the 180-degree view of downtown Austin; and the swimming pool, the indoor movie theater with staggered, stadium seating and the fifty-five-inch flat-screen TV; the enormous eat-in kitchen covered in dark granite countertops and gleaming, stainless-steel appliances. I dream that I'm taking a bath in the master bedroom's bathroom, the one with the huge Jacuzzi-style marble tub, big enough to swim in.

It's a bit jarring when I wake up to find myself still in my cramped airplane seat in coach, and worse, my entire left leg has gone numb. The closest thing to Jacuzzi jets are the spit bubbles threatening to dribble onto my shirt from the woman sitting next to me. She must have tired of stomping on my self-esteem and fallen asleep somewhere over the Atlantic. I close my eyes and try to conjure up Ted's house again. I think it's quite possible I miss it more than I miss him. To be fair, while we were married, I saw it more than I saw him.

The real tragedy is that I was good at being rich. This is due in large part to the fact that I am lazy. I'll admit it. I don't like to work. Who does, really? Sure, there's that whole self-esteem thing from accomplishing something. But all of my jobs involved work that a blindfolded monkey could do, so the sense of accomplishment from my temp/data entry jobs pretty much amounted to "Wow, I've accomplished something a lesser-evolved primate is capable of doing, except I did it without throwing feces."

So, okay, I was pretty psyched when it turned out my loser rock star fiancé (who at the time had to borrow money from me constantly for cigs) hit it big. Who wouldn't want to win that lottery?

Money can't buy happiness, but it can sure buy you a lot of other really, really nice stuff.

The only thing worse than being poor is being poor, then rich, then poor again. This is because you actually *know* what you're missing. It sucks. Trust me. But I understand it's also obnoxious. I'm not going to go on the *Today* show and whine about how poor I am since I had to give up my $1.5 million vacation home in Vail, like a certain Enron executive. I don't expect pity. I just want a very large divorce settlement. That way, I won't be bitter, and I can still afford weekly facials.

I arrive at Heathrow, jet-lagged and feeling more than a little nauseous, the airport a blur of people and stale-air smell. My hair is limp and greasy, and I smell like those dirty flannel blankets on the airplane. I need a shower or a drink. Or maybe both at once. On my way to baggage claim, I stop at a group of payphones. These days, I always stop at payphones. They're the perfect means of prank calling Ted.

I glance at my watch. It'll be about 4:00 A.M. L.A. time, which means that he'll just be going to sleep about now.

I got his new cellphone number by accident. It came in a piece of mail from Verizon sent to the old house. And I know he won't change it again, because he's probably given it out to too many groupies. And he always answers a strange call, because he never knows when it might be a booty call.

A groggy-sounding Ted answers. Bingo. I woke him up. I feel giddy.

I put on a German accent and ask for Dieter.

"Fuck off!" Ted shouts, and then hangs up.

I call back three more times, just to make sure he doesn't fall back asleep. To answer your question: Yes, I have the emotional maturity of a thirteen-year-old, and yes, I am a bad person.

I grab my overstuffed suitcases and head to customs, where an agent who looks like John Cleese asks me about my business in London. I am very tempted to tell him I'm a political exile— after all, fleeing American pop culture counts as some sort of political statement, I'm sure.

"I'm here to see a friend," I say.

John Cleese nods, holds my passport up to a scanner, and scans it.

He looks at me a long time without blinking. I'm starting to get nervous, and then I realize it's probably because I still look like a rock star's wife. My light brown hair sports platinum highlights (courtesy of the Four Seasons) and falls to my shoulders; I'm wearing big, aviator-style Fendi sunglasses—which I tell myself I'll probably have to sell soon. I've got on an as-yet-unreleased pair of Lucky jeans, Dolce & Gabbana suede boots, and a matching suede blazer. Underneath it, I've got on a simple T-shirt with Elvis on the front. And beneath this I'm wearing La Perla underwear (of which I have more than a dozen matching sets), which cost more than my entire wardrobe in college.

Not that I paid for any of it.

Some of it came from the *Entertainment Weekly* shoot. They did a spread called "Desperate Rock Wives." That's where I met

Heather Mills (Paul McCartney's wife) and Rod Stewart's wife (number three or four, I forget). Other clothes came from designers hoping that I could convince Ted to wear their clothes by giving me some, too. This is how famous people afford to be famous. People keep giving them free stuff, so they can fritter away their hard-earned royalties on more important things like entourages and filling their swimming pools with Cristal.

Beyond customs, Carter is waiting for me, looking, as usual, very well groomed. His hair is perfectly spiked in a deliberately messy, just-out-of-bed-if-your-pillow-had-a-styling-gel dispenser sort of way. It's a thrown-together look I imagine too Carter somewhere near an hour to create with a minimum of three styling products. The upside of Carter's hair obsession is that he always smells really good. His face breaks out into a warm smile when he sees me, and he immediately envelops me in a tight hug. I get a good whiff of something sweet and clean. Ex-boyfriends should not smell this good.

Carter tries to pull back, but I keep hugging him. I don't want to let him go.

"Uh, Lil? You okay?" he asks me.

"No, I'm not okay," I say, squeezing him harder. I suddenly have a violent urge to cry. This would not be good, because Carter doesn't do well with tears. He so hates to see women cry that he says this is why he never breaks up with them face-to-face.

"I know what will make you feel better," he says, stroking my back. "Rebound sex with me."

I pull away from him and give him a playful punch in the

arm. "Ow," he says. "You know you really want to rip my clothes off."

"Is that your new pickup line? Because it needs work."

Carter scoffs at me. "As if I would test my new material on you," he says. "You'd just laugh at me and undermine my confidence."

"You have plenty of confidence to spare, I think," I say. "Last time I checked, you had more than enough savings at the ego bank."

"Did you spend the entire flight trying to come up with that one?"

"Maybe."

"It shows," Carter says. "Come on. I've got a car waiting."

Carter looks down at my four Louis Vuitton duffel-size bags.

"Louis Vuitton?" Carter asks, quirking one eyebrow.

"If you're going to have serious emotional baggage, you might as well carry it around in designer luggage."

Carter reaches for the bag I'm still holding and inadvertently touches my hand. I get a minishock from the touch, and I wonder if it's static electricity or just the feeling of Carter's skin on mine.

I have flashbacks of the last time we had sex—Carter on top of me, telling me how beautiful I am. He stared at me so intently, touched me so gently, as if he couldn't believe how lucky he was. The memory makes me feel warm in all the right places.

I shake my head to try to clear it. That was then. This is now.

Sex was never our problem. Carter's roving eye was the problem. Also, Carter's inability to say "I love you"—an even bigger problem.

Luckily, Carter is busy with my bags and doesn't notice that I'm blushing. Carter grunts, picking up three of my bags—one in each hand and one over his shoulder. I take the smallest one, a cosmetics case. "Couldn't you have packed your emotional baggage a little more lightly?"

"Why would I do that when I know you'd carry them for me?"

"How did you know I would?" he asks, making an exaggerated show of lugging my bags out of the door.

"The tarot cards told me," I say.

Carter makes a face and rolls his eyes. "Don't tell me you're still doing that. You know it doesn't mean anything." Carter is a doctor and a man of science, so anything remotely nonscientific strikes him as ridiculous. This goes for tarot cards, astrology, feng shui, and reality shows like *America's Next Top Model.*

I sling my purse over my shoulder. It's got practically my entire life from the last year in it, including the small fortune of freebies I stole from Ted's Grammy presenter gift basket when I left him five months ago: his iPod, the two-carat diamond stud earrings, an array of outrageously expensive hair/bath/beauty products, and a Juicy Couture jogging suit— pink, size zero. I can't fit into it, but it's bound to be worth something on eBay.

If I were a good person (which it's well-documented I'm not), I'd donate these items to a charity, but at the moment, the only charity I feel like giving to is the Ex-Wife Without Credit Cards fund.

Carter leads us to his car, a silver Audi. He's very proud of it because it's a stick shift, which he learned to drive after he moved to England. Learning a clutch while remembering to drive on the left-hand side of the road, Carter claims, is more challenging than hip-replacement surgery. He also insists that sitting for the driver's test in England requires more studying than the MCATs.

"There are a few things you should know now that you're here," Carter says as he turns the key to the ignition and checks his rearview mirror.

"You've got a psychotic girlfriend and need me to lie and tell her you're gay?"

"For the record, I only asked you to do that once," he says.

"That you even asked once speaks volumes."

"Stop distracting me. Now, being in London, there are a couple of things you should know. First, everyone here smokes and everyone here drinks like fishes, so you should blend right in."

"Thanks for giving me the lung cancer and alcoholic vote," I say.

"Second, don't throw your gum on the sidewalk. You'll get fined a hundred pounds. Cigarette butts, however, are fine. Toss away."

"Good tip."

"Third, no matter how much you may be tempted by the Krispy Kreme donuts in Harrods—avoid them. They aren't as good as the ones back home, and they'll just make you sadder that you had them."

"Is that it?"

"Lines are queues. Cigarettes are fags. And a stone is fourteen pounds."

"That means I weigh . . ." I pause, trying to calculate.

"Don't hurt yourself."

My phone chimes the dual-phonic ringtone of "These Boots Were Made for Walking," one of ten bad breakup songs I'm rotating through my phone as a source of inspiration. I dig around in my purse for my slim-line flip phone (another freebie, since Motorola was Ted's tour sponsor) and look at the caller ID. It's my mother.

Reluctantly, I pick up. I'd been avoiding all calls from Mom. Every time I speak to her I feel like I've failed her somehow; that it is somehow my fault that Ted decided he preferred being with Melanie Slate than being married to me. It isn't anything Mom says, exactly, just the pitying tone she uses when she asks, "How are you holding up?" as if the blow to my self-esteem is so great that I'm about to crumble at any moment. I'm not going to crumble, for heaven's sake. I'm not some delicate flower. I have a tattoo. I'm going to be fine.

"Hi, Mom."

"How did you know it was me, dear?"

"Caller ID." I've attempted to explain the concept of caller ID to both parents for years, but neither one seemed able to grasp the concept. It's no wonder, since both of them are techphobic. They are the only people I know who don't own a DVD player. Dad once called me from a Wal-Mart when he made the heart-stopping discovery that some mobile phones now have cameras in them. That was a month ago.

"Hello? Hello!" shouts Dad, picking up the other line.

"Frank! Don't shout, for heaven's sake. Lily can hear you just fine."

"Landed all right, pumpkin? 'Allo guvner and all that?" Dad is putting on an atrocious English accent.

"Yes, I'm here with Carter. Everything's fine."

"Ask Carter when he's going to come over for another poker night," says Dad. "I've got a new strategy this time Carter can't beat."

"I don't think Carter wants to play poker."

I look over at Carter, who is shaking his head furiously and mouthing "no—no way."

Carter made the mistake of attending one of Dad's poker nights some years ago. Poker night at Dad's involves Dad and his three lovable but clueless neighbors, Tom, Bill, and Marshall. All of them claim to be poker experts, except that in Texas Hold 'Em, they call the "river" card the "stream" and they insist on playing with pennies.

Because Carter actually does know how to play, Dad has it in his mind that Carter is some sort of poker champion, and keeps asking him back to test whether or not he's improved his skills. Carter hates to play them because he says it's like robbing blind men, and then he ends up with a jar full of pennies he doesn't want.

"Why not—he's got to give us a chance to win our money back," Dad says.

"Dad, you lose every time you play him. Just give up."

"Frank, I don't think discussions of gambling are appropriate at the moment," Mom says.

"I'm just trying to—"

"Frank. Please." Mom draws a deep breath. "How are you holding up, dear?"

I sigh. There it is: *that tone.* The one that says that Mom has the suicide hotline on speed dial; the one that tells me she's mentally checking off the signs of depression she clipped from *Redbook* and is trying to diagnosis me.

"I'm fine, Mom. Really."

"You don't sound fine."

"Mom—I am. Really. Fine."

"Quit bothering the girl," Dad barks. "She said she was fine."

"Frank, I'm her mother. I think I know when she's not fine."

"Look—I'm *fine.*" I am trying not to shout.

"If you want, I'll call Ted and have a few words with him—man-to-man," Dad says. Dad has been offering to do this since he heard we were getting divorced, as if a philandering husband is like a rude prom date.

"No, Dad. That's okay."

"Well, we just want you to know that we're here for you," Mom says. "I don't want to make the same mistakes I made when your sister got divorced."

After my sister, Lauren, left her ex-husband (for, among other things, screwing her neighbor on their new couch), Mom tried for months to get the two back together. But since learning that Brad cheated on Lauren, she's finally come around to the idea that divorce isn't an evil word. Unfortunately for me, this means that Mom feels the need to call every day to ask me how I'm doing. Her call usually comes during the fifteen or so minutes in the day when I manage not to think about Ted.

"I mean, yes, it is a burden that *both* of my daughters are now divorcées, but I realize that times are different today and marriage is just a different thing."

"Mom . . ."

"I mean, I *understand*. I bought that book *The Starter Marriage*. And I think I understand what you're feeling."

I'm pretty sure Mom has no idea what I'm feeling.

"And even though I never liked Ted—"

"Now we promised we wouldn't get into that," Dad interrupts.

"What I was *going* to say is that Lauren says that you've just got to let yourself heal," Mom adds.

Great, I think. Mom has been talking to Lauren about me. I have a sudden image of my sister and mother spending hours on the phone discussing every detail of how I've managed to screw up my life—again. Being the "problem child" means you always feel like other people in the family are talking about you. Usually because they are.

"Mom, I'm not going to take Lauren's advice," I say. She was a complete basket case for more than a year after her divorce. For the first six months, she didn't even get out of bed, and I'm supposed to take her advice? Not to mention, she's married to a wonderful guy (Nick), and she's still so insecure about men that she lives in mortal fear that he's going to cheat on her even though he worships the ground she walks on.

"I have good news for you, dear," my mother is saying now. "I double-checked with Emily Post and since you were married for a full year you get to keep your gifts. You don't have to send them back."

"Thanks, Mom." I sigh. My mom is semiobsessed with Emily Post. She had a particularly hard time finding out the etiquette for announcing my Vegas wedding, but she managed. Apparently, Emily Post provides for every one of life's awkward occasions. "It's nice to know that while I don't have Ted, at least I have a matching set of place mats from Pottery Barn."

"Lily! Be nice. Your aunt and uncle sent you those because they thought you'd like them," Mom chides. "Anyway, I can tell this is the depression talking. Maybe you ought to see a professional."

"Let's leave the girl alone. I'm sure she'll be fine," mumbles Dad. He sounds like he's eating something.

"Frank! Are you eating my brownies? I told you not to eat those. They're for our church group. Frank, for heaven's sake! Lily, I have to go."

Abruptly, the call ends.

"How's Emily Post?" Carter jokes, referring to my mom.

"She's doing fine, and apparently has a statute of limitations on wedding gifts. But luckily, I'm just under the wire."

"You know I would let you keep the fondue set I gave you anyway," Carter says.

I have to laugh. "Thanks," I say. "Mind if I?" I ask Carter, tapping a cigarette out of my pack. If there is one thing worse than eating that can make me crave nicotine, it's discussions about my emotional health with my mother.

"You really should quit." Carter gives me a disapproving look. This is his doctor's face. I've seen him pull it on people who Rollerblade without knee pads, or who bicycle without helmets. But beyond my health, I know Carter is thinking about himself, too. He doesn't like anything that threatens the smell of his hair. This includes cigarette smoke.

"I quit pot smoking," I joke. "Isn't that enough?"

Carter doesn't laugh. "You don't have any drugs on you, do you?" Carter looks worried.

"No. Why does everyone think I'm a druggie?"

"I just figured you'd be like Courtney Love," Carter says.

"You thought I'd marry Ted and wind up with a heroin addiction?"

"That was the best-case scenario."

I laugh, exhaling smoke into Carter's pristine interior and dangerously close to his hair.

Carter frowns.

"This is just one more thing I can blame on Ted. I can let him live or quit smoking. Not both."

I feel the calming fuzz of nicotine seep into my brain and I feel entirely less homicidal. I catch a glimpse of Big Ben out of the cab window, and lean into the door so I can see more of the city. It's early October, much cooler than the Austin I left (of ninety degrees), and everyone is wearing tweed or sweaters, looking extremely English, down to their black umbrellas. The sky, however, is clear. I take this as a good sign.

"You know, if you want me to, I'll beat Ted up," Carter says.

"What? Is this fourth grade?"

"I just felt that, as a man, I ought to say it."

I think of Ted on the sidewalk in the fetal position outside the Iron Cactus.

"Thanks, but I think I did a pretty good job already of beating him up."

Four

REASON #4 TO DIVORCE A ROCK STAR:

Because "Do you know who I am?" is a surprisingly good pickup line.

I first met Ted at La Zona Rosa, one of Austin's best spots for live music, even if it did used to be a Mexican restaurant (explaining its very Southwestern pink/blue/pastel decor). I liked La Zona Rosa mostly because it had one of the longest bars in town, which meant you didn't have to wait hours for a beer when you saw a show.

Ted saved me from a particularly dull group of my coworkers' sorority friends, who were busy comparing engagement rings and talking about Ralph Lauren paint chips. At the time, I was working as a temp at a local ad agency, trying to find myself after taking five and a half years to fail to get my bachelor's degree.

I was beginning to think I should be like some of my coworkers' sorority friends and marry rich. They had enough carat weight between them to rival the Hope diamond, and enough designer labels to start their own runway show. One of them, Colleen, had married a rich lawyer during her junior year of college (he was fifteen years older), dropped out, and now was living in a giant house, complete with maid service, a cook, and two convertible BMWs—one white and one black—so she could properly coordinate her car with her outfits.

Given that I majored in women's studies, I realized that marrying rich would probably not win me any points with my former professors. Then again, I doubted a women's studies degree would ever earn enough money to have two BMWs. All of my professors drove secondhand Beetles.

There were other problems with marrying rich. For one, I didn't know any rich people. The men I dated tended to wear uniforms to work: waiters, valets, and police officers. I hadn't been on a single date that involved linen napkins for more than a year, which didn't bode well for my marry-rich career plan.

My coworker Mindy turned all that around by setting me up on a blind date with a twice-divorced stockbroker. He claimed to be forty, but looked closer to fifty. We'd had two dates involving linen. We hadn't slept together, yet, since I was trying to work up the courage to see him naked. He said that people told him he looked like George Clooney, but I thought he looked more like Bob Barker. That is, if Bob Barker wore Hawaiian shirts and bragged about not needing Viagra.

I'm shallow, I'll admit. But it turns out I am too shallow to marry just for money. I was having grave second thoughts about the stockbroker's loose chin skin and the hair plugs dotting his receding hairline.

Enter Ted.

He was bartending at La Zona Rosa, serving me vodka sodas and trying to impress me by giving us free shots. It worked. Drinking was the only way to get through the deadly combo of my coworkers' friends and the steady hum of lousy cover songs being played in the background.

Ted was cute, but nondescript. He eavesdropped on my conversation with my coworkers and singled me out as the girl he wanted. This was probably because I was the only one not wearing Burberry plaid or an engagement ring. We shared conspiratorial glances and rolled eyes. He could tell I wasn't one of the others—the married or about-to-be married, the women who look through men without seeing them.

They left, eventually, but I stayed.

"I've got a band," Ted said, giving me another free Jägermeister shot. "I'm Ted Dayton," he added, as if I might know the name. "My brother and me, we've got a good band. One day we'll be famous."

In Austin, every boy you meet is in a band. They call the city "the live music capital of the world," but it should be "the cover band capital of the world."

I didn't intend to go to the show, but I wound up there anyway. I was avoiding the aging stockbroker, who wanted to take me out for a steak dinner. I figured that given his age, the steak dinner, and the fact that this would be our third date, he'd be expecting me to put out afterward, and I wasn't sure I'd be up for the task.

Ted came alive onstage. Nondescript Ted suddenly became

the sexiest man I'd ever seen. There's such a thing as stage light-ing, I know, and the fact that if you put a guy in front of a gui-tarist, a bassist, and a drummer then he automatically looks ten times sexier than he would sitting in front of a Cinnabon at the mall food court. It's what I call the Mick Jagger effect.

Let me explain.

If you had Mick Jagger working in your office, there's no way you'd ever want to sleep with him. No way. Can you imag-ine? Big-lipped and skinny, making lewd innuendos while you tried to get around him to use the fax machine? He'd be the weird guy who struts, whom everyone avoided direct eye con-tact with or rides in the elevator. You'd never in a million years ever find him attractive. You'd be busy listening to the rumors that he downloads porn in the office. But you put him onstage before twenty-thousand screaming fans, and he does his little strut dance, and women start taking off their shirts, and before you know it, you're fantasizing about him ripping your clothes off.

Voilà.

So there's Ted. If you saw Ted by the fax machine, wearing those leather pants and stubble, you'd say, "Who is that loser wearing leather pants in Austin when it's ninety-five degrees out?" But onstage, where he looks so comfortable, where he doesn't seem at all nervous, just in his element, exuding indif-ference, as if he couldn't care less if you even appreciate the song, his singing, or anything else. He was too busy singing, looking sexy, working the microphone, and working the crowd. He didn't even strut, he just swayed back and forth, mop in his eyes, sending out one message with every beat of the music: *I Am a Rock God, Worship Me.*

He had it. The Mick Jagger effect. And it would be what everyone would notice later—the band's first manager, the first record producer, the legions of groupies, and the audience at the Grammys. Anyone could see he was born to be a rock star. Like all musicians do, he had that devilish bad-boy mojo working from the start.

Not to mention dating the aging stockbroker had made me weak for boys anywhere near my age group. When Ted offered to buy me a drink on his free bar tab, it was like being offered cheesecake after a steady diet of rice crackers. I felt like I'd been given a second chance at love, and I was too weak to resist.

Now I know that it's more like Stockholm syndrome. If you're in a bad enough relationship, just about anyone will look like husband material. Even Ted.

Five

REASON #5 TO DIVORCE A ROCK STAR:
You can stop pretending to like his music.

"J ust what the hell do you think you're doing?" asks my lawyer on the phone. He's called my mobile just as Carter is in the process of parking in a space the size of a lawn chair. In the last five minutes, a storm has blown in from nowhere, and there's a steady drizzle of rain falling from the gray sky. I'm standing on the curb with my bags, trying to keep dry under a nearby awning.

My lawyer, Larry Sullivan, speaks in a Texas drawl and sounds a bit peeved at me. This is probably because he's defending me against the assault charges Ted filed against me.

"I just heard from your mother that you're in London, *England.*" Larry is nearly shouting. "Did you forget you have a little thing called an assault charge pending? A little thing called a 'trial' on December fifth? Or did you forget? That's just over five weeks away."

"I didn't forget," I say, sighing.

"I realize it's just a little old misdemeanor, Lily, but you still aren't supposed to just up and leave the country without checking with your lawyer first. Besides, I thought you turned over your passport to the bail bondsman."

"I used my sister's passport to come to London," I say.

"And she let you do this?"

"She doesn't know. I just took it, okay? It's not like she's ever going to use it." Lauren is the only person I know of, except for Sandra Bullock's character in *While You Were Sleeping,* who has a passport with no stamps in it. She's never gotten a single stamp. She's never even been to Mexico.

"That was a poor decision on your part," Larry says.

"What about your history with me suggests that I make good decisions?"

"That's true, but, Lily, this is a really, *really* bad decision."

"But I only plan to stay a few days." I stamp out my third cigarette on the wet concrete. "Besides, the tarot cards said it would be all right."

This is a lie.

Actually, before the trip to London, I drew the Wheel of Fortune card, but upside down (meaning: an inescapable descent due to fate or karma. Misfortune, failure, and a chaotic series of events set into motion by an action of the past that cannot be undone), but I didn't take it too seriously. Tarot cards never give good news. They're like having a really cynical and pessimistic grandma. They're always going to tell you to expect the worst.

"Oh, did they? And did they also say you're going to jail? Because that's what Judge Leopold is going to do to you when he finds out you've skipped bail."

"I'll be back in plenty of time for my court hearing. That's not for weeks. I'm only doing this to prevent future crimes."

"How so?"

"You know I'm not a violent person. But if I had stayed in the country one more hour, I would've killed Ted. Do you know how often they play his songs on the radio? They already have a Muzak version. I heard it at Walgreens, for heaven's sake."

Larry sighs. Larry is used to dealing with oil magnates committing white-collar crime. Rock star wives are new to him.

"Lily, we can't turn this lemon into lemonade. I'm telling you, you'd better get your butt back to the States, pronto," Larry says. "How am I supposed to plead this case out when you're across the Atlantic? I have a meeting with the prosecutor next week. What am I supposed to tell him? My client's AWOL?"

"I'll be back way before then."

"And what about the community service I told you to do to help win over the judge?"

I think about this a moment.

"I can do it here."

"May I remind you that you aren't even supposed to be there? We can't tell the judge in Austin that you are doing volunteer work in a city you aren't even supposed to be in."

"I think that's a technicality," I say.

"Lily, you are going to put me in an early grave."

"But . . ."

"Just come home, all right? Come home, now." With that, he hangs up.

"Who was that?" Carter asks me, shaking off the rain. I notice that the water beads on his well-gelled hair. I want to put my fingers in his hair. Ruffle it a bit, like I used to do when we would sit on the couch cuddling. It doesn't seem so long ago. Why is it that with Carter I always want to touch him?

"My lawyer. He wants me to do volunteer work," I say. I don't mention that he wants me to do that volunteer work in the United States.

Carter scoffs. "You? Are you sure he's got the right number?"

"I can volunteer," I say.

Carter looks skeptical. "Lil, you don't even like to work when you're getting paid for it," he says. "I think I'll have a heart attack the day you actually do something for free."

I squint at him, but say nothing. He has a point. I may be a bit self-absorbed. This might explain why I didn't notice Ted was a narcissist. If I'd been a bit more outward looking, I might have caught the warning signs, like the first love song Ted wrote about me. He called it "The Me in You," which was pretty much a graphic sex song. It's proof that he can't even write a love song without putting his penis in the title.

At the thought of Ted, my heart feels squeezed, as if someone has placed a book on my chest or about three tons of bricks. Why do they never tell you that heartbreaks *actually* hurt your heart physically? Sometimes the pain is so intense, I feel like I can't breathe. The only way to get rid of the hurt is to get mad. That's why prank calling feels so good.

Carter's apartment is in Notting Hill, one of the most expensive neighborhoods in London, which would be impressive except that his entire apartment would fit into my parents' living room.

He tells me location is everything, also pointing out that he lives down the street from Stella McCartney, which makes him one degree of separation from his favorite band in the world, the Beatles.

"Not to mention, I can't get chicks to come to a huge flat in the dodgy part of London," he says.

"Did you just use 'flat' and 'dodgy' in the same sentence? You've been living in London too long."

"I'm thinking of adopting that fake Madonna lilt next."

"That would go well with your hair, I think."

"Let's face it, everything goes with my hair," he says. He gives me a wink. I have to laugh.

"Are you sure you're not living a double life as a gay hairdresser?"

"I am not gay—not that there's anything wrong with that," Carter says.

Inside Carter's apartment, I see a large redheaded man sitting on the couch playing video games. He's wearing a shirt that has a swastika on it with a big slash through it on the front. On the back, it says I HATE F*#!ING NAZIS.

"The fixture on the Xbox is Ian, my roommate," Carter says, by way of introduction.

"Naycetomeetcha," he mumbles. "Awveeardawotboutcha."

"What?"

"Awveeardawotboutcha."

I can't, for the life of me, understand a single word he's saying, his accent is so thick. This isn't a Sean Connery accent, or even a Mike Myers impression; it's so thick it's like another language.

"I'm sorry—what?"

Ian throws his hands up in the air, as if he gives up. "Achebludeeyawnk."

"It just takes a little time," Carter tells me. "Trust me, you'll start to understand him after a while."

Ian shrugs, and goes back to his game, involving shooting zombies with laser guns so that their guts explode on the screen.

"Thanks for helping with the bags," Carter says.

"Chayrs," he says, raising his beer bottle.

"Ian's a documentary filmmaker. He's making a movie about video games, but instead of filming it, he just sits around and plays them all day," Carter says.

"Eearddat," Ian says.

Carter's apartment, aside from the two-foot radius around Ian, which is littered with empty chip bags, is in good order—pristine and well-furnished. Everything is sleek, modern, and expensive. There's even a strange square chair that looks very mod in the corner by the television. I start to put my purse on it, when Ian makes a strangled sound.

"No!" Carter shouts, nearly tackling me to prevent me from touching it.

"That's the Lennon chair. John Lennon once sat in that chair. I got it at a charity auction sponsored by Abbey Road Records."

Ian shakes a warning finger at me. "June Leeennon," he says, which I understand.

"You haven't sat in this chair?"

"God, no! That imprint, right there, could be Lennon's butt print."

"And that's worth saving?"

"Do you know anything about John Lennon? Hello. He is a legend. He could've written 'All You Need Is Love' in that chair."

"Or Yoko could've just sat in it naked."

"Don't ruin it for me, Lil," Carter warns me.

Next to Carter's prized Lennon chair, there's a giant stereo. It practically takes up the entire living room, and nearby in shelves lining the walls are his extensive CD and vinyl LP collection. He looks as if he's trying to single-handedly create his own rock library archive. Carter is most definitely a frustrated musician. He once tried to play guitar, but it turns out he's completely tone deaf. He couldn't even tune the guitar properly. The next logical step, of course, was medical school.

In Carter's apartment, there are three bedrooms, thankfully, and he shows me into the windowless one. I notice, sadly, that it is smaller than the changing room in Ted's pool cabana.

"I think I need a drink," I say.

*   *   *

Carter takes me to the appropriately named Hung, Drawn, and Quartered Pub, which is what I feel like has happened to me on the cross-Atlantic flight. He orders me a pint of Caffrey's ale, which you can't get in the States. I don't know if it's really, really good beer, or if I'm just starved for a drink.

"Hey there, slushy, slow down or the next stop for you is Betty Ford," Carter says, as I finish my second Caffrey's.

"Are you going to lecture me about liver damage now?" I ask him.

"Ach, drinkeedooyagwodeetweel," says Ian, who has followed us to the pub. He slugs down his beer in one seamless gulp, as if he was pouring it down the sink. He burps and waves his hand at the barmaid.

"I like the way you think, Ian," I say, as he orders another round for the two of us. "When you get divorced," I tell Carter, "then you can tell me I'm drinking too much."

"I have to get married first," Carter says. He's very prudently drinking soda, as he's on call and might be summoned to the ER at any moment. "And anyway, it's been five months. You should be beyond shotgunning drinks by now."

"Is that your expert medical opinion, doctor?" I ask him, teasing.

"Yes, as a matter of fact."

Ian slams his second beer, and then wanders off in search of a dart game.

I tell Carter about the *US Weekly* woman on the plane.

"You mean you didn't just kick her? I thought you Tae Bo-ed anyone who offends you."

"I didn't have a good range of motion in my coach-class seat, so I had to resort to Diet Coke. Anyway, it's a difficult day. And I probably won't be getting much of a divorce settlement."

"You don't need a divorce settlement," Carter tells me. "You can make a fine living on your own."

"Doing what?"

"Being a phone psychic?"

Fran "Sheba" Holman tried to convince me to join her as a phone psychic. I considered the job. It would be a step up from my other failed career enterprises: waitress, bartender, and administrative assistant. But I do have a problem: I'm not a psychic.

Fran, however, told me that the papers she signed to work for her company said that customers who called into psychic hotlines couldn't "reasonably expect to talk to an actual psychic." According to Fran, this meant that I could be a phone psychic without any actual psychic powers.

Fran worked for a company called Third Eye. They had a series of late-night infomercials involving a woman speaking in an Eastern European accent and wearing a jeweled turban.

The barmaid puts down two more beers in front of us.

"What you ought to do is finish your degree," Carter says. He's always bugging me about the two credits I lack for my bachelor's degree. He's a walking public service announcement for staying in school.

"Ted says I'm better off learning how to be a stripper than finishing my bachelor's."

"Ted's an asshole."

Carter has never liked Ted. Other than the fact that Ted doesn't have a "list," he also seems to rub Carter the wrong way—literally. When Ted first met Carter, he put his hand in Carter's hair and gave him a dry swirlie, messing up two hours of primping.

It's probably no mistake that Ted and I eloped. If we'd had a real church wedding, Carter might have talked me out of it.

"Tell me again how much you hate Ted," I say.

"Worse than granny drivers."

"And when did you know you hated him?"

"The first second I saw him and he put his greasy hand in my hair. You should have listened to me. A man who doesn't respect hair isn't going to respect wedding vows."

"You're right," I say, and sigh.

"And of all the people to . . . I mean, Melanie Slate? She's more silicone than human." He makes a face.

This is why I love Carter. He knows the exact right thing to say to cheer me up.

"I'm glad I'm here," I say, giving him a smile.

He smiles back. "Me, too," he says.

Carter's mobile phone chimes. It plays the theme song from *The Good, the Bad and the Ugly*—his favorite movie of all time.

"It's Brigid," Carter says, looking pensive.

"Is this the latest love of your life?" I ask him.

He silences his phone. "She's a nice girl, but she's turning into something of a stalker."

"How can she be nice and be a stalker at the same time?"

"It's complicated. She's a little . . . unhinged."

"And that's different from your other girlfriends how?"

"I don't always date crazy women."

"You have dating Alzheimer's." Carter is the only one I know who makes worse dating decisions than I do.

"Okay, maybe *sometimes* I date crazy women, but you know why."

Carter says loons bring out his paternal instincts, but I know he dates the criminally insane only because he thinks they are completely uninhibited in bed.

"Anyway," Carter continues, "we're in a cooling-off period."

"Have you told Brigid about this?"

"Not exactly."

"Let me guess. You told her she was the most beautiful/smart/funny girl in the world, and then you realized she was actually a felon/drug addict/psychopath and stopped calling her, and now she's stalking you and you don't understand why."

Carter puts down his beer and his eyes widen. "God, you know me so well, it's scary," he says.

"I know you better than you know yourself," I say.

"That's for sure, because I don't spend any time at all getting to know myself."

"That's because you're too busy getting to know poor unstable women who you love and then leave," I say.

"Okay, okay! I forgot how much of my conscience you are. Sheesh."

"It's a dirty job, but someone has to do it," I say. "You know that all women deserve a good face-to-face breakup. We need closure."

"Even the crazy ones?"

"Especially the crazy ones."

"Och, aye, weeemon," Ian agrees, wandering back to the table.

Carter sighs and slumps his shoulders. "I know—I know. But you women scare me. With the tears and the slapping and the knee-to-the-groining. Look what you did to Ted when he gave you closure, for heaven's sake. And you're not insane, like Brigid."

"Yes, but Ted deserved it and so do you. You ought to take your knee to the groin like a man."

"I'm not good with pain," Carter says.

"At least send her a letter or an e-mail."

"A Dear John e-mail! What kind of advice are you giving me here? That's awful."

"So is not returning her calls," I say, as Carter's phone lights up again. It's Brigid, calling back. She calls back four more times in the span of the next fifteen minutes.

"I told you she was a stalker," Carter says, sighing.

Later that night, I lie in my room, listening to the sound of Carter speaking on the phone. I've finally convinced him to break up with his mystery girl. Carter knows I'm good for him. I help him be a better man even though he won't admit it.

Even louder than Carter is Ian, who is playing some kind of zombie video game.

I pull the covers over my head.

They're not Carter's nicest sheets, probably because this is the guest bedroom and rarely gets used. All of Carter's guests likely sleep with him, if at all.

I start crying, suddenly and without warning, which is what happens to me a lot these days, which is probably why Mom thinks I'm suicidal. The other day, I broke out crying right in the middle of Target, and I never cry—not even when I broke my arm when I was eight after falling off the jungle gym.

As suddenly as they come, the tears stop, and I feel about a split second of peace and then I'm back to wanting to rip Ted's head off. I hate that Ted makes me cry. I hate Ted period.

Because I can't sleep in my current state of Ted Hate and because I'm jet-lagged, I boot up Carter's computer and check my e-mail.

There's an e-mail from Ted's manager, Ed Reiner. No subject. I almost delete it without reading it, but curiosity gets the best of me. I want to know if Reiner has learned how to spell.

To: Lily0903
From: ereiner@Daytonfive.com
Lil,
Thought you'd like to know that your screwed. I just

signed Ted for a $10 million endorsement contract for
The Gap. Since it happened after you're separation,
the money is all his.
Cheers,
R
P.S. By the way, we're going to find some way to
press charges for that billboard stunt.

I take a deep breath and count to ten so that I don't rip out
the computer from the wall and hurl it out the window. I take a
few calming breaths and then I write back:

To: ereiner@Daytonfive.com
From: Lily0903
Reiner,
Your (y-oo-ur) adj. Possessive form of the word "you."
Sample sentence: "Your client's assets earned in the
last year and a half are half mine by law."
You're (y-oo-ur) Contraction of the words "you are."
Sample sentence: "You're an asshole."
Cheers,
Lily

After hitting Send, my blood pressure is still dangerously
high and there's only one way to calm me down. I sign Ted up
for the Tampax weekly preteen e-mail newsletter and an hon-
orary membership in NAMBLA, the North American Man-
Boy Love Association.

I put both Ted and Reiner on a list for gay porn. They are both homophobes, so I know it will get to them. After that, I feel much better.

Me = bad person, in case you forgot.

I drift off to sleep to the sounds of the shrill cries of the undead falling before Ian's machine gun fire. I imagine me shooting Ted, over and over and over again, blasting holes through his zombie corpse. Perhaps I do need counseling. Something, clearly, isn't right with me.

Six

REASON #6 TO DIVORCE A ROCK STAR:
His idea of a romantic date is you, him, and thirty thousand screaming fans.

On our second date, after we'd spent an hour making out in the back of a dark bar, Ted admitted to me that he had a "sort-of girlfriend." By "sort-of girlfriend," he meant a girlfriend he was no longer attracted to, but who lived with him and paid his rent. I understand now that it's just Ted's way of having relationships. He doesn't break up with one girl before he moves on to the next. It's just like car shopping. You don't sell the car you have until you know which new one you want to buy.

I should've pushed him off the barstool right then and headed for the door, but I was deep under the spell of the Mick Jagger effect and about three blue moons. And I had a sort-of boyfriend, too. The aging stockbroker, who still called and left me strained but upbeat messages on my voicemail, asking me for that elusive third date. Granted, I wasn't living with the aging stockbroker, nor had I ever had sex with him. But he was a "sort-of" date and a "sort-of" love interest.

So I listened to the stories about how Ted's sort-of girlfriend was a drug-using maniac who once sold his car to get a fix and recently got arrested for hitting a cabdriver and then refusing to pay the fare.

If I'd been sober, and not reeling from the Mick Jagger effect, I might have picked up on two (now obvious) warning signs:

1. A guy with a sort-of girlfriend who's a drug addict means he *also* is an addict. You don't date a coke fiend and refuse your share.
2. A guy who uses the phrase "sort-of girlfriend" will one day use the phrase "sort-of wife."

"Pick a card," I told Ted then at the bar, offering him up a stack of tarot cards. "I'll see if I ought to date you."

Ted drew the Sun card (freedom from restraints, creative inspiration, success, and happiness). I took that to be a good sign.

"Your turn," he said.

I drew the Fool.

"We're made for each other," Ted said, and grinned.

I toss and turn for hours, unable to sleep. I hear noises in the living room, and decide Ian's probably still up, even though it's 4:00 A.M. Thirsty, I head to the kitchen to get a glass of water, where I nearly trip over a bag full of CDs and Xbox games. I grunt and look up and see that it's not Ian making the noise, but a strange woman wearing a black track suit who is trying to dismantle Ian's Xbox.

"Who the hell are you?" she says, eyes narrowing. It's dark, so I can't quite make out her features, but I know she's thin and very pale. She's got sharp blue eyes and jet-black hair.

"Uh, I think that's my question," I say.

It takes me a moment or two to understand what's happening—she's a *thief*. She's *stealing* Carter's and Ian's stuff. I look in the bag and see my tarot cards, as well as my wallet.

"Hey! These aren't yours!" I cry and try to rescue some of my things, but only am able to get my tarot cards before she snatches the bag away from me. She gives me a hard shove, sending me backward over the couch. I hit the floor with a thud, and by then she's already out the door.

"It was Brigid," Carter says, when I describe her. "Did she look like this?" he shows me a picture of his ex-girlfriend, and it's an exact match. Same blue eyes. Same rail-thin frame.

Brigid is one of those waifs who Carter always seems to find so attractive. He goes for the Mary-Kate or Ashley Olsen type—young and pixielike with big blue eyes and shoulder blades that could cut glass. Except this one looks like Lara Flynn Boyle. She might be skinny, but she exudes an air of danger and a slight mental imbalance.

Ian—upon hearing that his Xbox was almost taken and that I helped save it—gives me a long hug and says something I don't understand, but that Carter says is his pledge to protect whatever is most important to me in return for keeping his prized Xbox safe from Brigid's clutches.

"But how did she get in?"

"I gave her a key," Carter says and shrugs.

"You gave her a key! Before or after you realized she was a felon?"

"Before. Seemed like a good idea at the time."

Brigid cleaned out the living room, including a large chunk of Carter's CD collection, a couple of Ian's games, and my Louis Vuitton bucket bag, which I'd left on the couch, containing, among other things, five hundred dollars in cash and my sister's passport.

"Are you happy now?" Carter asks me. "This is what happens when you give girls closure."

"No," I correct, "this is what happens when you give girls keys to your apartment."

"She could have killed me," Carter says, rubbing his throat. "I'm a sound sleeper, you know."

Never mind that Carter weighs 185 pounds and is nearly six feet tall and can probably bench-press me.

"Och, aye—eech—dehd," Ian says, making a slashing throat signal.

"She probably would've just cut off your pecker, but left you alive."

Carter turns white.

"That's even worse," he says.

"I'm just kidding," I say. "She probably just sat in your bedroom and watched you sleep."

"Oh God! Stop it. I won't be able to sleep for a week."

"You really are a little girl sometimes," I say.

I look up and see Ian—wearing only a pair of Christmas boxer shorts and a shirt that says SOD OFF!—throwing down his game controller and jumping on the couch, pumping his fists in the air like Tom Cruise.

"He's saved the world again," Carter explains to me.

"Too bad he couldn't save my bag," I say. "I need a smoke."

Carter sighs. "At least she didn't touch the Lennon chair," he says, getting down on one knee and rubbing the arm of the chair. He looks like he's about to propose to it.

We file a police report, but are told that it's unlikely we'll be seeing either Carter's CDs or my sister's passport again. Carter refuses to tell the police Brigid is the thief because he fears retribution. He is a total coward. Ian, wearing a SPAM T-shirt and carrying a camcorder to record what he calls "police brutality," is disheartened by the news that he won't be seeing his Resident Evil game anytime soon. He nearly starts a fight with some police officers and mumbles something that I'm pretty sure is "dumbfookinEnglish." Carter has to then explain to me that all Scots have a burning hate for the English that goes back further than William Wallace. Scots don't much care for Americans, either, but they're better than the English, which is why Ian doesn't mind living with a Yank.

"Why is he in London, then, if he hates the English so much?" I ask Carter, who shrugs.

"With Ian, you just don't ask why," Carter says.

On the ride home, I try not to think about the fact that if I still had signing privileges for Ted's Platinum American Express that I could go straight to the Ritz-Carlton and order my weight in caviar. Unfortunately, Ted cut me off from his credit cards shortly after he got the bill from the Four Seasons. I figured the least Ted owed me was keeping me temporarily in the lifestyle to which I'd grown accustomed. I figured that included room service.

Carter heads to the hospital to work, and I sit down to break the news to my sister that some crazy woman now has her passport.

"How could you let your passport be stolen?" my sister Lauren says on my phone—one of the few things that wasn't stolen. Luckily, I keep my mobile phone nearby, just in case I get the urge to prank call Ted.

"Considering that I was sleeping at the time, there wasn't much I could do," I say.

My sister, Lauren, is older and more put together than I am (classic Virgo). She's also extremely bossy (wedding planner) and freakishly neat (she's the only living person I know who actually has a closet that looks ten times neater than the ones in the catalogs from The Container Store). She also has to plan out everything meticulously in advance. When she and her husband Nick wanted to try for a baby, she had the whole bedroom covered in fertility charts. Only my sister would be able to plot her ovarian cycle down to the minute.

I love my sister, I do. But she's been trying to tell me how to live my life since I was four and she didn't approve of how I dressed my Barbies (with mismatched shoes).

We're just not the same. We have different life philosophies. I live in the moment. Lauren lives in her Palm Pilot.

"Why don't you tell me where you left the photocopy and I'll fax it to you," she's saying now.

"Photocopy?" I echo.

"You didn't copy your passport." Lauren sighs. I almost hear her put her head in her hands. "Lily, you're *always* supposed to do that. In case it gets stolen."

"I must have missed that little tidbit during the in-flight safety lecture." I clear my throat. "And, uh, well, it wasn't actually *my* passport. It was yours."

"That's impossible. My passport is in my top right desk drawer—"

"Behind your credit card statements, in that brown leather folder that also has your birth and marriage certificates in it," I finish for her.

There's a long pause on the line. "You stole my passport? Are you on drugs?"

"No! I'm not on drugs. Why does everyone think that? And *I* didn't steal your passport. Carter's crazy ex-girlfriend did."

"But you stole it first."

"I borrowed it," I say. "There's a difference."

Lauren sounds like she's hyperventilating, she's so mad. "Okay, I realize nothing you do makes sense, but can you tell me why you didn't just use your own passport?"

"Duh. I had to give it to the courthouse in Austin. I

wasn't, technically, supposed to leave the country before trial."

"I . . . can't . . . believe . . . this," Lauren chokes. "I can't be-lieve it. You are a fugitive and some crazy woman has my pass-port! Are you insane? Seriously. This is the thanks I get for looking after your dog, who, by the way, is totally destroying my house?"

Lauren is referring to my dog, Arnold the Chihuahua. He was a gift from Ted. Like Ted, he's got serious impulse control problems.

"I didn't think you could ever top burning down my house, but congratulations—you've just outdone yourself," she says.

"You know I didn't burn down your house. That was Michael, not me." Michael was my semipsychotic ex-boyfriend who didn't take well to me breaking up with him a few years ago. He burned down my sister's house because he thought I was in it. But no one died, and the insurance company gave her a check for $175,000, which she used to buy a bigger and better house, so really, when you think about it, it was all win-win.

"Do you think before you make these decisions, or is it just dumb luck that you always pick the worst possible thing to do? It's amazing you've lived this long. I'm amazed I haven't killed you yet."

"So I take it this would not be the best time to ask if you would send me another copy of your passport? I sort of need it to get back in the country."

"I don't have a copy."

"What about all that about photocopying?"

"I didn't think I'd need one, considering I didn't leave the country."

"You think you could have another one made?"

"Lily, I am so going to hang up on you right now."

"Lauren!"

"I mean it. I cannot talk about this now, or I will say something I will seriously regret."

"But the passport . . ."

"The next sound you hear is going to be a dial tone."

"Lauren—don't tell Mom and Dad, okay?"

But she doesn't answer me. Instead she hangs up. I take that as a no. I hang up and dial Lauren's favorite florist. Luckily, I've sent my sister flowers enough that the florist and I are on a first-name basis. She agrees to bill me.

"Lily—tell me you are back in the U S of A," says Larry Sullivan, when I call him the next day.

"No, not exactly," I say. "My sister's passport's been stolen."

"Sugar, you had better be telling me you're pulling my leg, or I'm going to have to slam my head against this desk right here and knock myself the hell out," Larry says.

"Not joking."

I hear a thump, sounding like Larry banging his head against his desk. He's definitely not taking this well.

"Lily, you give me more indigestion than a plate full of my mother-in-law's barbeque. You are going to be the death of me." Larry sighs. "And I heard something from Ted's manager about you *still* prank calling him. Lily, that's got to stop."

"I'm not prank calling him," I lie.

"Or signing him up for spam? For NAMBLA?"

"I have no idea what you're talking about."

"Just stop it, okay? It won't help us prove in court that you *aren't* insane. And I think that's an uphill battle already at this point."

"Thanks. How much do I pay you again an hour?"

"Not enough."

Seven

REASON #7 TO DIVORCE A ROCK STAR:

Because he will never treat you as well as he treats his guitar.

I have started asking the tarot cards the same questions. They are:

1. Will Ted come back to me?
2. If he doesn't come back to me, will Ted die soon?
3. If he doesn't die soon, can I kill him and get away with it?

The tarot is murky on the last two points, but on the first one, it's unequivocal. For that question, I always pull up the Three of Swords, the card with the heart with three swords stuck through it. That's my answer. Ted = three swords through the heart. One from him. One from Melanie Slate. And one from me for not seeing the first two before they were already in hilt-deep.

*   *   *

Ted and I dated five weeks before he decided it would be a good idea to move in with me. He had two reasons: 1) he loved me; and 2) he had nowhere else to go. He'd finally broken things off with his "sort-of girlfriend" and in response she'd kicked him out and set his belongings on fire in the Dumpster behind their apartment building. (Obvious Warning Sign You're Dating An Evil Narcissist #128: His drug-addicted ex-girlfriend gets mad enough at him to burn his stuff instead of selling it for drugs.) Ted arrived on my doorstep with the only things that survived the meltdown: the clothes on his back and his guitar, his most prized possession.

I quickly discovered what all girlfriends of guitarists know: You cannot, under any circumstances, touch his guitar.

I knew his guitar was important, but I had no idea it was a priceless artifact. For one thing, it was covered in stickers so old, most of them had peeled off and the ones that remained had a weird, unidentifiable gray sludge attached to them. On the back side of the guitar, there was a fossilized clump of someone's used gum. And there were more scratches on it than my beat-up Honda Civic.

Not to mention, he had a habit of getting drunk and then leaving it at a bar. The next morning, hungover, he'd drive around looking for it, like a lost coat or cellphone.

One night, he left his guitar on the couch and went out. I moved it, because that's the only place to sit in my living room. When he came back and found his guitar propped up against the wall, he went ballistic. Apparently, I was supposed to wait for him to return and move it, and until then refrain from sitting on my own couch or watching TV.

"This is my life. My *life*," he shouted at me. "Do you understand that this is my life? YOU CAN NEVER TOUCH IT. EVER!"

He stormed out of the apartment, his guitar in hand. He came home drunk, six hours later, without his guitar, and curled me up in his arms.

"I'm a dick. I'm sorry. Why do you put up with me? I love you. I love you more than anything. I love you more than my guitar. I love you that much."

I should've known that how he treated his guitar—his most prized possession—would be the way he would treat me. He'd neglect me, too, and abandon me in seedy bars. But if someone else tried to touch me, he'd shout and rant and rave.

I can't find my tarot cards the next morning, and, well, I freak out.

"What are you *looking* for?" Carter asks me, as I toss everything I own that wasn't stolen by Carter's ex out on his guest bed, frantically turning over everything in sight.

"My *cards*," I sigh, as if it's obvious. I feel like I can't breathe, and I'm sure this isn't a good sign. I realize I probably have an unhealthy fixation on the tarot cards, but they're so confident in their decisions, and I am, well, not at this point. I need impartial advice, and if it comes from a deck of cards designed in the nineteenth century, so be it.

"You realize they don't *actually* tell the future," Carter tells me.

I throw some jeans across the room and slump on my bed. I feel like crying again. Why do I always feel like crying? The tightness in my chest turns into the old familiar heart squeeze. It feels like my heart is shrinking.

"I know, but . . ." But they're the only way I seem to know what's going on with Ted, especially now that he's gone. I feel so lost, and well, they seem to be able to point out a direction to me, even if it is a bad one. They are also the only thing that can answer the question: why. Why did Ted leave me? Why is Ted an asshole? Answer: Because we told you he was an asshole in the first place. Not to mention, I need the tarot cards to tell me if I'm going to jail or not.

"They help me make decisions," I say.

"You can make decisions on your own," Carter tells me.

I try to think about the last time I made a good decision. The only one I can think of is leaving Ted.

"Here they are," Carter says, grabbing the box of cards. They were poking out from under my bed. I guess I hadn't looked there yet.

I feel my lower lip start to wobble. Carter shakes his head. "Don't cry! There's no crying in my apartment, okay?" he says, wrapping me up in a hug. It feels good. Too good. Has Carter been working out? His arms feel stronger and firmer. I fit so perfectly in the crook of his arm. I just want to stay here forever.

Carter pulls away first.

"I know what will cheer you up," he says.

Rebound sex? I think, but don't say. I am half hoping that's what he has in mind. Carter's skin on mine seems like a good idea, which probably shows me just how out of sorts I actually am. I'm seriously considering sex with Carter!

"What?"

"Sightseeing," Carter says, sounding excited. I try not to be disappointed. A tour of London is probably just what I need.

Carter is being so good to me, I feel like I have to tell him the truth about my fugitive status.

"What the hell," Carter shouts when I fess up and tell him that he might be harboring a fugitive (me), since I've broken the terms of my bail. "You didn't see fit to mention this *before* you crossed the Atlantic Ocean. Jesus Christ, Lil."

Carter, who doesn't break the law, even to jaywalk, is visibly upset.

We're standing with a tour group of mostly Americans at the Tower of London. I can tell they're Americans because half of them are wearing fanny packs, and all of them have on bright white tennis shoes. Our guide is dressed like the Beefeater Gin guy and is in the middle of a story about Anne Boleyn.

"What were you thinking?" Carter shouts, louder than he intends, causing others in the group to turn to look at us. He lowers his voice to a whisper. "Seriously, what were you thinking?"

"Look, I just thought I'd pop over and then pop back, no big deal," I say. "I didn't expect my passport to get stolen."

"Right, but it is a big deal," Carter says. "You could go to jail."

"Not if you help me get back that passport."

Carter turns white.

"I'm not going to contact Brigid."

"You have to—I'll go to jail!"

"Lily, you don't know what she's capable of. She's already committed a *felony.*"

The Beefeater Guy sends us a dirty look. The rest of the tour group is trying to separate themselves from us.

Carter lowers his voice. "Anyway, what makes you think she didn't burn that passport? You think she'd want to keep the passport of one of my exes around?"

"Maybe she'll use it for voodoo."

"Great. Just great. That's probably the cause of the stabbing pain in my chest."

"No, that's just your fear of confrontation."

"Look, I'll think about it, okay? I'll *think* about it. Now, let's listen to the tour. People are staring at us."

The Beefeater Guy is telling us about how Henry the Eighth married his second wife, Anne Boleyn, in the tower and then had her executed at the same location three years later.

"That's a lousy settlement," I say.

The Beefeater Guy lowers his voice and tells us that Anne Boleyn's ghost still walks the tower today.

"Women are crazy even after they're dead," Carter says.

"But her husband killed her!"

"Yes, but can't she just move on? She's dead, for crying out loud. Yes, he was a homicidal maniac, but I mean, stalking him after death? That's a little too obsessive, isn't it?"

"What are you talking about? Henry asked for it. He could have at least had the decency to execute her at a place *other* than where she had her wedding reception." I feel my blood pressure rising.

"Lil—calm down. I am kidding. You remember kidding? Anyway, back off from your donkey stance. I don't want to be kicked here."

I guess I have that tense, ready-to-spring look.

"I'm not going to kick you," I say.

"That's a relief."

"Yet, anyway."

The rest of the tour gives us more dirty looks. Apparently, we're like those people who just won't shut up during the movie at the theater.

"Let's go to Madame Tussaud's," Carter suggests. "That's more our speed."

Ted's manager accused me once of being a gold digger, which is ironic because when we first dated, Ted had about ten dollars to his name.

He liked to split his time between borrowing money from me and telling me what he'd buy me when his first single went platinum. My friends called him Rock Star Ted—ironically, because he was broke and mostly played cover songs.

"I'd settle for a loan repayment," I joked.

"Daddy will pay you back in diamonds," he'd say.

Ted often referred to himself in the third person, specifically as "Daddy."

"Daddy's working now," he'd say, even when he wasn't, even when he was watching *The Daily Show* on Comedy Central. He would say, "Daddy likes" when I made him a grilled cheese sandwich, or when I'd offer to rub his shoulders. Every once in a while, he'd save it and say it during serious moments of foreplay—and every time, it would make me laugh.

"That's so wrong," I'd say, laughing so sharply I'd snort.

"You mad at Daddy?" he'd ask, innocently, making a funny face.

When I shut my eyes, I can see Ted as I last saw him, the day I moved out. He looked contrite, sad even, as he said, "I guess Daddy's really messed up this time."

I find myself thinking about Ted because we're standing in the middle of the Chamber of Horrors exhibit at Madame Tussaud's Wax Museum, and Ted bears a striking resemblance to the masked torturer who is about to boil in oil a very nice-looking girl accused of witchcraft. But then again, maybe I'm being too harsh. Ted would never boil someone in oil. He doesn't, after all, know how to boil water, much less an actual person.

"You'll find someone a hundred times better than Ted," Carter says, interrupting my thoughts. He puts his hands on my shoulders and rubs the spot that always gets tense, my upper left shoulder. He rubs it gently, and instantly, the tension leaves me. He remembers my spot, I think. I wonder what other spots he remembers.

I shake myself. I must be sex-starved to be salivating over Carter.

"How did you know I was thinking about Ted?" I ask him.

"You were looking like you were contemplating ripping that wax figure's head off."

"That explains it."

"Seriously, I mean it. Don't be down. You'll find someone better."

I find getting love advice from Carter ironic, considering his ex-girlfriend just burglarized his apartment.

Carter glances over my shoulder and suddenly looks stricken.

"Why don't we get out of here?" Carter seems a bit nervous.

"Why? Is Brigid stalking us?"

"No, but I'm bored with this place. Why don't we go?" Carter has his hand around my elbow and is steering me to the door.

"Carter! If it's one of your exes, you're going to have to learn to deal with them like a . . ." I've turned around to see who is making Carter so nervous, and that's when I see them.

Ted—in wax form—standing next to . . . Melanie Slate. They're *holding hands.*

She looks even skankier in wax form. She's wearing too much lipgloss and not enough skirt.

"They're a wax couple now?" I say. Even to myself, I sound sad and defeated. Seeing them in a museum makes it seem so official somehow.

Carter now has one arm in front of me like he's trying to protect me from a car crash or prevent me from running forward and knocking off their heads. The idea of playing soccer with them holds some appeal. But the thought of being arrested in Great Britain with the tabloid headline of "Dayton Ex Goes Wild on Wax Melanie" doesn't.

I take a deep breath.

"Are you okay?" Carter's coifed hair droops a bit in concern.

"Yes, I'm fine," I say. "You can let go of me now."

"You sure? You still have that psychotic I'm-going-to-vandalize-private-property look in your eye."

"I'm fine, really."

"You sure you don't want to go kick Ted? He's a standing target."

"It doesn't give me the same satisfaction if he's not rolling on the ground cursing at me."

"Remind me never, *ever,* to piss you off."

Eight

REASON #8 TO DIVORCE A ROCK STAR:
Rock star is the only profession where it's okay if you show up to work inebriated.

The thing about dating a borderline drug addict is that it's not boring. Ted had severe mood swings. One day he would love me with a kind of scary, fixated passion, like I was the only person in the world. He'd call me five or six times in one day. He'd beg me to call in sick to work and spend the day with him. The next day, he would disappear for hours and not tell me where he went. Or he'd go into violent rages (typically against our furniture) when he faced any of life's minor setbacks, including parking tickets or canceled gigs.

Unlike Nancy Reagan, I never had a strong stance on drugs. I'd dabbled in pot in college, but never anything more serious than that. Ted, on the other hand, sampled them all. He particularly liked coke. He said it made him feel invincible. I tried coke once, but I didn't like it. My sinuses went numb and I felt like me, only me as an asshole.

I never thought much of it, although I should've. But I expected a musician to dabble in mood-altering drugs. If you have a really talented rock star, he's got to be a little unhinged. That's part of his rebel charm. Who wants a mild-mannered, well-adjusted rock star? They're rock stars. If they don't destroy at least one hotel room, it's like they're just not serious about their careers.

The thing is, I liked Ted's mood swings. I liked not knowing which Ted I was going to get. I always felt off balance being with him, and I liked it. What's the fun in having a safe, predictable guy? That's why you date a rock star and not an accountant.

And Ted didn't seem like one of those people in the downward spiral of drug movies where he would get so desperate for a fix, he'd sell his own mother's TV and then his mother herself to feed his habit. Ted got drugs when he had the money and when he didn't, he went without.

But I suppose now it seems logically that there's no such thing as a mild drug problem.

At Carter's apartment, I am so furious about the wax figures that I really feel the need to kick something. That's how it always is with Ted. First, I feel sad, then hurt, and then I get so angry that I want to commit a violent act. Clearly, I'm better off without him.

It doesn't help that when I log on to check my e-mail there's a reply from Reiner. Ted's manager never knew when to quit:

To: Lily0903
From: ereiner@Daytonfive.com
Subject: Stop Spamming
Lil,
I don't know what you mean to prove by stalking Ted, but you're e-mails have got to stop. We know your signing Ted up for spam. I'm writing to let you know he's changed his e-mail address and if you insist on trying to overload the Dayton Five website with spam, we're going to have to find a way to press charges.
R

Despite the single-minded stubbornness of Reiner's poor grammar, my chakras are at a boil, and I doubt even the downward facing dog position is going to help me. It's really just the last straw. There's only one thing to do. I start working on a bogus press release.

URGENT—FOR IMMEDIATE RELEASE
Contact: Ed Reiner, Manager, Dayton Five

Dayton Five Singer Admitted to Hospital for Rare Strain of Genital Herpes

Award-winning pop sensation the Dayton Five have suspended their upcoming tour dates since Ted Dayton, singer and founder of the band, was hospitalized yesterday with a rare and highly contagious strain of genital herpes. Doctors have quarantined the Austin native to run a series of tests.

Scientists believe he may be suffering from a new and treatment-resistant strain of the virus. Band manager Ed Reiner said he believes the band will be back on tour in three weeks. "We're hoping he doesn't need surgery, but the band will stand by him, whatever the case."

I send it off from a bogus Hotmail account to a few of Reiner's magazine contacts (he once made the mistake of giving me part of his media contact list). I think it's well-established by now that I'm a bad person. I can live with that.

But, after the anger fades, I'm left, as usual, in a deep depression.

I spend the next few days on Carter's couch consuming my weight in (British-style) Cadbury chocolate.

I'd been doing so well and now, here I am, on the couch, unable to move. It's official: I've fallen off the rebound wagon. Even worse, I'm back to watching Melanie Slate movies.

It's slow torture, and I don't know why I do it to myself, I really don't. I'm watching her in perfect makeup, her thin arms and perky, gravity-defying boobs, and all I can think is: That's why he left me. Those boobs. That butt. Those lips. That come-hither smile. I'm pretty sure I know Melanie Slate's body better than most of her best stalkers. And no, it doesn't make me feel better that she probably has a team of specialists to help her look the way she does (makeup person, hair stylist, personal trainer, and, of course, plastic surgeon). What does make me feel better is listening to Melanie recite stilted dialogue that sounds as if English is her second language.

"I'm worried about you," Carter tells me a few days later when he comes back from his shift at the hospital to find me, once again, in front of the television, with tarot cards scattered across his coffee table.

Ian left hours ago, when it became clear that my tarot cards could not properly predict the winner of his Xbox tournament. "Are those cards telling you to get off your butt and do something constructive?"

"No, they're saying what they always say—that I'm on a path to self-destruction and that I'm doomed."

"Nice and upbeat, those tarot cards."

"I know."

"Why is it that you use them again?"

"Because I can't be trusted to make my own decisions."

"Oh, yes, right—I forgot," Carter says.

The TV is tuned to *House of Screams*—one of Melanie Slate's earlier films, where she plays a teen sex addict who is sliced to pieces by a psychotic axe-wielding murderer who doesn't believe in premarital sex.

"Not this again," Carter says, slumping into a chair next to me.

"But this is my favorite scene," I say, speeding up the DVD to the point where Melanie Slate—mascara streaking down her face—is running in the dark woods screaming her head off.

"Listen, there is something seriously wrong with you. Why do you want to watch her get killed over and over again?"

"Um, as if that isn't obvious." I watch as Melanie falls into a muddy puddle and ruins what's left of her makeup. "Actually, I don't even care about her death scene. I just like it that she looks like crap. Her hair is a mess, and she has snot coming out of her nose."

"But she's also in a wet shirt and she's not wearing a bra." Leave it to Carter to point that out. I give him a sharp look, and he shrugs. "What? I'm just saying. Guys won't be looking at her hair."

I frown at him and click off the TV. Watching Melanie Slate get an axe to the skull normally cheers me up, but seeing it from Carter's guy-vision perspective has sucked the joy right out of it.

"Look, I know you're depressed, but don't you think you ought to get dressed? I think you've been wearing the same pajamas for four days." Carter is close to using *that tone*.

"Well, it's not like I can go anywhere since I don't have my passport. Have you called Brigid?"

"You mean your sister's passport. And Brigid is not returning my calls, which is probably the first sane thing she's done since we broke up."

"That's not like one of your love-sick puppies," I say.

Carter shrugs.

"Don't change the subject. We were talking about your clinical depression. Seriously. Get dressed, why don't you?"

"I don't have anywhere to go."

"Come with me to the hospital tomorrow. Didn't you say

you needed to volunteer? Trust me, there are plenty of people who need help there."

"I'll probably accidentally kill one of them."

"Only if you practiced your Tae Bo."

I'm left with no choice but to go with Carter. I suppose it couldn't hurt my karma. And the way I'm going, I'll probably come back in the next life as a mole on some teen pop star's ass. I'm not sure whether or not it would be a step down from my current life, and that tells me I'm definitely in a bad spiritual place.

Carter wakes me up at what feels like 3:00 in the morning, even though it's much closer to 7:00. I'm still a little jet-lagged even after a week in London, and even before that, I wasn't used to getting up for a regular job. I'm not sure how Carter is supposed to be able to operate on people when all I want to do is swim in a giant bucket of espresso.

After some time standing in front of my open suitcase, I realize that being a rock star's wife didn't properly prepare me for the working world. I have far too many red-carpet outfits and not enough regular clothes.

I settle on my most conservative outfit, which is somewhere in between Sheryl Crow and Paris Hilton.

Outside, the morning is bright and cold, and I'm underdressed because in Austin there is no such thing as fall. There are two seasons, summer and December. My suede coat with the pink fake-fur trim isn't designed to keep me either warm or dry.

I've got on my oversize aviator sunglasses, which are hiding my bloodshot and puffy eyes, but are making it difficult to see in the cloudy, overcast day. I ate my weight in fish and chips the night before, and so my clothes are tighter than usual. I wish I had sunglasses for my ass. My jeans are pinching into my sides, and my chakras feel like they're retaining more water than the Hoover dam.

We squeeze into a subway car, where Carter pushes his way fearlessly into the corner.

"Elbow anyone who comes into your swiping radius," Carter instructs. "Otherwise, they'll get you first."

I'm sandwiched in between some men in suits and a woman whose breath is so bad I think she must have eaten road kill for breakfast. I'm tempted to try to offer her an Altoid, but it's far too cramped for me to even think of getting to my purse, and so I just hold my breath and dream about the stretch limo with the full-service bar that ferried me off to the MTV Music Awards.

I miss the limo so much that I'm thinking that I'm starting to miss Ted, too.

As soon as this thought bounces into my head, I squash it like a roach. I can't afford to let thoughts like that nest and multiply.

We arrive at the hospital around 8:30. It is interesting to see Carter in that white coat. He's got everything but the stethoscope, which he said he abandoned because doctors who fix broken bones look pretty silly with a stethoscope around their necks. You can't listen to broken bones.

Even in England, where medicine is socialized, doctors still get a lot of respect. All the nurses seem particularly in awe of them, and more than a few nurses, I notice, seem to have crushes on Carter. After a quick survey of the other doctors (mostly old and tired-looking versions of Tony Blair), I can see right away why he's got most of the attention. He's the Hot Young Doctor, which is a catch no matter what side of the Atlantic you live on.

Carter introduces me to the desk nurse to get settled for volunteer duties. Her name is Becca, and she looks almost exactly like Baby Spice, complete with platinum pigtails in her nurse's habit and boobs that want to spring out of her nurse's uniform. She looks like a walking centerfold.

"I don't date doctors, yeah?" Becca tells me right off.

I'm not sure what to say to that. I look at Carter, who only shrugs.

"I just want you to know, yeah?" Becca continues. She ends every sentence with "yeah" so that everything she says sounds like a rhetorical question. "There's nothing going on between Dr. Henry and me, yeah? He dates a lot of crazy birds, so I don't want you to go into a jealousy frenzy or anything."

I see his reputation has caught up with him, even here.

"We're not dating," I point out.

"Well, it's Dr. Henry, so you never know. But, believe me, he's all yours, yeah?"

"Thank you, Becca," Carter says.

"Dr. Henry would be the only man in London you wouldn't date," says another woman, who emerges from the file closet. She's not wearing a nurse's uniform. She's dressed in plain clothes: a puke green argyle sweater, a forest green plaid kilt, and rubber clogs.

"Shut it, Sal," Becca growls.

"Nice to meet you," the walking fashion disaster says, shaking my hand with a firm grip. "I do the paperwork around here, but only to have something to do until my parents leave me their fortune. My family owns an estate in Wiltshire. It once belonged to the Duke of York."

"Maybe five hundred years ago," Becca adds.

Sal wrinkles her nose at Becca and trots off to the restroom.

"I'm so bloody sick of Sal's Duke of York crap," Becca says, rolling her eyes. "Her family's rich, right? But she's working here? Doesn't make no sense, does it, though, yeah? Don't bother trying to borrow anything off of her, right? She's megaskint, yeah? But somehow she manages to travel halfway 'round the world every summer? Exactly. S'pose that's how they get all that money though, init? By being right tight buggers the lot of 'em. I mean, look at the queen. She eats off of Tupperware. It was in the *Daily Mirror,* so it has to be true, yeah?"

Becca talks so quickly it's like she's doesn't have to breathe.

"On that note, I'm off to make my rounds," Carter says. "You think you'll be okay?"

"I promise I won't kick anyone," I say.

"That's a good start," Carter says, smiling at me.

"So, it's true about you and the lead singer out of Dayton Five, yeah?" Becca asks, the minute Carter has gone.

"Bloody typical. Dr. Henry said we weren't supposed to say

anything." Sal frowns at Becca as she returns to the desk.

"You guys know of the Dayton Five?" I ask.

"Only because of Melanie Slate. She's more popular than Sienna Miller around here. Is it true you got into a fight with her?"

I sigh. "Yes."

"Nice one," Becca adds. "I reckon she's a right tart, me, and not even that fit, really. That slapper would shag Alan Partridge if she thought it'd make the glossies in *Hello!* magazine."

"You're one to talk," Sal says.

Becca throws a pen at Sal, but she dodges it easily.

"So? Tell us, what was it like?" Becca says. "You know, being married to a rock star, yeah?"

I think about the time that Ted came home from his first tour. He hurled a plate of spaghetti across the room, missing me by inches, splattering the wall with shards of glass and pasta strands. He claimed he hated marinara sauce. If I loved him, I would've known that.

"No different than being married to any other kind of narcissist," I said.

"But what was it *like,*" Becca insists.

There are lots of answers to this question. None of them are what anyone wants to hear. The truth is: You wait around a lot. You wait while he's on tour. You wait while he's being interviewed. You wait while he talks to fans. You wait while he practices. You wait while he writes songs. You wait while he records songs. And then you wait around while he cheats on you.

And then you wait until he leaves you.

But that's not the answer people want.

"I met Sting and I got lots of free clothes," I say.

"Wicked," Becca says, eyes bright. "Go on. What kind of clothes did you get, yeah?"

Nine

REASON #9 TO DIVORCE A ROCK STAR:

They can write love songs and breakup songs about you.

The tabloids said that Ted proposed to me in Las Vegas after hammering tequila shots in the bar at the Hard Rock Hotel. The truth is far less romantic.

Ted proposed to me in the emergency room after getting his stomach pumped. It was a week before he would be going to Las Vegas for his first opening set for the Killers.

He'd been out with the band and made the mistake of taking Valium he thought was speed, along with a bottle of Jack Daniel's. The band's drummer, Terrance, asked me to come pick him up because he couldn't stand up. It was three in the morning and I'd been at home sleeping.

I knew it was bad because four shots of antifreeze wouldn't have fazed him. Ted could consume more alcohol than Slash and still manage to perform a roadside sobriety test with frightening precision.

Ted passed out in the passenger seat of my Civic, and when he wouldn't respond to me shaking him, or shouting at him, I drove him straight to the hospital. Later, the doctor at the ER told me that, along with the Valium, Ted had had traces of alcohol, pot, cocaine, and some speed. His heart rate was through the roof.

"You saved my life," he'd said when he woke up. "What would I do without you?"

The thing about dating an addict is that they *need* you like no one else needs you. No one ever needed me as much as Ted. It's why it's so fulfilling being an enabler. No one was as grateful to me as Ted was. No one in my life ever depended on me before. I was the irresponsible sister, the out-there friend. But Ted trusted me to look after him. He was the only one.

"Lily, no one cares for me like you do. Marry me. Be my wife."

"You can't be serious."

"Why not? Don't you love me?"

"Yes."

"Then marry me."

"No."

"You don't love me! God, I'm going to die."

"Of course I love you."

"Say you'll marry me, or I'll die," he said. "Say yes, or I'll literally die without you."

"Yes," I said.

I realize now that accepting a proposal in the emergency

room is not the smartest thing to do. I also realize that codependency is not, as much as it seems, a good foundation for a relationship.

Becca shows me around the hospital and gives me a running commentary on all the patients.

"That's the room with Patrick, John, and Celia. Patrick's an arse and hates everybody. Celia's a sweetheart, but can't remember where she is, and John is a vegetable. A total mess, poor bloke."

So much for patient confidentiality.

"That's Clint, who's a hypochondriac, who also happens to have a bad case of blood poisoning. And Denise, who had hip replacement surgery this week, yeah?"

We come to a room with a guard outside.

"And this," Becca says, her voice building into an urgent hushed whisper, "is Sean Gates's room."

"Who?"

"Sean *Gates. The* Sean Gates." My face must look blank because she frowns. "Oh, bollocks. I forgot I'm talking to a bloody Yank, yeah? He's a striker for Arsenal. Broke his foot last Saturday. Was in for surgery yesterday. Your Dr. Henry helped on that, yeah?"

"Arsenal?"

"Football club, dear God, but you really don't know anything, do you, yeah? No one's supposed to go in, but it doesn't keep the paparazzi from trying. We had one sneak in here as a curry take-away bloke, if you can believe it."

"So he's famous?"

"More than the queen," Becca says. "And bleedin' gorgeous, as well. Makes David Beckham look like Rowan Atkinson."

I must look blank again, because she says, "You know, Mr. Bean, yeah?"

"Oh, right," I say, nodding, but she just shakes her head at me, appalled by my abysmal British pop culture knowledge.

"He's going to be here at least a month, the doctors say."

"His injury is that bad?"

"No, his behavior is. Arsenal's manager wants to make sure he heals properly, and that means twenty-four-hour surveillance. The team is paying for the room. They want to guard their investment." Becca nods at the room. "So that room is off limits, but you can go about anywhere else."

"So what should I do with the patients?" I ask.

"What can you do?"

"I can read tarot cards."

"Let me see them," she says, grabbing the cards and leafing through them. This is a tarot no-no. You're not supposed to let other people manhandle your cards. It messes up the cards' energy or aura or something. Becca digs into the pack and picks out the Death card.

"We had a bad experience before," she tells me.

My first patient reading is Patrick, an elderly man who had his hip replaced. He tells me the cards are "bloody rubbish," but listens intently when I tell him he might soon lose all his money.

He looks so disappointed that I quickly start making up good news, just so he doesn't think that the hospital, as he put it, is "robbing him blind."

After that, I decide just to lie for the readings. Whatever cards come up, I say they are positive.

"That's a very ugly card," says Denise, one of the patients who can't get out of bed. She's looking at the Devil card. It has a menacing horned devil with a naked man and a woman chained to its feet as slaves.

"It means you're going to have visitors very soon," I say.

"Demon visitors?"

"No, people you like. Your grandkids," I say, but not very convincingly. The chained slaves don't look like children. "By the way, is there a smoking lounge in here somewhere?"

She blinks at me. "We're in hospital," she says. "They generally discourage smoking."

By the end of the afternoon, I've talked to a woman who has breast cancer, a man who fell four stories and severed his spinal cord, and two stroke victims. I feel like, compared to these people, my problems are about the size of an iPod nano.

I wonder if this newfound perspective means I'm becoming more mature. For the record, being mature sucks. Having perspective makes me feel like total crap.

While I'm contemplating this fact, a very frazzled-looking Carter walks quickly past me, oblivious. He has the fear of God on his face.

"Carter! What are you . . ."

He looks back at me, startled, and then quickly puts himself behind me, putting a chart up to hide his face.

"Brigid," he hisses at me, nodding toward the folder, in the direction of a petite, well-dressed woman in her late twenties. Said woman is busy having a conversation with Sal at the nurse's station.

"What's she doing here?"

"She, uh, works here. She's sort of a hospital administrator."

"Carter! You didn't date someone from *the hospital.*"

"Technically, she's the hospital's director. Almost everyone reports to her."

"Even worse," I say.

"I'm here all the time, Lil. Where else am I going to meet people? Besides, it's better than dating a patient."

"Only slightly better."

"Crap! Here she comes. I've got to hide." Carter ducks behind a nearby medical cart and out of view.

Coward.

I turn around, ready to face a psychotic ex. I've met plenty of Carter's exes, one of whom threw a brick through his windshield (while he was in the car), but this one—Brigid—actually shoved me over a couch, so it's a bit personal.

She looks less insane than when I last saw her poking around Carter's living room and trying to steal Ian's Xbox.

She looks put together in a black suit and heels. She definitely looks capable enough of running a hospital. She also looks like she could do some serious damage with those stilettos. I can see why Carter chose to hide. But then again, in daylight she's also pretty much drop-dead gorgeous. I feel a pang of jealousy. Why do all of Carter's girlfriends have to be so gorgeous, and so . . . thin?

"Brigid?" I call, and she turns her head.

"Yes? May I help you?" She's all professional. She could anchor a desk at the BBC.

"We met in Carter's living room? When you were stealing all his stuff," I remind her.

"I'm sorry?" she says, her face a perfect mask of confusion. She's pretending like we never met.

"You are Carter's ex-girlfriend. The one who stole his CDs? Look, I understand. I do. If I still had a key to my ex's house, I would take a U-Haul to it. But, the problem is, you stole my passport and I need it back."

"I'm afraid I don't know what you're talking about."

"Uh, maybe this will help?" I put my hair back, and I strike a pose as if I'm about to fall over a couch. She still refuses to recognize me. "Look, my name is Lily and . . ."

Brigid's well-polished veneer shows a tiny crack. "Lily?" she says, instant recognition flitting across her face. She's not happy to see me. "I've heard a lot about you." She gives me a once-over. "Carter talks about you all the time." Brigid frowns. "He didn't say you were so . . . uh, stylish . . . and curvy."

Brigid says the word "curvy" as if she really meant to say "morbidly obese."

"Carter is here," I say. "He'd like to talk to you."

I reach around the medical cart and grab Carter and pull him up to his feet. Carter spins around as if he's expecting

Glenn Close to jump out of a bathtub with a butcher knife.

"Brigid! Um, hi, I didn't see you there." Carter looks like a cornered animal. His eyes are darting back and forth, looking for escape routes. "I was, uh, tying my shoe."

Brigid and I look down at his shoes. They're loafers.

Carter clears his throat.

"Carter wants to apologize," I tell Brigid, who quirks an eyebrow.

"I do?" he squeaks.

"He does?" she says, skeptical.

"He does," I say. "Because he's been an ass. He led you on, and for that he's sorry. He deserved to get his apartment burglarized. He also wants you to give my passport back."

Carter starts to say something, but I step on his foot.

"I didn't burgle his apartment," Brigid says.

"I saw you," I say. "You were there."

Brigid looks at me.

"I really don't know what you're talking about." You have to hand it to her. She's really tenacious when she wants to stick with a lie.

"Can I have that passport back now?"

She frowns at me. "I didn't burgle your apartment," she says, looking at Carter, who shrugs.

"I never said you did," he says.

"Carter," I cry, looking at him. What? Now I've just *imagined* that I found Brigid in the living room and that she shoved me over the couch?

"Is it true? Are you apologizing?" Brigid asks Carter.

I step harder on his foot. He grunts and nods, unable to speak.

"I think you guys have some talking to do," I say. I push them both into a nearby supply closet and shut the door, holding the doorknob so Carter can't get out.

He tries, but I hold firm.

"Are you trying to leave?" Brigid asks on the other side of the door.

"No, no—why would you think that?" Carter says.

"Get my passport back!" I shout through the door.

"What the bloody hell?" Becca says, walking by.

"I've got Brigid and Carter in there," I whisper. "I'm making them talk things through."

"Dr. Henry? He's *talking* to an ex-girlfriend? Has hell frozen over?"

"I know."

"Can you hear what's going on?"

We both strain to listen, but we hear only low murmurs. Sal trots by then.

"What's up with you two?"

"Dr. Henry and Brigid are in there. They're talking," says Becca.

"Talking to an ex! Call Guinness Book of World Records," Sal says.

"I know!" Becca presses her ear to the door.

"Did he run out of hiding spaces?" Sal asks me.

"I outed him," I say.

"Bloody brilliant," Becca says.

"Maybe he'll finally have a mature breakup with someone," Sal says.

"No, I'm guessing he'll take the easy way out. He'll get back with her," Becca says.

"You think?"

"I'll bet you ten quid."

"Done," Sal and I both say.

Half an hour later, the door opens. We all scatter, back toward the nurse's station, and pretend to be minding our own business. We shouldn't have bothered. Brigid and Carter are wrapped up in themselves and oblivious to the world.

We watch as the two of them kiss and Brigid ruffles Carter's hair.

I don't believe it. Carter is even more of a coward than I thought. And I was putting him somewhere between the Cowardly Lion and Fraidy Cat.

"You both owe me ten quid," Becca cries, holding out her hand.

"So? Dinner later?" Brigid asks Carter.

"Wouldn't miss it!" Carter calls after her.

Carter ambles over to us, while Brigid takes off down the hall. Carter watches her walk away.

"Did you get back together with her?" I cry.

"Of course! What did you expect to happen if you locked us in a room? You know I'm scared to death of her."

"You agreed to get back with her because you were afraid to say no?"

"She robbed my apartment, Lil. She's not stable. You're not supposed to provoke the insane."

"That's not exactly a good relationship foundation," Sal points out.

"Well, she is pretty hot," Carter says: "And you know that crazy women are totally uninhib—"

I nudge him, hard, with my elbow.

"What?" he asks me.

"You have lipstick on your face," Becca says.

Carter frantically wipes at his face. "Is it gone?" he asks.

"You're pathetic," I say. I'm unreasonably annoyed that he and Brigid have made up and made out, it seems. What did I expect? Locking Carter in a room with an attractive and clearly mentally unbalanced woman would lead to only one conclusion—sex. Still, I'm irked. Pissed, even.

"Did you at least get my passport?" I snap.

"It, uh, didn't come up," Carter says, grinning at me.

I frown. It's not funny. Not at all funny.

"You are completely and totally worthless," I say.

"I second that," Becca says.

"Third," agrees Sal.

The day goes downhill from there. Carter skips out on me for dinner to go out with Brigid. I take the tube home alone, squashed next to an adolescent listening to Dayton Five's album at the loudest possible setting, so that her earphones are acting like minispeakers, booming Ted's voice directly into my ear.

I hear Ted singing, *I'm drowning in your love; drowning in your soul; drowning in your hair, drowning . . .* The song makes me want to poke out my eyes. I'm filled with an irrational rage.

I should've known it would be only a matter of time before the Dayton Five landed on this side of the Atlantic. I guess I was holding out hope that the British would have better taste than everyone in North America. Now I realize it's just more evidence that no matter how far away I move, Ted will always manage to follow me.

"Your earphones are too loud," I say, pointing to her ears. I would move away, but I'm wedged where I am between the girl with the earphones and a guy with an umbrella that he periodically uses to poke me in the shin.

She turns away from me, ignoring me. I tap her on the shoulder again. "EARPHONES," I shout, pointing to my ears. Other people on the tube, who are remarkably quiet, start to stare at me.

The girl with the earphones says, "Sod off," and turns back to her corner of the train, just as I hear the next Dayton Five song cue up. It's not just a random single, it's the *whole damn album.* I feel that same pent-up, pre-Hulk transformation rage that came over me the night I kicked Ted. And I know, with crystal clarity, that this is all his fault.

I get off the train three stops too early and start walking home. I stop in an Internet café. I am filled with Ted rage. I decide to write a letter to *The New York Times.*

> *Dear Times Editor,*
> *I read your piece on Civil Unions for Gay and Les-*

bian Couples with some interest, since I, myself, am gay.
With the strong support of Melanie Slate, I finally have
the courage to come out of the closet, and I want to ap-
plaud The Times *for taking the issue of homophobia so*
seriously. It is my hope that one day we can all live as
equals.

> *Sincerely,*
> *Ted Dayton*
> *The Dayton Five*

I start to e-mail the letter and realize that perhaps I should listen to the heart chakra. That's where forgiveness lives, Fran used to say.

My heart chakra is telling me that Ted's an asshole. After all, if he wasn't homophobic in the first place (he often says someone or something is "gay" if he doesn't like it), then the letter wouldn't bother him, would it?

I hit Send and immediately feel calmer.

At Carter's apartment, I find a box sitting on his stoop.

I lean down for a closer look and see the box says CAUTION: LIVE ANIMAL on the side.

I look inside and see the tiny, cowering figure of a Chihuahua.

Crap.

It's Arnold, the dog that Ted gave me as a wedding gift. This is Lauren's doing. I guess she's still pissed at me. The flowers I sent did no good, I see. She must have shipped Arnold across the Atlantic. I don't know how she got around customs, but I don't think I really want to know.

Time to start taking some responsibility, Lauren's note reads. I wonder how much it cost her to ship Arnold here.

I pick up the dog kennel, and a small dribble of dog pee leaks out onto the toe of my shoe. Arnold is incontinent and more neurotic and needy than I am. After my separation with Ted, I left him in the backseat of Ted's Porsche 911. I'm sure he drenched those leather bucket seats.

The thought of Ted's car reeking of Chihuahua pee makes me feel a sudden fondness for Arnold, and I take him out of his plastic cage. He's a lot heavier and fatter than I remember. He's definitely put on weight. I doubt he'd fit in any of my small handbags anymore.

He's shaking uncontrollably and looking like he's suffering from post-traumatic stress syndrome. It's either the long flight or being left alone with Lauren, who probably tried to have him house-trained. As I'm holding him, another dribble of pee leaks out of him and drips down my arm.

Arnold, sensing my disapproval, licks my face.

"I'm no attorney, Ms. Crandell, but I'm going to say that I don't think you can get child support for a dog," says Larry Sullivan's secretary, Paulina. I can't get my own lawyer on the phone, so I'm resorting to asking advice from anyone who will talk to me in his office.

"But he's like a child—he cries all the time, especially if you put him down for longer than one second."

Arnold, who is the only creature on earth lazier than me, doesn't like to walk. He prefers being carried, preferably in a designer bag. If you put a leash on him and put him on the ground he just stands there and looks at you with one tiny paw in the air until you pick him up again. And if you put him in anything that isn't genuine leather, he'll pee all over it, and he'll be sure to save a few dribbles for your sleeve.

"I'll tell Mr. Sullivan you called—again," Paulina says. "And I'll tell him about your, uh, Chihuahua-support problem."

I detect even more sarcasm in her voice than usual.

I look down just in time to see Arnold yak all over the cuffs of my favorite pair of Lucky jeans.

Ten

*Because you want to see your husband in person and
not just on MTV.*

Carter was the first person I told that I'd gotten married,
and his response was: "Are you pregnant?" My sister said,
"Are you high?" And every other relative and friend had some
variation on either of those questions.

My mother added, "But you're so young!" as if marriage is
an affliction only for old people.

No one liked Ted. Perversely, this only reinforced my belief
that no one understood him except me. It made me that much
more convinced that Ted really *did* need me.

My poor judgment can be blamed on the drugs of love—
hormonal endorphins that short-circuit logical thinking in the
brain. I once read that after a climax, women produce twice the
amount of the hormone oxytocin in the brain, the chemical
that makes you want to cuddle and go pick out china patterns.
It's no wonder that we make so many poor choices. Men come,

and then they have just enough oxytocin in their blood to want to fall asleep. Women come, and their brains start obsessing about baby names. It isn't fair.

If I ran the world, I'd have Breathalyzers for oxytocin. I would make it illegal for any woman to consent to marriage if her blood oxytocin levels are higher than .10.

A month after Ted and I eloped, "Drowning" hit the charts, and everything changed. Ted went on an extended tour. I had to work two crappy jobs to pay rent on our place, since he didn't yet have his first royalty check. After Ted had been on tour for six weeks, he sent me a "guard dog" to keep me company. Arnold was his wedding gift to me.

"He can't stay here," says Carter the next morning, leaning over me with his hands on his hips. I fell asleep on the couch watching some full-frontal show involving a barmaid and a police officer. Arnold is curled in a ball on my stomach.

Every time I see Carter, I'm reminded how good looking he his. It's always a bit of a surprise. As if I can't quite imagine that we really did date. We did—for three months before Carter moved to London to study abroad his senior year of college. The romantic side of me says that it feels like thwarted destiny—Carter meeting me in June in summer school, just three months before he planned to flee the country in September. But the cynical side of me says I was lucky to get out with Carter on good terms, given that I am (at three months) his longest relationship to date.

Besides, at that time I was eighteen and he was twenty. We

weren't nearly mature enough then to make a go of a real relationship. And come to think of it, I'm not sure we would be mature enough now, either.

Carter, I notice, is wearing the clothes he wore yesterday. This means he stayed with Brigid all night.

Not that I care about that. Or the fact that he has a giant red hickey welt on his neck. Correction: freaking huge love bite. Okay, maybe I do care.

"Is that a hickey on your neck?" I cry, pointing.

Carter puts his hand up reflexively. "Don't change the subject. We're talking about Arnold, the dog rat."

Arnold stands and stretches, and I feel like the wind is being knocked out of me.

"God, Arnie, you've put on weight," I tell him, gently nudging him off me. I put him down on the floor and he sits upright, but his belly is so fat that his legs sort of spread out beside him, so he can't quite sit up normally.

Ian, who stumbles out of his room in his bathrobe, shouts when he sees Arnold.

"Blowdyhwlfookinratsdar," he cries, and jumps on the couch.

"It's not a rat, it's a dog," Carter says. "Lily's dog."

"Doog? Aye, fookinratseetallya," Ian says, carefully climbing off the couch and holding out his hand to Arnold, who sniffs at it. "Ooglybooger."

"Agreed," Carter says. "Even Ian thinks he should go," Carter says, pointing at the door.

"I can't just abandon him. He's a pain in the ass, but he's got feelings, too. What would he eat on the street?"

"It looks like he has quite a bit of reserves there," Carter says, poking at Arnold's potbelly.

Arnold lets out a low whine and looks at Carter as if he's an abusive husband who's been drinking.

"Why is he looking at me like that?"

"Because you're about to kick him out. He can sense when people don't like him."

"I have leather furniture, Lil. It doesn't mix with dog. Not to mention, my Lennon chair. That's priceless. It's a collector's item."

"I know. Look, I promise to keep him under control. Let him stay for now. I'll try to figure out how to send him home to my sister."

"You have one week. And he stays in your room."

Right after Carter jumps in the shower, Arnold hops off me, does a little half turn, and then raises his leg to pee on Carter's prized Lennon chair. I snatch him up just in time to save the chair, but not Carter's rug, as Arnold leaves a trail of dog pee straight to the kitchen until I can get him over the kitchen sink. I let him dribble until I think he's done and then I put him on the ground, where he promptly christens the cuffs of my wool pants with a fine misting of dog pee.

Ian finds this hysterical and can't stop laughing. "Ooh, boogerstays, aye."

"Dammit," I curse, looking down at Arnold. "If you don't behave, I am going to send you back to Ted."

Arnold shivers a bit and whines.

I look through the kitchen, trying to find something that will pass for breakfast for me and Arnold. Carter's refrigerator is empty except for odds and ends. There's some awful-looking stuff called Marmite in the fridge, which Carter says is supposed to be like peanut butter, except it looks like the remains of someone's failed liposuction and tastes like ass. I settle on marmalade and toast. I feed Arnold some cold cuts.

Arnold, sensing something is off, starts yipping at a frequency usually reserved for bats and submarine sonar.

"Is he going to do that all day?" Carter asks me, emerging from his room.

"He might."

"Well, he can't. I didn't put down a pet deposit. If my landlord hears him, well, you'll owe me one hundred fifty pounds."

"I don't have one hundred fifty . . . well, whatever it is in dollars."

"Then that dog can't bark."

Arnold is giving me his "don't leave me alone or I'll bark up a storm" look.

"I can't take you to the hospital with me," I tell Arnold, trying to be firm. Arnold preferring my company to staying in the apartment is almost tantamount to suicide, since I'm likely to forget he's in my bag and leave him on the tube.

"You're right, you can't take him," Carter says. "I work in a hospital. Arnold isn't sanitary. Maybe Ian will watch him."

Ian shakes his head vigorously. "No weeeh," he says, and lumbers back into his room and shuts the door.

Arnold yips.

"I guess I can't leave him, either," I say. "I'll figure some-thing out."

I stuff Arnold in my oversize Hermès bag. He barely fits, he's gained so much weight. The bag straps cut into my shoulder.

"If you get caught at the hospital with that thing, I don't know you," Carter says.

The hospital is as grim as usual, and sneaking in Arnold is a lot easier in theory than in practice. Arnold's gotten too big for me to stuff his head in the bag and zip it up. I'm slightly worried about the possibility of suffocation. And it doesn't help that he now weighs somewhere in the neighborhood of twenty pounds. And that's quite a lot when it's hanging from straps on your shoulder. I give up trying to hide him.

"Oooooh, she's soooooooooo cute," Becca purrs. "Let me hold her! Go on, yeah!"

"She's a he," I say, "but you can hold him."

Becca takes Arnold and coos at him as if he's a baby or David Beckham.

"God! What is that? A rat?" Sal cries, appalled.

"No, it's a dog, which is more than I can say for you, init?" Becca says, cuddling Arnold.

"We can't have dogs in hospital," Sal says.

"Then how did you get in here?" Becca quips.

Sal ignores her. "Besides, I'm allergic." As if to prove her point, she starts sniffling.

"I'm allergic to that jumper you've got on, but you don't

hear me complaining," Becca says, referring to Sal's murky brown wool sweater. It seems that yesterday's outfit wasn't an anomaly. I wonder if all of Sal's clothes come in varying shades of brown or hunter green—the color wheel for vomit.

"This is a place where we take care of sick people," Sal says. "We can't have dirty animals running about."

"Then we'd better get rid of some of the patients 'round here, they're filthy." Becca scratches Arnold behind his ears and cuddles him closer. "Bollocks!" cries Becca suddenly. She drops Arnold to the ground. "He's pissed on me!"

There's a wet spot the size of a grapefruit on the front of Becca's shirt. Sal bursts out laughing.

"I've changed my mind, he can stay," Sal says.

A few fans of Sean Gates come by then, sniffing around for his room. You can tell they are his fans, because they're wearing extremely short skirts and low-cut shirts. Becca narrows her eyes. She clearly doesn't like the competition.

"I'm afraid you are going to have to leave," she tells them.

"But we're just visiting our uncle," one of them cries.

"I'll ring security." Becca picks up the phone, and the two of them scamper off.

"Um, hate to interrupt," Sal says, "but when a dog sniffs and circles, doesn't that mean he's about to . . ."

I look over and see that Arnold is, indeed, about to leave a little gift for us all.

"Arnold! No! Bad dog. Bad."

"Yes, bad dog. You ought to save that for Becca's shoes."

"Shut it, Sal."

"Would you guys quit arguing and help me catch him?"

Becca and Sal look at each other and then join in the chase.

Arnold, being fast when he wants to be even in his new pudgy state, eludes us all for several minutes. He sprints off down the hall, tail wagging, as if we're playing a lively game of tag.

I send Becca around one way and Sal down another, so that we might converge and corner him, when I see him dart straight into Sean Gates's room. His door is ajar, and the guard who's normally there seems to have wandered off. Great. Just what I need. An international incident.

I don't see Becca or Sal. I need to get in there and fast, or Arnold is going to lay a fat one in the room of one of England's most valuable, famous, and rich soccer players. Carter would kill me. No doubt about it.

I hurry over and glance in. I see one large room and one bed. It's the only room I've seen in this hospital with just one bed, and that includes intensive care. The figure in it has his foot and knee elevated on a stack of pillows and seems to be sleeping.

Arnold is sitting beside his bed, his little potbelly dragging on the floor.

I signal Arnold to come to me. He doesn't want to come. Worse, he scrunches himself under Sean Gates's bed and refuses to come out.

I have no choice but to go in. I look right, then left, and then creep into the room. Beside his bed, I hear his deep, rhythmic breathing. He's got bleached blond hair and a tan that's unusual for an English guy.

I get down on my knees and try to reach Arnold, but I end up doing more contortions than Madonna in yoga class. While I'm twisting to try to reach him, a button pops off my shirt, leaps off my chest, and rolls over near Arnold's front paw. Arnold sniffs at it and then eats it.

"Arnold!" I hiss. He eats anything in his path, which is probably the reason for his extra pounds.

It's in this position, on all fours, that I hear a man's voice.

"Oiy, what do we have here then, luv?"

My head whips up, and I look up and find myself staring into the face of a very awake and very alert Sean Gates.

Awake he looks a bit different than asleep. Awake he looks more like he ought to be an underwear model. Or starring in his own action movie with his shirt off. This is probably because his shirt is off and I'm getting a nice view of his very in-shape body. He's got sex appeal oozing from every pore, like Clive Owen or Russell Crowe. A kind of barely restrained aggression that only alpha males and men with six-pack abs have.

My inner slut, the one who likes to wear halter tops and too much lipstick, sits up and takes notice. *A solid 9.8 on the fuckable scale,* she tells me right off. My inner slut's fuckability scale runs from 1 (our high school math teacher Mr. Gary—a four-foot-nine, hairy little ball) to 10 (Brad Pitt).

I realize that, since Ted, this is the first man I've seen who broke a 7 on that scale. Not that there weren't objectively men who were higher than 7s. But I had no interest in them. This one is the first one I'd consider getting naked in front of since Ted.

I feel a strong urge to impress him, which I realize is going to be an uphill battle.

Offer him a blow job, my inner slut suggests.

My inner slut has the worst advice. It usually involves getting naked, doing tequila shots, or committing lewd sexual acts.

It's at this point that I realize, from the direction his glance is taking, that I am quite nearly hanging out of my shirt.

"Um, hi," I manage, as I sit up and straighten out my shirt. I'm pretty sure he's already seen most, if not all, of my pink La Perla bra.

At least it lifts and separates, my inner slut says.

"Either I'm still medicated, or I have woken up in heaven," he tells me, grinning from ear to ear.

I smile. *Hello? He is coming on to you. What are you waiting for—blow job! Now!* cries my inner slut.

He's got that confident way about him that Ted has. The one that tells me he has no trouble at all convincing women to take their clothes off.

"I've lost my dog," I explain.

You're losing him. Losing him! Flash your boobs. Quick, my inner slut says. She's tapping one of her clear plastic stiletto stripper heels impatiently.

His brow wrinkles. "I know I'm a bit out of it, yeah? But is that some sort of code I don't know?"

Arnold barks.

"What the bleedin' Christ . . ." He maneuvers himself so he can see over the side of the bed, where Arnold pops out and gives him another good-natured bark.

"Oiy. Who is this, now?"

I hold up Arnold, and let Sean take a closer look. He scratches the dog behind his ears and gives him a rough pat. "You are a right fat bugger," Sean tells Arnold, who whines and flinches under his rough but good-natured touch.

"This is Arnold . . . he's uh, my dog, and the reason I came in uninvited."

"With looks like yours, luv, you're invited into my room anytime." He winks at me. "But I have to say, I'm disappointed. I was hoping you were here to give me a sponge bath." He gives me a wicked smile.

If you don't jump him right now, I swear that the next time you're drunk I'm going to go to bed with the ugliest guy in the bar, my inner slut says.

"Sorry about waking you up. Your guard has left. I don't know if he's coming back or not."

"Useless tosser," Gates says. "I told him to piss off, yeah? He was getting in the way of me and me fans."

By fans, I'm assuming he means soccer groupies. Gates isn't so different from a rock star. He's got the same easy charm. The same sense of entitlement. In other words, the very last person on earth I should consider dating.

"I should probably let you rest." I say this, as I bound and gag my inner slut, who's thrashing around and squealing.

"Rest, darling, is the very last thing this bloke needs," Sean says. "Why don't you stay a while?"

Gates grabs my wrist and nods toward the chair by his bedside. Against all my rational instincts, I sit down.

Over the next ten minutes, Sean tries to convince me that I actually *have* seen him somewhere, when I haven't. He's amazed that I really haven't seen any of his games, or his endorsements, or anything.

"But I've been in *People,*" he said. "I was on their eligible bachelors list."

I shrug. "Sorry," I say. "Musicians are more my thing."

"Musicians! They're rubbish," Sean says, making a face. "A footballer is what you need, luv. We're strong. We can outlast musicians any bloody day of the bloody week."

Becca appears at the door, catching me talking to Sean. "What's going on here, then?"

"Um, nothing?" I say.

Sean looks back and forth between us.

"You'd better come out of there," Becca tells me. She sends a flirty look to Sean.

"Aw, but we were just getting acquainted," Sean says.

"Off with you," Becca says.

I get up, pick up Arnold, and head to the door.

"Laters, luv!" Sean calls out after me.

"Are you sure you don't know who Sean Gates is?" Becca asks me, sounding suspicious.

Outside his door, we run straight into Brigid, who doesn't look at all pleased to see us. Her lips are pressed into a thin line.

"You know that room is off limits." She frowns at me. And glares at Becca. Becca glares back.

"Is that a *dog*?" Brigid cries, putting up her hand to cover her mouth as if Arnold smelled bad. "There are no *dogs* allowed in this facility, Ms. Crandell. You were well informed of that when you signed the volunteer consent papers."

"I . . ."

"You must take him out of here immediately, and if I see him again, I'll have to have your position terminated."

"Okay . . ."

"And another thing, *stay out of Sean Gates's room.* This is your first and last warning. Just because you're a *friend* of Carter's, doesn't mean you get any special privileges around here."

Becca has walked around where Brigid can't see her and is making a face at the back of her head.

Brigid glances down at my shirt and frowns.

I see that the top of my La Perla is still showing.

"Wardrobe malfunction," I say.

Eleven

*Because he might be a rock star, but he's not
England's most eligible bachelor.*

My old neighbor Fran "Sheba" Holman said that
most people find themselves attracted to the
wrong people.

She believes that we seek mates in this life who represent
unfinished business in the previous one.

A bad relationship with your father or mother, for example,
could mean you end up marrying them in the next life and
fighting your way through all your unresolved issues. What you
think is love at first sight might just be your soul saying,
"Haven't I seen you somewhere before?"

Fran attempted once to expand her telephone tarot reading
business to face-to-face sessions. One of her tricks involved re-
gressing people to discover their past lives. Fran used hypnosis,
a crystal on a string, and Enya music to set the mood. She of-

fered a couples regression package around Valentine's Day.

She gave up the practice after she regressed a couple from Wisconsin, and the wife came out of her hypnotic trance screaming that her husband had been the man who drowned her in a river in colonial times.

"People think they know the difference between hate and love," Fran would say. "But most of the time you just can't tell."

I spend an hour or so Googling Sean Gates. I discover:

1. He's worth twenty-five million pounds.
2. He's had more girlfriends than George Clooney and is currently in an on-again, off-again relationship with British-born Victoria's Secret model Tanya Richards.
3. He has hundreds of fan dedication sites and more than one offer to carry his baby.
4. He is very likely another egomaniac that I ought not to touch with a ten-foot pole.
5. None of the above facts hold sway with my inner slut, who keeps telling me I should volunteer to give him a sponge bath. With my tongue.

I decide to ignore my inner slut. The last time I did what she said, I ended up married to a narcissist rock star with a borderline substance abuse problem. My inner slut has the sense of a tube of body glitter.

*   *   *

The next morning, I wake up with the smell of burning pancakes in my nose. I stumble out to the living room to find Brigid, wearing nothing but Carter's sweatshirt, making breakfast. Carter has his hands wrapped around her and they're kissing. I feel like I might vomit. I notice with irritation that she has very nice legs. That is, if you like chopsticks. Her legs are skinnier than my arms. Instantly, I'm annoyed. This seems to be the reaction I have to Brigid whenever I see her. It may have something to do with the fact that she's a felon. That or her inability to keep her hands off Carter.

"Hey, Lil, want some pancakes?" Carter asks.

I look down at the black blobs burning on the stovetop. "No thanks," I say.

"I'm not much of a cook," Brigid admits. "But I have other talents."

Right before my eyes, she reaches down and squeezes Carter's crotch. I lose what little appetite I had for breakfast.

"Wharesdebloodyfeer?" cries Ian, coming out the door. His shock of red hair is sticking up and he looks startled.

"There's no fire," Carter says. "We're just making breakfast."

Ian, seeing Brigid, widens his eyes. He looks left, then right, and slowly backs out of the kitchen, careful not to make any sudden movements, as if he fears Brigid will knock him flat and run off with his Xbox.

Arnold trots out by my feet and barks.

"Oh! What an adorable little dog!" Brigid says as she stoops to pick up Arnold. "You should bring him to the hospital."

I squint. Didn't Brigid, just yesterday, see Arnold and order me *not* to bring him to the hospital?

"It would cheer up the patients," Brigid says, blinking fast. She smiles at me. It's like she's possessed. Yesterday she looked like she wanted to rip my head off. Today she's acting like I'm her best friend. Cuckoo for Cocoa Puffs. I look over at Ian and see him meticulously checking his stacks of Xbox games to see if any are missing.

"You're so generous," Carter says in a baby voice to Brigid, pulling her close. "Always thinking about other people."

Brigid beams at his praise. I want to yak. Ugh.

"Carter? Can I speak to you for a minute?" I drag Carter into the living room.

"Isn't she great?" Carter says, once we're out of earshot. "I mean, I was really crazy to let her go."

"You do realize this is the woman who just last week you feared was going to skin you alive."

"Shhh. Keep your voice down. We're really trying to make things work. I think she might be Mrs. Henry material."

"What?! No!" I cry, without even intending to do so. The words just pop—unedited and uncensored—straight from my brain.

Carter gives me a funny look. "But I thought you wanted us back together."

"What?! No," I say, shaking my head furiously. "I wanted my passport—that's all."

"You locked us in a closet together to get your sister's passport back?" Carter seems skeptical. I agree, it seems pretty lame.

But I swear, I didn't think they'd actually get back together. She's psychotic, even by Carter's standards.

This is leading down a path I don't want to go. Carter is getting that look he always gets when he thinks I want to have sex with him.

"And did you get the passport?" I ask, changing the subject.

"She says she doesn't have it."

"Ian saw her in your apartment. She took it. She must know what she did with it."

"She said she didn't."

"And you believe her?"

"Lily, a relationship has to be built on trust."

"Relationship! But I thought you were scared of her! How can this be a relationship?"

"That was before we had sex again," Carter says, giving me a wink. "I'm not scared of her anymore."

"Sex! That's what this is about? Sex?" I am so mad at Carter right now, I want to scream. Seriously.

"Can I join the party?" Brigid asks, coming into the living room and giving me a wary look. Carter draws Brigid close to him. She giggles and then they start nuzzling noses. While I watch, Brigid takes two of Carter's fingers and actually sucks on them, right in front of me. I think I'm going to be sick.

They wind up in Carter's bedroom, and I get stuck on the couch with Ian, who is saving the world from alien invasion.

He's wearing a shirt that says I'LL TRY TO BE NICER, IF YOU TRY TO BE SMARTER.

"Wannashoot?" he says, which sounds very close to something I can actually understand.

"Did you ask me if I want to shoot?"

"Yeah," he says, nodding.

"That's the first thing you've said that I actually understood." I can't believe it. I've officially been around Ian long enough to understand him.

"Och, aye, 'bout bloody time, Yank," he tells me, and smiles. Arnold whines, and Ian gives him a rough pat on the head. I've noticed Ian taking a much greater liking to Arnold of late. It's probably because, like Ian, Arnold doesn't mind spending hours sitting on the couch.

We hear Brigid moan and wail from behind Carter's closed door.

Ian turns up the volume on the TV.

"Och, lad has lost his bleedin' marbles," he says about Carter. "An' he's lookin' fer 'em up his arse."

Ian attempts to show me how to play some of his video games, but there are too many buttons and I keep running my guys into walls. I think this is probably symbolic of something, but I'm not sure what.

A half hour later, Brigid emerges from Carter's room dressed and ready for work. She's got an early-morning meeting and won't be able to escort Carter to work, holding hands like he'd so hoped. I think this is a good thing, until I am witness to the long, drawn-out, sickening sweet good-bye.

They kiss. And kiss some more. I mean, at this rate one or both of them are going to suffocate.

"So I'll see you for lunch?" Brigid says, pulling away at last.

"Of course you will."

"I miss you already," Brigid says.

"I miss you more."

"No, I miss *you* more."

"I miss you even more than that. . . ."

And so on, and so forth.

Blech.

I look at Ian, and he puts a finger gun in his mouth and mimes pulling the trigger.

At the hospital, even Becca and Sal notice Carter's new condition.

"He's lost his head—again," Becca says.

"He always gets like this," I say.

"Tell me about it." Becca snorts. "He's a total knob when he's in love. Thank God it doesn't last long."

"Maybe this one is the *one.*" Sal glances up from her calculator. "You never know."

"Wanna bet?" Becca says. "Twenty quid he's off her in one month," says Becca.

Carter walks by humming "(Love Lift Us) Up Where We Belong."

Becca and I glance at each other as Carter disappears into a patient's room.

"It's a good job he isn't operating on me today," Becca says. "He's in a right state, wouldn't surprise me if he attached someone's arm to their arse."

*   *   *

I've got a knot in my stomach and, for once, it doesn't have anything to do with Ted. Why am I so bugged about Carter and Brigid? I guess it's got to be the fact that my best friend in the world is with a psychotic criminal who isn't afraid of resorting to violence. That's a big part of it, but maybe there's more. It doesn't help that she's skinny and gorgeous. Too skinny, I remind myself.

Maybe I ought to just let it go. Maybe I've just overstayed my welcome and it's time for me to really think about going home. I don't even know what I'm doing here. I took the trip on a whim, thinking I'd just figure it all out once I got here, but I still don't really know. It just *seemed* like a good idea to come and get away from it all, but given the fact that Ted's song is everywhere, it's not exactly getting away. And when Brigid manages to annoy me more than Ted, clearly this isn't what I need.

Since I will probably never get Brigid to admit to stealing my passport, much less give it back, I try to call my sister again (who doesn't answer) and then, worried about what damage she may or may not have done by telling the parents about my current problems, I call Mom.

"Are you in trouble?" Mom says, when I call.

"No, why would I be in trouble?"

"You only call if you're in trouble," Mom says. "Did you get arrested again?"

"Mom—no, I'm not in jail."

"Are you sure?"

"I'm sure."

Mom sighs. "Good. Okay, then."

When not being in jail is an accomplishment, you know your family members have extremely low expectations.

"How are you holding up?" She's using *that tone*.

"I'm fine."

"You don't sound fine."

"I'm *fine!*"

"There's no need to shout. I'm your mother, for goodness sakes. When do I need a license to care about my daughter?"

I sigh. "I'm sorry."

I can tell that Mom will be no help with my passport.

For one thing, she doesn't exactly know about my assault charges. I led her and Dad to believe that there was a settlement pending, and neither one knows I'm not supposed to leave the country. So in order to enlist her help I'd have to admit to being a fugitive, which will only reinforce her suspicion that I only call her when I need something, and will lead to an even longer lecture than the one I got from Lauren, which I don't need. I know I screwed up. Let's move on.

Mom continues.

"I never cared for Ted's music," Mom says. Mom listens only to Neil Diamond and, occasionally, Barbra Streisand.

"Have you talked to Lauren lately?" I ask her.

"No," she says. "I'm a bit worried about her, to be honest. She's in one of her jealous fits again."

My sister sees a *Jerry Springer* episode around every corner of her relationship. Whenever something doesn't feel right, she just assumes it's because the man in her life is lying to her. And yet, her husband, Nick, is the most straight-as-an-arrow Boy Scout who ever lived. He'd never cheat on her. I doubt he could even tell a straight-faced lie. But he's also gorgeous, and there are plenty of girls who throw themselves at him. But that doesn't mean he's interested. Nick isn't like Ted. But you can't tell Lauren this, especially now that she's pregnant with baby number two. She's convinced he's cheating. Last month her suspicions were focused on their baby-sitter. I think it's a problem of her planning too much. She's so intent on making elaborate life plans that she also envisions, in detail, how every one of those plans can go wrong.

"She thinks he's interested in one of the firefighters he works with. A girl," Mom clarifies. The idea of women firefighters is still new to Mom. "She's convinced there's something going on with those two."

"Tell her she's insane," I say.

"I do, but it doesn't help."

After talking to Mom, at least I know that Lauren hasn't gone so far as to tell my parents that I'm a fugitive from justice. This is a good thing. It means she isn't quite as angry at me as she could be. There's hope, yet, that she'll get me the passport.

In the days that follow, Carter is a walking love zombie. Brigid and Carter are nearly inseparable, and when they are separate, Carter spends all his time talking about her. I swear, sex gives Carter a lobotomy.

"Brigid is so delicate, you know," Carter says.

"You mean she doesn't eat," I say, watching her on her twig legs walk down the hallway at the hospital.

"No, I mean she's *sensitive,*" Carter says.

I watch as Brigid shouts at a nurse and berates her for not wearing her hospital pass. Then she snaps at an orderly for leaving a wheelchair in the hallway.

"Oh yes, a delicate flower," I say. Carter misses the sarcasm.

"She needs someone to look after her," Carter says.

"I think she needs someone to make her eat," I say. "Have you ever noticed that people who don't eat are *extremely* grumpy? I would be, too, if I was that hungry all the time."

Carter ignores me, walking off to catch up with Brigid down the hall. Becca appears on my right. "We've got to save him from the bony wench," she says.

"What is it that you have against Brigid, anyway?" I ask.

"Not really much to like, is there?" Becca exclaims. "Like how she bollocked me for wearing a push-up bra or for being thirty seconds late for my shift? She docked my wage once because I was one minute late."

"She's evil," Sal agrees, stopping in the hall with her arms full of files.

"What did she do to you?"

"It's what she doesn't do. She doesn't do her work. I do it. I'm the one who puts together the budget. Brigid is the one who puts it in a nice-looking folder and gives it to the hospital board."

"But she takes all the credit," Becca says, arms crossed.

"I actually feel sorry for Dr. Henry. Never thought I'd say it, but there it is."

"Speak of the devil," Becca says, watching as Brigid and Carter part ways in the hall, and Brigid comes marching toward us, a determined look on her face.

"Lily!" she calls. "Lily, I need to talk with you."

In her office, she stares at me a long while.

"How long do you plan to stay with us?" she asks me.

"I'm not sure, really. I can't travel, as you well know. I need my passport. And my wallet."

Brigid clears her throat. "Well," she says, tapping a pencil on her desk. "It's not exactly *your* passport, is it?" She gives me a slow, calculated smile.

"So you do have it, then." And here I'd almost started to believe she just had split personalities and really didn't remember breaking into Carter's apartment. Now I know she's not just crazy, she's evil. Pure evil.

"Are you going to tell me who 'Lauren' is? Or shall I guess?"

"My sister," I admit.

"Now that is strange," she says. "Traveling with your sister's passport."

"I like her picture better than mine. Now, are you going to give it back to me?"

"I will give it back, only if you promise to leave. Carter and I are in a very delicate part of our relationship. I'd rather him not have any distractions. Like you. He needs to focus right now."

I don't particularly like how Brigid talks about Carter as if he's a toddler who needs her guidance. I also don't like to be told that I have to leave. I don't like to be told what to do in general, especially by a crazy person.

"Maybe I'm not in a hurry to go anywhere," I say evenly. "Maybe I'll take in some sights firsts."

Brigid frowns at me. She seems to be losing her composure. I can see the frantic wheels in her brain turning. She tugs hard at her jacket and presses her lips in a straight line. Frantically, she starts stacking up papers and restacking them.

"I'd appreciate it, *Lily,* if you found somewhere else to stay. I don't think you spending so much time at our place is appropriate, if you plan to stay long term."

Our? Since when is Carter's apartment Brigid's, too?

"Ian doesn't mind me there."

"I do," Brigid says, through grinding teeth.

"I don't have my wallet. I can't check into a hotel."

"Maybe Carter would like to know what you were up to in Sean Gates's room the other day?"

"I wasn't up to anything. And Carter wouldn't care if I was."

"We'll see about that."

She frantically starts rearranging more stacks of paper on her desk.

If I only sort of regretted my part in bringing queen of the crazies back together with my commitment-phobic ex, I now realize it was the *worst mistake in my life,* next to perhaps marrying Ted. Who is this psycho?

"I'd appreciate it if you'd leave now," Brigid says. When I don't move fast enough she shouts, "LEAVE!" like a demon possessed.

I have to be honest and say that I don't see the second go-round of Carter and Brigid lasting, either, if she keeps up this possessive streak. Carter doesn't like being crowded, and if I had to guess, I would say she's probably already picking out new curtains for his apartment. Bad move.

Then again, I've been wrong before. It's usually because I really underestimate Carter's weakness for the insane.

And then, as if unable to control herself, she grabs the first thing in her reach, a letter opener, and hurls it at my head. It sails by and imbeds itself into the doorframe, missing my head by inches. The handle vibrates as it swings back and forth.

I'm not certain, but I'm pretty sure Brigid just tried to kill me.

"I told you she was a right crazy bitch, yeah?" Becca says when I tell her and Sal later about the exchange.

"Yeah, I got that impression when she threw that knife at me," I say. "She could've taken out my eye. Or killed me."

"I don't think a letter opener is a knife," Sal says.

"It's sharp enough," I say. "Still could've killed me. It did a number on the door."

"Anyway, someone should talk some sense into Dr. Henry, before she starts hurling sharp objects at him, too," Sal says. "Why don't you do it, Becca?"

"I can't tell a doctor who to date," Becca cries. "I like my job, thank you."

They both look at me.

"What? No way. I can't do it."

They don't blink.

"Let's take a vote," Becca says. "All in favor of Lily going to save Carter's arse from Brigid the bitch, raise their hand."

Becca and Sal both raise their hands.

Twelve

REASON #12 TO DIVORCE A ROCK STAR:

Because "for the band" can be an excuse to cover all indiscretions, including staying out all night, forgetting your birthday, and sleeping with groupies.

The first time someone told me Ted was cheating on me, I didn't believe them. The news came from a girl I used to work with who saw him early one morning after one of the many nights he was supposed to be out practicing with his band. Janice Jamison was a do-gooder who filled her cube with signs like GOD DOESN'T GIVE US THINGS WE CAN'T HANDLE and COMMIT RANDOM ACTS OF KINDNESS! Her e-mails all had a gauzy pink graphic overlay to them, and she always used too many exclamation points like, "Thanks!!!! Lily!!!! For the copies!!!!!!" She was always a little too perky, a little too peppy, and a little too eager to point out other people's shortcomings to human resources in the name of helping them "improve."

Janice called me over to her desk on my last week at my temp-that-had-turned-into-perm job. She put her unnaturally pink acrylic nails on my knee and frowned. "I am so sorry to be the one to tell you this, but I think it's important for people to know these things."

I got the impression she wasn't sorry at all to be telling me she'd been out in the yard with her two kids on Saturday morning when she saw Ted stumble out of her neighbor's garage apartment and kiss her neighbor's daughter (age twenty) in a manner "not appropriate for an audience of young children."

"I have tissues," she told me, "if you need to cry. You just go on and let it out."

I walk beside Carter on our way home and I think about Janice Jamison. I told her to mind her own business and then I told her she ought to get a life. Janice reported me to human resources for "hostile language," but by then I didn't care. I didn't believe her. I refused to believe that a woman who had a Cathy mug that said ARRGGGH! PMS! on it could possibly have an insight into my marriage.

Beside me, Carter is humming "Islands in the Stream." He always hums easy listening tunes when he's infatuated with someone. And I hate that he's infatuated with Brigid, who may, quite possibly, be capable of real physical violence. I hate that a little sex can make Carter lose his mind.

And I wonder why he didn't try harder to have sex with me. He gave up pretty easily. He didn't even try to get me drunk straight off the plane and have his way with me. And then I wonder why I'm thinking that at all. Do I want Carter to try to be scheming to get into bed with me?

I remember suddenly that glazed-over, wondrous look that Carter always got during sex. It was as if every time was the first time for him. Unlike Ted, who approached sex like a sloppy, but enthusiastic Labrador retriever. He had all the finesse of an animal without opposable thumbs.

I glance up at Carter and realize I've been imagining him naked. Oh dear. That's not good. I try to erase that image from my head, but every time I look up at Carter I remember the feel of his chest under my hands. This is not what you should normally feel about exes, is it?

"Carter, stop humming. We need to talk," I say, trying to focus on the task at hand.

"Stop what?"

"Humming. It's driving me insane."

"I'm not humming."

"You are. And worse, you're humming 'Islands in the Stream.'"

Carter laughs. "I am not."

"You are. Now stop it. You know very well that when you go all mushy for a girl you start humming a selection of easy listening music from the seventies and eighties."

"That's ridiculous," Carter says, but sounds slightly unsure.

Arnold, who is tucked away in my purse, whines.

"Did I tell you that Brigid likes Dolly Parton? Isn't that funny."

"Carter. Seriously, focus here. If you start humming, I'm going to pinch you. That means you have to stop. I have something to tell you."

"Can you believe someone from London likes Dolly Parton?" Carter says in his dreamy, "I'm infatuated" voice. "Brigid is so funny that way—ow! What did you pinch me for? I wasn't humming."

"But you were being annoying, and that's the same thing."

"You know, I have you to thank. If you hadn't made me see Brigid, *ow!* Would you stop pinching me? That hurts. You know I have a low threshold for pain."

Arnold whimpers a little, popping his head out of my bag.

"Even Arnold agrees you're being obnoxious. Stop it with the Brigid stuff, okay? We have to talk."

Carter wrinkles his nose as if he smells something bad.

I open and close my fingers in front of him. "Don't make me use these again."

"Okay, okay. Uncle, all right? I can't believe you're so bent out of shape about my girlfriend!"

Good Lord. He's using the G word. This has got to stop. There is no cause for the G word. Carter is simply not fit to date.

"Carter, you are my best friend, but if you mention Brigid one more time, I am going to have to end our friendship."

"I don't mention Brigid's name that often. Just because Brigid happens to come up in conversation doesn't mean I'm obsessed with Brigid."

I stare at him for a few seconds. He checks out his hair in the reflection of a nearby window.

"Carter, you just mentioned Brigid's name three times in less than three seconds."

"I did not," he says, then he thinks about it a moment. "Anyway, I know a lot of people don't like her, but she's different when we're alone."

"How so?"

"She *really* needs me. You know? Do you know what that's like? When someone can't live without you?"

I sigh. I do know what it's like. It's exactly how I felt about Ted.

"I know this is hard to hear, but I'm not sure Brigid is, well, sane," I say. "And, honestly, she does need to eat. Does she ever eat?"

Carter frowns. "Are you jealous?"

"What? Me? No!"

"You are! You're jealous. You're jealous of Brigid."

"I'm not. Believe me, I'm not." Am I telling the truth? I wonder. I was just thinking about Carter naked.

I don't know which I dread more—that I might still have feelings for Carter or that Brigid could be right to be jealous of me. Do I have a crush on Carter? I'm not sure, although he does look good enough to eat. And he smells a little like vanilla candles. I think it's his hair wax.

"Admit it. You're still in love with me." Carter leans into me, so close I can see his pupils. I have a strong urge to put my hands in his hair, to pull him closer to me and kiss him on the lips.

Now I know that Ted must have seriously messed me up. I'm imagining making out with Carter! What am I thinking? Carter is a friend, I tell myself. *Just* a friend.

Carter raises his eyebrows at me and gives me his best Chuck Woolery from *The Love Connection* look. This is his way of being somewhat mysterious and sexy, even though there's nothing mysterious about Carter, except how he manages to put so much product in his hair without it breaking off at the roots.

"You so want to sleep with me," Carter says.

"I don't," I say, but I can't help a smile from creeping up at the corners of my mouth. What is Carter's hold over me? Is it that I *know* he's so absolutely toxic?

"You sure?" Carter's eyebrows dance.

"I'm not going to sleep with you. Give up now."

"Just checking. I'm a guy. It's my responsibility to check."

Carter seems to drop the subject and I'm surprisingly disappointed. One minute, I don't want him teasing me about it, and when he stops, now I suddenly do? I have clearly got issues.

"I guess if you're looking for pity sex from me, you're not in love with Brigid after all," I say.

"First of all, I would be the one taking pity on you, not vice versa, let's get that straight," Carter says, his eyes glinting. "Second, didn't I just remind you that I'm a guy? Now, what was it you wanted to tell me? You have my full attention, I promise."

Carter stops and looks at me. His hair is perfectly in place. The crisp air has put color in his cheeks, and his lips are half-turned up in a smile. Why does he have to look so adorable and so happy right before I'm supposed to crush his heart like a tomato under the wheel of a Hummer?

"Um . . ." I say, faltering. Your girlfriend is a lunatic who stole my passport, threw a knife at me, and is trying to bully me out of your apartment. And there's probably a good reason for that, because there's a strong possibility that I really, really do seriously want to jump into bed with you.

"I'm waiting," he says. "Come on. Spit it out."

I think about telling him everything. I see Carter turning against Brigid. I see him jumping into bed with me. I see us having fantastic, sweaty, mind-blowing sex, and then I imagine Carter the next morning, when he gets that look of panic. I don't want to see him try to gnaw off his own arm to get out the door. Or even worse than that, pretend that nothing ever happened. Because, let's face facts, sex with exes is not a good idea. Aren't they exes for a reason?

"When are you going to take me to the London Eye?" I say, flaking.

Carter laughs. "Is that all? I thought you were going to tell me I had ear hair or something really awful," he says. "How about this weekend?"

"You didn't bloody tell him!" Becca cries. She puts her hands on her hips, where her uniform hugs and leaves little to the imagination. Becca likes to wear spandex leggings with her nurse's scrubs top.

"We were counting on you," Sal says.

"Well, that settles it then, you're going to have to shag him," Becca says.

"What," I cry, wondering if it's obvious to everyone but me that I have the hots for Carter.

"You're his friend, and as his friend, you cannot let him continue to date that nut, yeah?" she says. "Besides, I've seen the way you look at him. You still fancy him, I reckon."

"I don't," I say, but even I think my denial sounds weak.

"Who in this hospital doesn't fancy him?" Sal says. "He's shagilicious."

"Did you just use the word 'shagilicious'? You can't be serious," Becca says, frowning.

"You're asking me to break them up."

"Why not? In the end, he'd thank you." Sal eyes the small tattoo just visible on Becca's lower back between the seam of her shirt and her tight-fitting leggings. "Is that Garfield on your back?" she asks Becca.

"Bloody well right it is. I love that tabby, yeah?" Becca says.

"That's the most ridiculous thing I've ever seen," Sal says.

Brigid walks by and we all cease our conversation. She sends us all looks that make us glad she doesn't have heat vision.

I watch as she walks by on her toothpick legs.

"Has anyone ever seen her eat?" I ask.

"I saw her smoking once," Sal says.

"That doesn't bloody count, you sod," Becca says.

"Shhh! Here she comes," Sal says. We watch as Brigid swivels and heads back in our direction. I swear she moves with the same eerie precision as Michael Myers in *Halloween*. She turns her head and glares at me.

"Lily? Would you do me a favor tomorrow? Sean Gates asked to see your dog, Arnold, again. Would you mind visiting his room. Tomorrow at two?"

"Sean Gates? Are you sure?" Didn't she threaten to fire me if I ever went in his room again?

"Yes, I'm sure."

"Can I come, too?" Becca asks.

Brigid narrows her eyes at Becca. "No," she says.

"Bollocks," Becca says under her breath. "Does Brigid like you all of a sudden?"

"I don't know," I say, wondering. "I really don't know."

Thirteen

REASON #13 TO DIVORCE A ROCK STAR:

Rock stars don't do their own dishes.

The first time someone recognized Ted, he was standing in the frozen food aisle of the grocery store. The fan, a girl with pimples, big cheeks, a pig nose, and green hair, said she and her sister had seen him in concert a couple of nights before.

"You were pretty good," she said. " 'Drowning' is like my favorite song ever."

Ted came alive. You would've thought he had won the Nobel Prize. He talked about it for weeks after. I started joking about Ted's "one fan." But, after a while, it got annoying. He wouldn't stop talking about her. About his first groupie.

"You can't be attracted to that girl," I said at the time. She was, even by Ted's low standards, unattractive. And probably younger than eighteen.

"No, of course, not," Ted said, but his face got that far-away look, as if he was reliving the moment when a strange girl had approached him by the Tater Tots and told him he was "pretty okay." He was a Leo. It didn't matter what the girl looked like. What was important was that she liked him and said so.

A month later, the single "Drowning" hit the radio stations and started its march to number one. And then Ted's fans came out like water from a faucet, first at a dribble, then at a pour.

Fran "Sheba" Holman warned me not to marry Ted because he was a Leo, and Leos only think about themselves. Fran was a big believer in the zodiac.

She said the zodiac could explain every mistake in my love life.

Let's review:

I dated a Scorpio in college, who also turned out to be a stalker who wouldn't take no for an answer and eventually burned down my sister's house. His most-used line: "I'm only doing this because I love you."

Dated the Taurus police officer (who arrested my Scorpio stalker), who kept harassing my ex-boyfriends (including Carter) and issuing them bogus parking tickets. Said Taurus also tended to run through red lights and drove drunk since he felt like he was above the law. His favorite line: "Who's going to arrest me? I'm a cop!"

And, then, the Leo rock star. You know how that one turned out.

Sadly, my healthiest relationship to date is with Carter, and he keeps his ex-girlfriends tucked away in his Palm Pilot, along with their unique features ("double-jointed yoga instructor, no gag reflex"). He won't let me see what he put next to my name, but I'm pretty sure I don't want to know.

I wonder if my poor dating history means that my stars are out of alignment, or if it just means I have really low self-esteem.

That night, I get an e-mail from Larry telling me that they're close on the divorce settlement. Ironically, each new offer seems to get less generous instead of more, as if we're negotiating backward.

My lawyer's letter outlining Ted's new offer reads like a laundry list of prizes I haven't won:

Ted gets: the house in Austin (which was in his name), all the furniture (bought with his credit cards), all future rights to his songs, his Porsche 911, the condo in L.A., the concert proceeds, and all future rights and royalties on all Dayton Five merchandise and endorsements.

I get: Arnold, my wardrobe, and $30,000 (minus the hotel bill from the Four Seasons). This puts my net settlement at one dog, some spiffy duds, and $10,000 of credit debt.

"You can't expect more than that," says Larry Sullivan on the phone. "We've been over this, Lily. You were only married a year, and Texas is a no-fault divorce state."

"But he earned more than sixty thousand dollars last year."

"Yes, but your actual assets in the bank are only that

much," Larry says. "And you have no retirement fund. That's it, Lil."

"But . . ."

Larry continues. "Not to mention what is this I hear from Ted's attorney about you harassing him? You realize that they *know* you've been sending out bogus press releases. Did you think you'd get away with that? Do you *know* how desperate that makes us look? How can I negotiate a tougher settlement when you're acting like a hearbroken teenager?"

I feel ashamed suddenly. I've taken a step beyond a bad person. I'm now a pathetic person. It hits me suddenly that Ted is probably laughing at me. That he probably thinks I'm still in love with him. He always did have a problem discerning anger from love, or correctly identifying any emotion. Bipolar people and sociopaths often have this problem.

"Lily, take my advice. Take this settlement and just *get on with your life.* You can't mourn him forever. Let's face it. He's just not worth it."

I sigh. My lawyer is right.

"In the meantime, I'm doing my best to keep your bony butt out of jail, which, may I remind you, is a real possibility."

"For calling my butt bony, I'll forgive you for this really bad settlement."

"For the record, I'm pretending that you're in Pasadena right now, so don't shatter my illusions, all right? You realize that barring an unexpected settlement, your trial is in a month."

"I'll be home by then," I say.

"You said you'd be home last week," he reminds me.

"I know. I just have some unfinished business.

I ask the tarot cards whether I should a) hire an assassin to kill Ted; or b) whether I should just sign the divorce papers and be done with him.

I turn up the Tower (which means I will experience a clean break that will help change me for the better, even if it requires suffering in the near future). It shows a brick tower being destroyed by lightning and a page falling to his death.

I hope the page is Ted.

I'd make a fantastic widow. It has such a nicer ring to it than "divorcée."

I imagine myself at Ted's funeral. I'd be the one sitting in the front row in a tasteful Dior morning dress, gently dabbing at the corners of my eyes with a handkerchief. I'd nod and cry silently while his manager would talk about how many lives Ted reached with his music.

Of course, I wouldn't know which of the women in attendance Ted had slept with. Given his criteria for a quick shag (between the ages of eighteen and forty, any height, weight, and/or body type), it would be impossible to narrow down the likely candidates.

I sigh. Ted can even manage to ruin his own funeral for me.

Later that day, my sister calls.

"I think I'm ready to talk to you again," she says.

"Good, because it would make a phone conversation difficult if you weren't," I say. "Besides, you saddled me with Arnold. It's punishment enough."

"Ha ha. You saddled me with him first. My house smells like dog pee, by the way. You deserve what you got. And because you are my sister, I am not going to kill you or call the police," she says. "But just because I am talking to you doesn't mean I've forgiven you. And I also think I have to tell Mom and Dad."

"Lauren! You can't do that. They'll freak."

"But they might be able to help."

"They'll just make things worse. And I've had enough bad news this week. My lawyer says my settlement from Ted is Arnold and a ten-thousand-dollar debt."

"That's nothing. I got eighteen thousand dollars of Master-Card debt from Brad and a herpes scare."

"Is this how divorces always are?"

"I'm a wedding planner, not a divorce lawyer. How should I know? So you're sure you don't want me to tell Mom about all this."

"No. She has enough to worry about. You, for instance."

"Why is she worried about me?"

"Because of your psychotic jealous rants," I say.

"They're not psychotic. They are based on the fact that my husband is a very attractive man and women want him."

"Like who?"

"Cori—the firefighter at his station. I don't trust her."

"You don't have to trust Cori. You have to trust Nick."

"I know. It's just that my ass is the size of a barn. A woman the other day thought I was at term already and I've got more than a month to go!"

Lauren is pregnant with baby two; the first one, Tyler, is nearly three.

Because she's early for everything, she doesn't wait for postpartum for her psychotic episodes. She's got partum psychosis. All the hormones in her system combine for a perfect storm of paranoia and jealousy.

"And you should see my nipples. I swear, they're like dinner plates."

Why is it that pregnant women always want to tell you about their bodies?

"Ew, I mean it. That's a bit too much information, thanks," I say.

Lauren sighs. "Do a reading for me."

"No."

"Come on! I'll call Fran if you don't."

"She'll charge you nine dollars an hour."

"I know. If you don't do a reading, I'm going to tell you some more about my nipples."

I sigh. "Okay, okay, I'll do a reading for you."

I spread the cards out in front of me.

"What do they say?"

"That you're being a total freak and need to back away from the edge. They also say you need to get a new passport for me."

"They do not. Lily, be serious."

"I am being serious."

"Will-wee!" I hear my nephew cry into the phone.

"Tyler, honey, Mommy's on the phone . . ." says Lauren. This is followed by what sounds like a death match struggle over control of the phone. Tyler is more hyper than a Jack Russell terrier on speed. Lauren's husband, Nick, seems to be the only one who can contain him, and that's usually because Nick has the endurance to give him a hundred airplane rides back-to-back.

Lauren has Tyler's feeding and nap schedule down to the second and freaks out if he's one minute late for his nap. I think part of the reason Tyler throws fits is that he's a toddler, not a Swiss train. Who can stand the pressure of keeping to that sort of on-time precision schedule? But what do I know? I'm the irresponsible sister.

"Don't pee-pee on Mommy's ficus! Tyler!"

Tyler has been on a tear recently, taking after the family dog by only peeing outside in the bushes or in potted plants.

"Tyler! Stop. Do you want to say hello to Lily? Come on, Tyler. Say hello."

This is my least favorite part of the conversation. This is where I wait for five or ten minutes listening to Tyler's heavy breathing. He never says hello. It's like being forced to listen to a prank call.

"Hi, Tyler, you bad boy," I say. "Are you going to say hello?"

He says nothing, but breathes more heavily than Darth Vader.

"Are you being a good boy?" I ask, but all I get for an answer is more heavy breathing. He sounds like an asthmatic.

Lauren comes back on the phone.

"Now be a good boy, Tyler. No, Ty. Big boys leave their pants on. No, Tyler! Wee-wees have to stay inside their pants. Tyler!"

"Lauren, if you need to go . . ."

"No, sorry about that. It's like Tyler has just discovered he has a P-E-N-I-S."

"Did you just spell the word 'penis'?"

"Well, you'd think he'd discovered the tenth wonder of the world or something," Lauren says.

"Isn't that how all guys feel about it?"

Lauren laughs.

"I don't know what I'm going to do with him. Mom says I ought to spank Tyler, but I'm *not* going to spank him."

"Yeah, I got spanked all the time and look how I turned out," I say.

"You're right! Good point," Lauren says. I can tell she's filing that away for the next time she and Mom clash over parenting tactics. "So tell me what the cards really say."

"They say things are fine. Nick is the King of Wands, which I wouldn't know anything about, but you would."

"Funny. What does that mean?"

"He's honest, good, and is not cheating on you."

Lauren sighs. "You're sure?"

"Yes. Now, are you going to get me my passport?"

"I looked into it. I can't get it earlier than a month. I went to the post office and they told me, even with a rushed order, I couldn't get it before a month."

"But I have to be home by the first week of December."

"I'm sorry. There's nothing I can do. I put in for it today. It'll be a month, they say."

"Dammit." I sigh. I don't want to go asking Brigid for my passport again. She'll just deny having it.

"It's not my fault you stole my passport," Lauren says.

"Borrowed! I *borrowed* it," I say.

"Same difference." Lauren sighs. "So what are you doing with all your free time?"

"I'm volunteering at a hospital, actually," I say.

Lauren laughs. "You? Work for free?"

"I'm just trying to improve my karma. What's wrong with that?"

"Lily, it might be too late for that already."

I decide not to take offense at my sister's negativity. She's the only one I know more pessimistic than the tarot cards.

At the hospital, on the day I'm supposed to meet Sean Gates in his room, I run into him in the hallway. He's out of his hospital robe and in some baggy pants and a crewneck sweater. He's leaning heavily on crutches.

"Oiy! I wondered where you had gone to, luv. I thought you were going to give me a sponge bath." He winks at me.

My inner slut still wants to jump him, but my rational self is wondering if he talks about anything other than sex.

"Do you ever say anything that isn't a sexual innuendo?"

"Nope," he says, and grins. "Footballers are randy. It's our nature."

"So, uh, you wanted to see Arnold?"

I hold up Arnold for his inspection.

"Um, all right then, I'll pet your pup," Sean says. "But I was more in the mood for a little pussy cat. If you know what I mean."

I think a deaf, dumb, and blind person would know what Sean means. Sean Gates is getting less sexy by the minute. He's coming on with the strength of a Buick.

"Wait, wait! You're not going to just leave me like that. I hear you're psychic," he says, giving me a mischievous grin. "So what am I thinking right now?"

Sean leans against the hospital wall, his considerable frame hovering over me, looking in his wool sweater like he'd be right at home on the cover of *Men's Health*.

"Judging by the look you're giving me, something lewd," I say.

"You *are* psychic! Amazing," he says, and leans in closer. "So what do you say we go back to my room and you give me a reading? And by reading, I mean let's shag, yeah?"

The only thing worse than a sexual innuendo is one that is spelled out.

"I think I'll pass, thanks." Sean Gates is handsome, but there's really nothing going on upstairs except a preoccupation with sex. Even my inner slut is starting to lose interest. I wonder if this means that I'm actually evolving in my ability to identify jerks before I marry them. I guess there's always hope.

"Oiy, you're breaking me heart, luv. Breaking it to pieces."

"I think you'll live."

"Yes, but what about my wanger? He might not survive."

"You have all the subtlety of a freight train," I say.

"Oiy, I've got the length of one, too," he says, and grins.

Wow. He really isn't capable of talking about anything else but his penis. That is really not a good sign. He's getting less attractive by the second.

"'Bye, Sean," I say. "Stay out of trouble, okay?"

Brigid finds me later that afternoon. She's furious.

"You were supposed to go to Sean's room at two P.M.!" she cries.

"I ran into him in the hall around one, so I showed him Arnold then."

"Unacceptable!" Brigid bellows. She's clearly got on her bitch hat at the moment. "Lily, I run this hospital and I do not want you disobeying an order from me. If you do this again, I'll have to have you fired."

"But you're not paying me anything," I remind her.

"Removed from the premises, then," Brigid says, eyes flashing. "Sean's been asking about you. He wants to have his tarot cards read."

"That's not all he wants," I say.

"Sorry?" Brigid says. I shrug. She continues. "He wants you to come to his room Monday afternoon. At two P.M. Don't be late."

She really does have a mental imbalance. And an anger-management problem.

"Have you eaten lunch today?" I ask her.

"I don't eat lunch," she snaps and strides off. She stops mid-step and swivels. "By the way," she says with a sneer, "I heard today that the Dayton Five are going to tour England. And Ted is bringing Melanie Slate. Won't that be fun?"

Fourteen

REASON #14 TO DIVORCE A ROCK STAR:

Because in his head, he's always going to be twenty-five.

Unlike other musicians who cling to the pureness of their art, Ted had no scruples about selling out. This is probably because Ted isn't a very good musician. I can't play guitar, and even I know he got through most songs by just strumming G major. But Ted had the Mick Jagger effect, and he also had a commercial vision, which included the band being featured on one episode of *7th Heaven* on the WB.

Ted didn't mind taking a hit in cool points if it meant selling more albums. Ted was the only musician I knew who didn't think Mark McGrath was a sellout for taking a job as a host of *Extra*. On the contrary, Ted admired McGrath's single-minded determination to stay "out front."

I didn't ask him "out front" of what. But now it's clear that whenever Ted said "out front," it typically meant "out front to earn a dollar, even at the cost of your dignity."

*   *   *

Seemingly overnight, London turns into Dayton Five territory.

Suddenly, everywhere I turn, I see Ted.

He's on the television in the waiting room at the hospital. He's playing on the headphones of nearly everyone walking in the street. He and his band drive by in an ad on a red double-decker bus. Every radio station seems to be giving away free tickets. In the music store windows there are giant posters of the Dayton Five. Ted stands there in his frayed jeans and skin-tight black T-shirt, staring out onto the street with his devilish smile. His shirt says DADDY LOVES YOU.

I look up news on E! online, and there it is, plain as day:

Dayton Five to Start European Tour in London
Ted Dayton is bringing hit sensation the Dayton Five to London, kicking off a twenty-city European tour sponsored by Enzyte. Rumors have it that the frontman's new love, Melanie Slate (*Beautiful, Model Report,* and *Bringing Up Daisy*), will be joining them on the Enzyte tour.

"The Enzyte 'Natural Male Enhancement' Tour?! There is just not enough irony in the world. That's it, Ted has officially used it all," I say.

"You have to admit that it's kind of funny," Carter says, as we stand by Sal's computer. I'm using it to surf the Web. "Just what is Ted trying to say about himself?"

"He's trying to say that he doesn't mind selling out to the

highest bidder, no matter the cost to his dignity, because he doesn't have any," I say. I sigh. "Can't I have one continent to myself, just one! That's all I ask."

"Can't you stop for one second obsessing over those two? So what that they're coming? London is a big city. You won't even know they're here. Unless you want to."

Is Carter jealous? He sounds jealous.

"Carter Henry. Are you jealous?"

"Maybe. Or maybe I'm just concerned about you. Maybe I can't figure out why you're still so obsessed with him."

"Sounds like you're definitely jealous," I say and smile.

Carter, cornered, just shakes his head and looks up at the ceiling. "Why are all women so insane?"

"Because we have to deal with men," I snap back. "You drive us crazy."

"Why don't you punch something? You'll feel better." Carter holds out his hands, like we're going to spar. I take a swipe at his palm and he yelps.

"Ow, Jesus, that's some right you've got," he says, shaking his hand.

"That felt good, can I do it again?"

"I think you broke my hand."

"I did not."

"You know I have a low threshold for pain," he reminds me again and pouts. "So while we're talking about your terrible taste in men, Brigid tells me you're interested in Sean Gates," he says. He looks worried. Even his hair seems tense.

Brigid? Who cares what Brigid thinks, I want to shout,

but don't. I'm too busy wondering just why Carter is so obsessed with my love life. First Ted and now Sean Gates? My stomach does a little dip. Is this more than just friendly intervention?

"I'm not interested in Sean Gates. He's got the subtlety of a porn video," I say. "Besides, I've had my fill of narcissists, thanks. I don't think I want to really jump into another relationship with one."

"Right, well, that's what I told her, but she doesn't believe me. She says you keep sneaking into his room."

"What! I'm not sneaking into his room. She's *asking* me to go in there."

Carter gives me a skeptical look. "I doubt Brigid wants you to bother the hospital's most famous patient."

"I know it sounds weird, but I swear, she's been asking me to."

"You, uh, don't like him, do you? I mean, not that it's any of my business, but . . ."

" 'Like him'? Is this fourth grade?"

"Just answer the question." Carter is serious.

"He's attractive, but he's got the IQ of a soccer ball," I say.

"Thank God," he says, and puts his hand to his chest. "He's my patient, but I can't recommend him as boyfriend material."

"Why?"

"He's about a million times worse than Ted. He treats women like shit," he says. "It's rumored he's fathered two illegitimate children. *Two.* With different mothers."

"I'm not that dumb, Carter," I say. "I know he's trouble."

"I know. But you're in a particularly vulnerable state. I don't want some playboy messing with your head."

Carter is handsome when he lectures me on sexual ethics.

"Aw, Carter. You do care." He does care and maybe cares more than just a friend would. Maybe this means he does have deeper feelings for me.

"I care about getting my place back to myself," Carter says suddenly, almost abruptly. "If you get into a bad rebound thing, then you'll stay on forever. And Brigid is always on me about you. She thinks we spend too much time together."

Ugh. Brigid. *Again.* She's known Carter for a month. I've known him eight years. Not to mention, she's a crazed psychopath and the last person on earth Carter should be trying to please.

You can ask tarot cards yes or no questions by laying out three cards in front of you. The position of the cards (upside down or right-side up) tells you if the answer to your question is definitely or probably yes or no.

The nice thing about this system is that you can keep doing it until you get the answer you want. After our trip to the Little White Wedding Chapel in Vegas, I tried four times before the cards told me "definitely yes" to the question: "Will I be happy with Ted?"

The first three times, the answer was "definitely no."

Now I ask them whether Brigid and Carter are going to break up. The answers: "probably yes": two times, "definitely yes": one time, "definitely no": two times, and "probably no": four times.

Sometimes I really hate these damn cards.

It doesn't help that everywhere I turn, I see Ted's smiling face. He seems to be rubbing it in. It's a wonder that I didn't notice before that his sexy smirk really looks like he's gloating.

I wonder where you go about hiring a professional killer? Is that the sort of thing you can find on Craig's List?

"I think he's not very nice at all," says Margaret, one of the patients in the hospital, who's had cataract surgery and can't read, so I've been reading her some tabloid stories every day. Today I can't help venting about Ted, because he seems to be in every one of her magazines, from *OK!* to *Hello!*

Another point—why do British magazines have exclamation points at the end of their titles? Why would you want your celebrity gossip shouted at you?

"He's not very nice. Not at all," I say. "Any one of you know where I can find a professional killer?"

"Lily!" gasps Margaret, who is easily shocked.

"I used to work in MI6," says Patrick, her roommate. Patrick is the grumpy old codger who Becca doesn't like.

"You were James Bond?" I ask him, amazed. He has about as much charm as a cigarette nub.

"No, I did *real* spy work," Patrick says. "I could have him killed for you."

"You could have Ted killed?" I ask, amazed.

"Not really, but I like saying I could," he says. "Bloody Yanks. You're so gullible."

"Don't mind him," Becca says, coming into the room. "Sorry about that wanker and his trollop," she adds, holding up the tabloid she's reading that has an article about the two of them coming to London.

"It's okay. I've almost come to terms."

I follow Becca out of Patrick and Margaret's room and stand with her at the nurses' station.

"You're not going to believe this," Sal says, coming out of her office. "I just saw Brigid steal a fork from the cafeteria."

"She what?" cries Becca, frowning.

"She *stole* a fork. And a Diet Coke. She put them in her jacket pocket and just walked out without paying."

"I don't know what's more surprising—that she stole a fork or that she was actually *in* the cafeteria," I say.

"I'm serious. What could she want with a fork?" Sal's brow wrinkles. "She doesn't *eat*. Does she plan to stab someone?"

"I heard from the salesclerk at the hospital gift shop that she's been known to nick a lip gloss or two, yeah?" Becca says.

"That explains why she broke into Carter's apartment then. She just can't help herself about stealing things."

"I've got it. Let's catch her in the act, yeah?" Becca says. "Get her sacked!"

"We could video her," Sal suggests.

"How would we go about doing that?" Becca asks. "I think she'd notice a camera."

"No, like a nanny cam. My sister has one. It's a camera hidden in a stuffed bear. You know, built for spying. We could put it in her office," Sal says.

"But she can't steal from *herself*," Becca points out. "What would we find in her office?"

Sal rolls her eyes. "She'd be unloading her loot, wouldn't she? Where do you think all those lip glosses and pens and forks go then?"

"I don't think stealing pens or forks is cause enough to fire someone," I point out.

Becca barrels on. "What if we can also put the bear so it's facing her computer, yeah? We could see what it is she does all day. It's certainly not working."

"Amen to that," Sal says.

"We could just leave the bear in her office. You know, pretend it's a surprise gift from Carter!"

"You both are insane," I say, shaking my head. I glance at the clock on the wall. It's time for me to see Sean Gates, aka Mr. I Never Met a Sexual Innuendo I Didn't Like.

Reluctantly, I head to his room.

"The psychic!" he cries, seeing me, his face lighting up. I'm beginning to suspect he might not know my name.

"Lily," I say.

"Right. Whatever. You come to give me physical therapy?" he winks at me. I sigh and hold up my tarot cards.

"I thought you wanted a reading," I say.

Sean looks up at the television, which shows some soccer match being played.

"Okay then. I'll quiz you, yeah? Ask the cards if I'm the best striker in England."

The cards say yes.

"Okay, good. That was, what do you call it?"

"A test question?"

"Right, that. So now for a real question. Tell me about who's gonna win this game on the telly? Come on, I've got a few quid on this game. Liverpool? Or Chelsea?"

I lay out the cards.

"The red guys are going to win," I say.

"Brilliant!" Sean says. "Thanks, luv."

He motions for me to come closer. "Come on, I won't bite. I just want to tell you a little secret, yeah?"

I sigh and lean in.

"Closer, yeah?"

Sean grabs my arm and tugs me closer.

"Hey," I cry out.

"You know, I'd heal faster if you gave me a kiss."

"Let go of my arm."

"Boy, but I love the girls who play hard to get," Sean says. "Come on then, give us a kiss first."

"No."

"On the cheek. Just on the cheek." Sean taps his finger against the side of his face. "My mum raised a gentleman."

"Just a kiss on the cheek, and then you'll let me go?"

"I give you my word."

I consider hitting him, but decide not to. I don't exactly want to assault the hospital's most famous patient. I figure a quick peck on the cheek won't hurt anything. And if he reneges, *then* I'll kick him. Besides, he's still attractive, even if he is dumber than a box of hair.

I lean in and give him a peck. He turns his face at the last minute, so I land the kiss straight on his lips. Before I can pull back, he's wrapped his hand around the back of my neck to deepen the kiss.

I'm struggling and fighting him, but he's got me in a lip death grip.

And then in perfect, movielike timing, a photographer jumps out from the bathroom like Kato trying to surprise Inspector Clouseau with impromptu karate fights. He snaps a few pictures.

"Oiy!" Sean shouts, realizing what is happening. He lets me go, and I'm caught like a deer in headlights.

"You wanker!" Sean shouts, struggling to free himself from the sheets of his bed. The photographer clicks another shot and then turns and sprints out the door. I shake myself from my temporary trance and try to run after him, but he's too quick and evades me down a flight of stairs.

Fifteen

REASON #15 TO DIVORCE A ROCK STAR:
*You never have to remember another record pro-
ducer's name again.*

I should have expected Ted to run off with someone famous.
He was obsessed with celebrity couples, and with getting
on the cover of *US Weekly*. There was, in Ted's mind, no greater
accomplishment than having photographers follow you around
everywhere you went.

He idolized Justin Timberlake for this very reason. He kept
count of the number of times Justin landed on the cover of *US*.
"I'm better looking than he is," Ted would say. "I can sing better. But I don't have Cameron Diaz."

Shortly after he came back from the Drowning tour, before
his contract with Pepsi, Ted started asking me to dress better. To
go out to parties with him. To mingle and meet celebrities in
posh, glossy bars where everyone wears black and no one has
any body fat.

I am not a Cosmopolitan/sushi kind of girl. I do not go to

trendy places. I like seedy bars where the most exotic thing on the menu is Jägermeister. And at that time, I couldn't tell a Gucci label from Prada, or why either of them was important to have.

Appropriately, the first pictures of him and Melanie Slate appeared in *US*.

It was a month after he'd spent time on her Austin movie set. I found out along with a million other people in America that my husband was cheating on me with a woman known for her breast implants and her complete lack of talent.

The photo showed the two of them kissing outside a Starbucks in Austin, a half mile from where I worked as a temp. Ted was wearing a ripped Sex Pistols T-shirt and Melanie Slate had on a low-cut halter top dress that had less fabric to it than a gym sock.

Ed Reiner, Ted's manager, told me not to worry, that Ted and Melanie were just friends.

"I don't French kiss my friends," I told Reiner.

"Maybe you should," Reiner said. "You'd get more places."

"You did what?" asks my sister Lauren when I tell her about the stealth tabloid photographer. I've tried to tell Carter, but he's being completely monopolized by Brigid. I barely say two words to him all day.

"I have to say, Lily, of all the messes you've gotten yourself into—and there have been a lot—probably hundreds, maybe even thousands . . ."

"Get to the point."

"This doesn't even seem like a problem. Some really hot and rich guy wants to date you and you're going to be in a tabloid. What's the problem again?"

"I may go to jail."

"Right. So maybe you should have fun with this Sean guy in the meantime. Before they send you up the river."

"Lauren. Be serious."

"Um, can you hang on a second? Paul, those roses do not go there!"

Lauren, as usual, is in the middle of planning someone's happily ever after. Since opening her own wedding planning business a couple of years ago, she's constantly at work.

"The florist nearly dumped the roses into the reflecting pool. Okay, what does Carter have to say about this?"

"Carter is not returning my calls. He's busy with one of his lady friends. A psychopath with borderline schizophrenia and multiple personalities."

"In other words, like every other girl Carter has ever dated."

"That's what I said!"

"I don't know what to tell you. Why not have fun with this guy Sean? It might be the last chance you get for sex with an underwear model."

"Lauren. You are not taking this situation seriously," I say. "I didn't mean to kiss him. I don't even like him."

"Right," Lauren says skeptically. "You just accidentally fell on his face."

"But what about my assault trial? If this gets out, then everyone will know I've skipped bail."

My future life flashes before my eyes. Me on the cover of a tabloid, linked to Sean Gates. Me going to jail for skipping bail. Me with hideous black roots and no makeup in a bright neon-orange jumpsuit and bad plastic slippers trying to fend off advances from a burly, hairy woman named Marcy who runs Cell Block Eight.

"Sometimes there just isn't anything you can do," Lauren says. "Paul!" she shouts. "Watch out for the runners." She sighs and comes back on the line.

"That's your advice for me? You, the perfect sister who always has all the answers? 'Sometimes there just isn't anything you can do'?"

"I'm a bit distracted at the moment, all right? I really wish I could talk, but this isn't a good time. I'll call you back, okay?"

"Aye! Lookee here," Ian cries, when I get off the phone. He's taught Arnold a new trick. "Roll over, aye? Roll over!"

We watch as Ian holds up a piece of chicken and Arnold rolls halfway over. His potbelly gets in the way of him making a full rotation.

"Good boy!" Ian says, clapping and tossing him another bite of chicken. "A smart pup, that."

On the way to the hospital the next day, the tabloids are full of pictures of Melanie Slate and Ted, but nothing about me or Sean Gates. I breathe a little sigh of relief. I never thought I'd be relieved to see Ted on the cover of the *Daily Mirror*. But there it is. The world is a funny place sometimes.

At the hospital, while I'm reading tarot cards for Margaret and Patrick, who swears that he *did* work for MI6 and that he *could* have someone killed if he wanted to (he just can't admit it in front of other people), I hear the telltale click of Brigid's heels on the hospital tile floor. She appears by the door, frowning.

"Lily? I need to speak to you."

"Bollocks, it was just getting good," Patrick says.

"I thought you didn't believe in tarot cards," I say.

"Aye, I only believe 'em when they tell me good news," Patrick says. "I'm an optimist at heart."

This causes me to laugh because Patrick is the farthest thing from an optimist. He says daily that he's dying, even though he just had a hip replacement and the doctors say he's strong as an ox.

Brigid clears her throat. "Now," she says.

In her office, Brigid pulls glossy color photos out of a manila envelope. They're the ones the sneaky photographer took. Me kissing Sean Gates. And you can't tell I'm trying to get away. This is mostly because you just see the back and slightly side view of my head.

"Where did you get these?" I ask her.

"I have my sources. The hospital is a very open place."

I look at her and then at the photos.

"I've found out that the photographer is currently trying to sell them to a couple different tabloids. He's got a bidding war going."

"He does?"

"He thinks they'll be out there by the end of the week."

"I see." I glance above Brigid's head and I notice a big brown teddy bear. It's holding a heart balloon that says YOU'RE BEAR-IFIC.

"Nice bear," I say, thinking of Becca and Sal. Is this their spy cam?

"Carter gave it to me," Brigid says and beams. "He won't admit it, but I think that's because he doesn't want to admit to being such a romantic."

On her computer, I notice that her screensaver is just a giant picture of Carter's head floating in black space. She also has three or four framed pictures of him on her desk. Can you say "creepy"?

"But about you and these pictures," Brigid continues. "I think it would be wise if you left the country. Carter told me about your, uh, legal problems."

He did? Great. He can't keep a secret at all. Especially when his pants come off. If he were a CIA agent, all the enemy agents would have to do is get him naked and he'd confess all our country's secrets.

Brigid opens her desk drawer and retrieves my blue passport. She slides it across her desk to me.

"The sooner the better," she says, smiling as if she's doing me a favor.

"You snogged Sean Gates!" Becca cries, when I fill her and Sal in on the exchange with Brigid and the photos of me and Sean.

"Not intentionally."

"What was it like? You have to tell us. I can't believe you

beat me to it, yeah?" Becca stares at me with grudging admiration.

"It wasn't something I planned," I say. "It just happened. And he's a decent kisser, except that he squashed my nose to his face. He's a little rough."

"Rough? Mmmmmm," Becca says in a dreamy voice.

"Would you stop thinking about sex for one second?" Sal snipes. "I know it's your only hobby, but let's focus on Brigid here. It's not like her to do you a favor. Why not just let the tabloids come out? Why warn you in advance?"

"Maybe she just wants to protect the hospital," I suggest.

"Or maybe she just wants you out of the way," Sal says. "She's already said she doesn't like you living with Carter."

"Did he use tongue, yeah?" Becca asks me.

"Becca! *Jaysis,*" Sal cries.

"What? For those of us who've actually kissed something other than our hands, it's relevant information, yeah?" Becca says.

"Sod off," Sal says.

"You only say that because I'm right."

"I've kissed a bloke. But unlike you, I've not kissed half of London."

"I guess I'll probably have to just go home," I say. "It's probably the smart thing to do."

Becca and Sal look sad. "We'll miss you, yeah?"

"That's at least one thing we can agree on," Sal says.

I use Becca's computer and look up flights. There's one out tomorrow. I decide that it makes sense if I take it. I've got to be back for court in a couple of weeks, and clearly, with Brigid around, I'm not exactly welcome in Carter's life at the moment, either.

Carter is distracted when I tell him I'm leaving. He's busy scribbling patient notes on a clipboard.

"Leaving so soon?" he asks, frowning at his clipboard. "What about your passport?"

"Brigid gave it to me."

"Brigid did what?" says Brigid herself, appearing out of nowhere.

"You gave Lily her passport?" Carter asks her.

"What do you mean? I never had your passport," Brigid says, eyeing me.

"Yeah, anyway," I say, looking at Carter, "do want to go out to the pub tonight? See me off?"

"He can't," Brigid says quickly, putting a protective arm across Carter's chest. "We've got plans."

"Oh," I say, looking at Carter. He shrugs. He's not making eye contact with me.

"Okay then," I say. I feel a stinging disappointment. I try hard to tell myself it doesn't matter, but even I don't believe myself.

Later, at Carter's apartment, Ian is more than disappointed to hear the news that I'm leaving and taking Arnold with me.

"Och, you canna go yet!" Ian says, hugging Arnold protectively. "Arnold's helping me save the universe."

"I'm sorry, but we definitely have to go," I say.

Ian sighs and then nods. "Och, aye, then let's go out and give you a proper send-off."

"Carter has a date with Brigid."

"Bollocks," Ian swears. "He's comin' out with us, and he's leavin' the head case at home."

"But he said . . ."

"Leave it to me."

At the bar, Ian orders us a frightening amount of scotch. Carter keeps glancing at his watch. Brigid is nowhere to be found.

"Have you guys seen my cellphone?" Carter asks us.

"Nope, mate, sorry," Ian says, giving me a wink, and then pulling it out of his pocket under the table so only I can see.

"You must really hate Brigid," I say to Ian, as Carter wanders off to the bar to see if his cellphone fell out there.

"No one touches my Xbox without permission, aye?" Ian says. "Besides, it'll do the boy good to get out of her clutches once in a while. Otherwise, she'll be tyin' his shoelaces before long."

"But isn't she just going to show up here?" I ask Ian.

"I told Brigid to meet us at a different bar."

I raise my glass and clink it with his. "Did I tell you I love you?" I ask him.

"Get in line, missus," he says and winks at me.

By the time we've had a few more rounds, Carter forgets about his cellphone. The topic of conversation is Carter's crazy ex-girl-friends. I'm telling Ian about the one who broke Carter's wind-shield and then slashed her own tires and had him arrested for it.

"You need to find a girl who's got her head screwed on straight," Ian says.

"What I need to do," Carter says, tipping his beer mug into mine, "is find a girl like Lily. She's practically a guy."

"Beg your pardon?" I ask.

"You are. Look, you don't spend hours talking about your feelings. And when you get mad, you hit something. Those are definite guy traits."

"And do I also have a five o'clock shadow you're not telling me about?"

Ian looks back and forth between the two of us. "I'll go get more drinks," he says.

I lean in closer to Carter and my heart speeds up. He's so handsome, so clean-cut, and his hair is perfectly in place.

"I didn't say you look like a guy. I said you act like one. For instance, you know all the rules of football."

"I grew up in Texas, Carter. Every Texas girl knows the rules of football."

"Not like you. Who's the best quarterback in Cowboys history?" Carter's hair is in rare form. Every strand is perfectly and professionally tussled. If he were on the make tonight, he'd definitely reel in a few unsuspecting chicks. As it is, I feel like he's reeling me in.

"Roger Staubach."

"And who bragged for months after meeting Ricky Williams in the 7-Eleven when he was still at UT?"

"I did."

"See? This is what I'm talking about. You're a guy. Embrace it. You even eat like one." Carter points to the fish and chips I've all but devoured in front of me.

"I told you that you should never trust a woman who doesn't eat," I say.

"Brigid eats," Carter says somewhat defensively. Then he pauses. "Of course, she doesn't eat much."

"See? Told you."

By the time Carter and I stumble home, we're laughing so hard that I can barely breathe. Ian has opted to stay at the bar, calling us amateur drinkers.

My stomach hurts from laughing so hard. I don't remember the last time my stomach hurt from laughing.

"I don't think I can laugh anymore, or my abs are going to burst," I say.

"Oh, I think you can laugh some more, Ms. Ticklish."

"No—" I cry, but Carter is already on the attack. He knows my weakest points, the sides between my ribs and waist.

"Stop, or . . . my bladder! Ack!"

In my anxiousness to fend off Carter, I fall backward on the couch and he follows me. Before I know it, he's practically on top of me. He stops tickling.

"Lil . . ." he says, suddenly serious. His eyes are so close to mine, I can practically see them dilate. "I don't want you to leave."

"You don't?"

Carter shakes his head. "Do you ever . . . ?"

"Do I ever what?" I say, heart thudding in my chest. Do I wonder what would've happened if we didn't break up? Do I ever want to rub my body against yours? Do I ever just want to rip your clothes off and let my inner slut have her way with you? The answer: definitely yes to all three.

"Do you ever . . ." Carter is staring at my mouth. " . . . wonder what it would be like . . ."

"To kiss you again?" I finish for him. My mouth parts slightly, anticipating a kiss.

It's one of those moments—the moments where it occurs to both of you that you've inadvertently crossed over that friendship threshold and into something more serious. You've got only two options: move forward or retreat. I'm suddenly very sober, not drunk at all.

I don't know if he moves first, or if I do, but all at once we're kissing, a soft, deliberate, exploring kiss. Carter is the one who deepens it, opening his mouth wider over mine. Carter is gentle but insistent, sensual and deliberate. He has his hands in my hair and is pushing his body into mine. It's everything I remember and more. It's just as good as I've imagined it would be. Better, even. I feel like I've come home.

I open my eyes and find that his are open. He draws back slowly and blinks.

"I didn't mean to do that," he says.

"You didn't?" I'm still dazed from the kiss. My body feels like a guitar string. It's humming.

"I mean, I did, but I didn't, uh . . ." he trails off. He runs his hands through his hair. Now I know that he's flustered, because he never deliberately messes his hair unless he's a bit unraveled.

He glances to the right, then the left, as if he's not sure what he ought to do next. He doesn't look at me as he gets to his feet.

"I think I'm, uh, going to bed," he says, rubbing his hair back and forth, completely annihilating what remains of the styling product in his hair.

"Carter, wait," I say, trying to grab his hand, but he's too quick for me. He's already sprung up from the couch and is heading to his bedroom.

His door clicks shut, and the moment is gone.

Sixteen

REASON #16 TO DIVORCE A ROCK STAR:
Because average, nonfamous guys can be just as confounding.

There's no mention of the kiss the next day. Carter pretends as if it never happened, and there's not even a conversation about it. I can't help but feel disappointed. It's like what's been at the back of my mind since I got to London is now front and center: I'm attracted to Carter. There's just no denying it. I want to jump him. Whether it's more than just sheer physical attraction, I don't know. But the fact that Carter seems to be able to forget about the heat in that kiss makes me wonder if he felt it at all.

Then again, the reasonable part of my brain says that it's better this way. I think my life is complex enough without opening the door to a self-admitted commitmentphobe who has to change his mobile phone number every three months to avoid the prank calls from the legions of pissed-off ex-girlfriends who have in one way or another been wronged by him.

Carter is sexy, yes. Carter is funny, yes. Carter also 1) has a girlfriend (even if she is psychotic); and 2) is also a hundred times more toxic than rat poison. No thanks. I don't see the point in risking a perfectly good friendship for what will probably be passable sex. From what I remember, there was a lot of fumbling. But isn't that how all sex is at eighteen?

And I know Carter. If I sleep with him, he'd be in New Zealand the next week talking about how it's not me, it's him, and how he needs to sort out his feelings, which is code for "sleep with someone else."

My friendship with Carter is far more important to me than an orgasm or two, no matter what my inner slut says. What would I do if I didn't have Carter to call the next time I saw Melanie Slate in *People?* I mean, I have priorities.

All in all, though, it's a good thing I'm leaving London. The drunken kiss just shows that things could get complicated with Carter, and the last thing I need in my life right now is another complication.

"Tell me you're still in London," my lawyer, Larry, says on the phone.

"I thought you wanted me back in the States. I got my passport back and I'm on a flight in about four hours," I say.

"Postpone it."

"What?"

"I don't know how it happened, but Melanie Slate got wind of you being there."

"How?"

"I don't know, but her people have been calling me all day. They want to cut a deal. Melanie Slate thinks she might be able to convince Ted to drop the assault charges if you sign the settlement papers."

"I don't want to sign the settlement papers. At least, not until the settlement is more balanced."

"Would you rather go to jail?"

"No. But, Larry—"

"I realize you never follow my advice, but as your attorney, I advise you to meet with Melanie Slate. Talk about the settlement. She's really anxious to have this divorce settled."

I have no doubt she is. It's extremely bad press if the number two female box office star in America is shacking up with a married man. The sooner Ted is divorced and the magazines stop running that Iron Cactus picture of me, the sooner I'll be forgotten and she and Ted can work on getting more red-carpet photos.

"If you don't want to meet Melanie, then how about her assistant?"

"No."

"If you don't do this, I'm quitting. Good luck finding someone else crazy or dumb enough to represent you."

"The abuse I get for three hundred fifty dollars an hour," I say. "Okay, when and where?"

Larry sets up a meeting with Melanie's assistant in front of the London Eye. I wanted a public place, in case Melanie's ulterior motive involves a hired killer. I ask the tarot cards about the meeting, and I turn up the Devil card. I assume this is representative of Melanie Slate.

If the meeting is no longer than a half hour, I might have an outside chance of still making my flight. That is, if there's not any traffic.

I wait at the base of the giant wheel, having no idea what to expect, and I'm not really sure what I'm doing here exactly. It has the feel of a James Bond movie. It's like I'm playing the hapless heiress being led into a trap.

Arnold pops his head out of my bag and whines.

"If someone tries to kill me, you'll protect me, right?" I ask Arnold.

Arnold yawns and then puts his head down on the edge of my bag and closes his eyes for a nap. Great.

My backup is a twenty-pound Chihuahua who sleeps twenty hours a day.

"Lily?" asks a woman in her twenties, wearing black-framed glasses, orange hair with bangs cut severely across her forehead, and a Sonic Youth T-shirt. She's American. "Hi, I'm Wendy. Melanie Slate's assistant."

"Hi."

"You want to take a ride? I've been dying to get on this thing, but Melanie is afraid of heights. Want to?"

Now I really am starting to think I'm in a James Bond movie. Is this where I get a poison dart to the neck and die?

"You're not going to kill me, are you?"

"God, no," she says. "I'm a Buddhist. We're pacifists."

Wendy has gotten tickets in advance, pulling strings as only an assistant to Melanie Slate can, so we get a London Eye car to ourselves, even though they can hold more than a dozen people standing at once. It feels like being in a giant, clear M&M. As we start to move, Arnold pops his head out of my bag and Wendy pets him.

"I'm here on a peacekeeping mission," Wendy says. "Think of me as a member of the UN."

"You mean the good members, or the ones who take bribes?"

"I just have a proposition for you," she barrels on, ignoring me. "Melanie wants to help you and Ted reach a compromise."

"Wendy, I don't mean to be rude, but I don't give a shit what Melanie Slate wants."

Wendy nods, as if she hears this argument often.

"Look, I'm going to tell you something that I hope you won't tell anyone else, okay? I work for Melanie, but I don't like her. I'm actually her first cousin back from Iowa, where we both grew up, and let me tell you, Melanie has stolen more than one of my boyfriends."

I wonder if it was Melanie who did the stealing, or if it was one of Wendy's three nose piercings that scared them away.

"So, look, I totally—totally—understand where you're coming from. I mean, fuck Melanie, right? Who cares what she wants, right?"

"Right."

"So here's the thing. What's best for you is what I'm saying. I mean, nobody wants you to go to jail for that Iron Cactus thing."

I think it's very possible that Melanie Slate does want me to go to jail.

"What will going to jail get you?" Wendy continues. "I think they're both evil, so let them be evil with each other, you know what I mean? You gotta move on."

Wendy whips out some papers from her messenger bag and inadvertently drops a couple of small Ziploc bags on the floor of the London Eye car. At first, I think they might be drugs, but as Wendy stoops to pick them up, I see they're carefully sealed wads of used chewing gum.

"Melanie's chewing gum," Wendy explains. "You won't believe how much it goes for on eBay."

"Who wants someone's used gum?"

"I don't know, and I don't want to know. I just get money in my PayPal account and mail off the gum. The only thing that sells faster is Melanie's underwear."

"That's more information than I needed."

I wonder if any of Ted's things could be auctioned off on eBay. I have a couple of his T-shirts and maybe a toothbrush. Then again, even I don't think I'd stoop that low. But I'm sure if Ted knew there could be money to be made on his discarded toothbrushes, he'd use a different one every night so he could sell them himself.

"Anyway, back to business. You sign these divorce papers, and Melanie will personally pay you one hundred thousand dollars because she feels badly about how this all went down."

Wendy makes my marriage sound like a heroin deal gone bad.

"This isn't about the money," I say.

Wendy throws her head back and laughs.

"This isn't about the money!" she squeals. "That's a good one."

"I would rather just have an apology."

"How about two hundred thousand dollars?" Wendy asks me, completely serious.

"Okay," I say, suddenly seeing reason. Maybe I can be bought. Or maybe this is just the "clean break" prophesized by the tarot cards. "Okay, I'll sign."

"You will?" Wendy seems surprised, shocked even.

She hands me the papers.

"Oh my God, I can't thank you enough. Melanie so would've fired me if I didn't get you to sign. I mean, Melanie has always been a bitch, but now that she's pregnant, oh my God, she's been firing people left and right like you wouldn't believe. . . ."

I pause, the pen on the paper.

"What did you say?" I ask her.

"About Melanie firing people? Oh yeah, she even fired her eyebrow waxer the other day. This is the same one who does J. Lo's eyebrows. She gets three thousand dollars an eyebrow, and Melanie called her incompetent."

"No, before that," I say. "About Melanie being pregnant?"

Wendy's face falls. "Did I say that? I wasn't supposed to say that."

I fold up the papers, crumple them, and look for a trash

can. I see none, and we're a mile up in the air. Instead, I stuff them in my bag.

"Oh shit, don't listen to me. I mean, who knows if it's even Dayton's—you can't be sure of that sort of thing with Melanie. Come on, please, sign! What about closure and moving on?" Wendy looks defeated. "I've blown it, haven't I?"

Seventeen

REASON #17 TO DIVORCE A ROCK STAR:
So you don't have to name your son Slash Jr.

When we were married, Ted insisted that he was not the fatherly type. As I had fewer maternal instincts than a blender, it didn't bother me so much. Besides, I wasn't even going to think about babies until at least thirty, so what did I care that he didn't want kids? I figured that was something we could discuss later, after he'd gone on his fifth or sixth world tour.

That all changed the month my period was one week late. My period is never late. I'm more regular than Big Ben, and that says a lot since I'm never on time for anything else in my life. But my menstrual cycle—well, you can time the Indy 500 by it. So I started considering the late factor, and the more I considered the possibility of pregnancy, the more I thought, well, it's not what I expected, but isn't life what happens when you're making plans (and all the rest of those clichés)?

Ted, however, didn't see it that way.

To say he freaked out is putting it mildly. First he threw a chair across the room. Then he stormed up to me, inches from my face, and began his red-faced shouting routine. He accused me of sleeping around, claiming if I was pregnant it couldn't be his. Then he accused me of lying to him about being on the pill and "entrapping" him.

And now, here he is, having a baby with Melanie Slate?

It's a kick to the stomach. I feel like I can't breathe.

"Why aren't you reacting to this news? Melanie is *pregnant*," I cry on the phone to my sister, Lauren. I'm in a cab and speeding to Heathrow. I'm pretty sure I'm going to miss my flight.

"I sort of knew about this already," Lauren admits.

"How could you not tell me!" This is urgent information. It's fresh fuel for my anger, and it feels good. Righteous.

"I didn't *know* know, but you know *US Weekly*? You know they do that 'is it a bump' thing—well, they've been doing that for Melanie Slate for the last couple of weeks. I didn't think you'd want the extra grief. Besides, I was hoping maybe she'd just had one too many bagels."

"You know Melanie Slate doesn't eat. She just injects herself with silicone now and again. Anyway, you should've told me."

"Look, I'm having bigger problems. I think Nick is having an affair."

"He's not."

"You haven't heard the evidence."

"Trust me, he's not."

"But . . ."

"Did you catch him with his pants down?"

"No."

"In a lie?" I ask.

"No."

"I rest my case. He's not having an affair."

"But, Lily . . ."

"I'm getting another call. It's Mom. I'll call you back, okay? Hello? Mom?"

"How did you know? Oh, never mind. How are you holding up?"

"Not so well, Mom."

"Is it because of Melanie's baby? I read about it in *People* magazine."

"It was in *People!*" I shout.

"Why else do you think I sound so concerned? I didn't think you might be having trouble coping with the weather in London."

My head hurts.

"You know I'm always the last to know what's going on with my children. I have to read about you in magazines."

"Mom, I didn't even know before *People* knew. And, anyway, you can't believe everything you read in those magazines."

"I don't know, Britney Spears says you can always count on *People*."

Since when did my mom follow the advice of Britney Spears?

"I just don't understand why you always have to go for the bad guys," Mom says. "You know you're so much better than that. Does it have something to do with self-esteem? I always thought I let you suck on your pacifier too long."

Only Mom would think a pacifier would lead me to date narcissists.

"Are you sure you're holding up all right? You don't sound like you're holding up," Mom says, using *the tone.*

"I'm fine, really."

"Well, are you coming home for Thanksgiving next week? You know it's not a Thanksgiving unless *both* my girls are here."

"I'll be there," I say. "In fact, I'm coming home today."

"That's the best news I've heard so far today," Mom says.

I get to the airport and stumble around with my many bags. I'm at the check-in counter when my phone rings.

"Where are you? Don't get on that plane!" cries the voice of Sal.

"What are you talking about?"

"Brigid set the whole thing up."

"She what?"

"We looked at the teddy cam," Sal says. "She's the one who told the photographer where you'd be and where to hide."

Of course. It makes perfect sense, doesn't it? Brigid has wanted me gone since the moment I arrived. She's also insane, so calling in the paparazzi probably makes perfect sense to her.

It also explains why she had the photograph prints before anyone else. I should've figured it out before now.

"You've got to help us keep the story under wraps," Sal says. "Carter's job may be at stake."

I inch forward in line. Arnold, in his doggy carrier, whines.

"You can't let her get away with this," Sal says. "If the story gets out, Carter might lose his job."

"Why?"

"He's the one who vouched for you as a volunteer, that's why. You think the hospital could take this kind of bad publicity without someone losing their job?"

"Brigid will protect him."

"You mean because Brigid loves him working at the hospital with nurses like Becca around in flirting distance. She'd love to have him home, under her thumb. She would love it if he was on the dole. Then she could keep an eye on him and control him even more. Trust me. You'll understand once you see the tape."

I think back to the Carter picture screen saver on Brigid's computer. It could be that she's a little obsessive. This might be plausible.

I've reached the head of the check-in line, and the woman behind the American Airlines counter waves me forward.

"You really think Carter's job is at stake?"

"Positive," Sal says.

"You really think I can help?"

"Absolutely."

I sigh.

"You can't let Brigid keep her claws in Carter," Sal says. "You can't let her win!"

I hesitate. Am I going to get on a plane? Am I going to leave, even after kissing Carter? Even after realizing that I am still attracted to him?

I glance over and see a couple standing at the security check-in. They're kissing, a long, passionate, don't-even-care-it's-in-public kiss, and at that moment I think about Carter, and how he'd done the same with me just yesterday.

I can't let him go on with Brigid without knowing the truth.

I realize that I can't leave. Not without knowing how he really feels about me. Not without knowing if we have a future.

It dawns on me that this is why I came to London. That I'd been wanting to know if there was something more than friendship here. If maybe Carter had feelings for me still. And I can't leave. Not without knowing if he does.

I cash in my ticket for a travel voucher and then head out of the airport.

First things first. I head to the hospital to help save Carter's job, even though I have no idea exactly what I should do to help. I decide to start with Brigid.

Brigid is in her office, wearing a dark suit and glasses. She slips them off when she sees me and frowns.

"What are you doing here?" she asks me, a panicked look on her face. "You're supposed to be on a plane."

"Call him off," I say.

"Who?"

"The photographer. Call him off. I know you hired him."

Brigid's face goes pale.

"I don't know what you're talking about."

"Get those photos back and make sure they don't go into any tabloids."

Brigid leans back in her chair, a half smile on her face.

"Why? You don't want your ex hearing about you and Sean?"

"There's no me and Sean and you know it."

"Look, I can't get the photos back. I don't own the photographer."

"You realize this could really hurt the hospital?"

"I think the best thing for everyone is for you to turn around and go back to the airport," Brigid says. "When the story breaks, I know Carter isn't going to want to see you."

"What does that mean?"

"You'll have to wait and see."

I don't know what Brigid is talking about, but I do know that I need to find Carter. I'm not sure what I'm going to say to him, exactly, but I think I'll figure out something. When I get back to his apartment, I'm disappointed to discover Carter isn't there.

Ian, however, is very happy to see me. Well, not so much me as Arnold.

"Wee pup!" he says, freeing Arnold from his kennel and spinning him around until he's in danger of yakking up kibble.

"Thanks for helping with my bags," I say, lugging up my heavy suitcases while Ian carries Arnold.

"I'm holding the pup, aye?" he says. "He's heavier than he looks."

"So let me get this straight," my lawyer says on the phone. "You turned down Melanie Slate's olive branch. You missed your flight *on purpose,* and now you will most likely be on the cover of every tabloid in England linked romantically to a famous soccer player. Is that right?"

"But there's something more important at risk here. This could be true love, don't you understand? I just need a few days to figure it all out."

"Oh great. First it was tarot cards and now it's true love. Next you're going to tell me you're shacking up with the Easter Bunny and unicorns are going to fly out of my butt."

"You are far too cynical for your own good."

"It's the only way to win court cases," he says.

"If it makes you feel any better, I have a plan. I'm going to catch a plane in a few more days. I'll still be back before the trial, okay?"

There's silence on the other end of the phone.

"Larry? Hello?"

"I need to start charging you more," Larry says.

I look for Carter everywhere, but I can't find him. He's completely MIA. I call his mobile phone, but it's turned off or he isn't getting a signal, because all I get is voicemail. I can't be more frustrated. I mean, whenever I don't want him around, Carter is everywhere, and when I actually have something important to say, I can't find him anywhere.

I wonder if Brigid has him held captive somewhere. Her jealous, psychotic rage might just be enough to tie him in her basement so that he can't come to see me. Just when I'm about to give up hope, Carter comes in. I have to restrain myself from running up to him, throwing my arms around his neck, and declaring my love.

Two seconds after he walks in the door, Brigid follows. My heart sinks. She glares at me, daring me to say anything.

I had imagined me telling Carter that I think I might love him and us spending a romantic evening, the two of us, in bed. Instead, I find myself sitting on the couch next to Carter and Brigid, while Brigid sticks her tongue in Carter's ear and he moans. I realize it's wrong to covet a boy who isn't mine, but wasn't he mine first?

"I'm going to bed," I announce.

"But it's only seven," Carter says.

I lie on my bed listening to the giggles coming from the living room, wondering if I didn't make a mistake. Maybe I should've gotten on that plane. Admitting to Carter that I have feelings for him is going to be a lot harder than I thought.

Arnold wakes me up at 5:00 A.M. with a paw to the eye. It's his way of letting me know he has to pee. This is one step up from just drenching my comforter, so I drag myself out of bed and grab Arnold's leash.

If taking care of a baby is one-hundredth the hassle of dealing with a dog, then I'm never having kids.

It's chilly outside and Arnold is shaking. He sniffs at every passing tree and every tiny crevice in the sidewalk, but apparently none are good enough for his business. I wonder what exactly he's looking for: a written invitation, I guess.

"Come on, Arnold. It's crap, not a buried treasure. Just leave it anywhere," I say. I look around on the sidewalk, seeing evidence of other dogs. Unlike in the States, here there seems to be dog poop everywhere. I guess there's no bag-it law. "Look? Everyone else did."

Arnold whines at me and shakes some more. "I know it's cold," I say. "That's why you ought to go right now so we can both go back to sleep."

I light up a cigarette and puff on it furiously. The cold air makes it look like I'm exhaling twice the usual amount of smoke.

It's nearly 5:30. I'm wondering if it's possible to sleep standing up when I notice a man across the street taking a picture. He's aiming the camera right at me.

I feel a sudden chill at the base of my spine. Is he paparazzi? Have they figured out where I live?

I get a sudden feeling of creepiness. Like the time shortly after Ted was featured on MTV's *Cribs* and a woman followed me around in the grocery store. As I waited in line, she approached me and asked me if I was "Lily Dayton," and that's when I noticed that her grocery basket was identical to mine. She'd been copying my every move and picking up one of everything I picked up. It took me a few days to lose that lingering feeling of ickiness.

I've got that same prickly sensation at the back of my neck as I watch the photographer across the street. Luckily, Arnold does his business behind a trash can, away from the photographer's lens. I pick up Arnold and walk quickly back to Carter's apartment. I will myself not to run. Paparazzi are like bears or mountain lions. If you run, it just brings out their predator hunting instincts.

That's when I walk past the newsstand and see it. The latest edition of the *Sun*. The headline reads, "I'm in Love with Sean Gates: Our Love Bloomed in Hospital." And there's a picture of me, locking lips with Sean Gates.

> Lily Dayton (former wife of Ted Dayton) says she's fallen in love with Sean Gates while volunteering at the hospital, where he is recovering from foot surgery. "I didn't mean to fall in love," Lily told the *Sun*. "It started as a quick shag, but it's moved on to something much more. We're ready to declare our love."

I read, transfixed. How is this possible? I didn't talk to any reporters. I never said any of these things. I don't even use the word "shag." Hello? I'm American.

The hamster wheel in my head turns.

Brigid.

This is her doing.

She's set me up. She called the *Sun* and pretended to be me! I can't believe she's sunk so low. I can't believe she's so threatened by me that she's called up a tabloid and had an entire interview pretending to be her boyfriend's ex. She's seriously mental.

I continue reading.

> Gates was unavailable for comment but friends of his on-again, off-again fiancée, Tanya Richards, the lingerie model, says Tanya is considering calling off their wedding.

He's engaged? He didn't say anything about being engaged. And neither did Brigid, for that matter. I read on and discover that Tanya is not only his fiancée, but she's also pregnant with his baby. Very pregnant, by the look of her in pictures.

You wouldn't know it the way Sean came on with all the subtlety of a man just out of prison.

Are all men bastards? Seriously, I want to know. You tell me. Really. Because from where I'm sitting they all sure *look* like bastards. I'm pissed and I didn't even *like* him. Now I know where Lauren gets her trust issues. I mean, how often can you be taken advantage of before you just snap?

The rest of the article goes on about how Sean, the incorrigible womanizer, has met his match in me, the spitfire ex of a rock star who has serious anger-management issues and a history of violence. On the inside pages there's the picture that won't die. Me outside the Iron Cactus in Austin, makeup smudged, looking unhinged and dangerously close to a mental breakdown.

This is the sort of press that Ted would kill for. Instinctively, I know that this is a story that isn't going to go away. When a big celebrity and a small celebrity hook up for a scandal, it's like when warm gulf air meets cold Canadian air. Separate, they're fine. Put them together and you've got an F-5 tornado. I can already hear the mobile homes being tossed around like Pez dispensers.

By the time I make it back to Carter's apartment, the photographer who has followed me is now sitting across the street. I assume Brigid told him where I live, too. Why not? If you're ruining someone's life, why do it halfway?

Inside Carter's apartment, I find Brigid cuddling innocently in the kitchen with Carter while the two of them make tea. I'm so angry my hands are shaking. I haven't felt this furious since I caught Ted with Melanie.

"Would you like to explain this?" Brigid asks me, stealing my very question, the moment I walk in the door. She has the tabloid and has been showing it to Carter, because he looks up and gives me his best disappointed face.

In an instant, I know how bad this must look, and I also know that Carter's been brainwashed by his psychotic girlfriend and there's little or no hope at this point that he'll be able to listen to reason and believe my side of the story.

"It's all Brigid's fault," I sputter to Carter, and I sound like my nephew when he's trying to blame the cat for eating all the cookies in the house.

"It's what?" Carter asks, skeptical.

"Lily, why in the world would I do that?" Brigid says, eyes wide. She is giving an Oscar-caliber performance. She is one hundred times the actress Melanie Slate is.

"You *told* me something like this would happen," I said. "You told me to wait and see what came out in the tabloids. How would you know that if you didn't set this whole thing up?"

Brigid wrinkles her brow in confusion. And I'd like to thank the Academy and my nemesis, Lily Crandell, for making this possible, I think.

"No, what I told you was that if you kept up your relationship with Sean that something like this would happen," she says evenly. *"That's* what I said."

"Lily, is this true?" Carter asks me. "Are you in love with Sean Gates?"

"No, of course not. I told you. He's not my type." And I'm infatuated with someone else, I want to add. You! You, moron! Can't you see it on my face?

"But you're kissing here."

"I didn't mean to kiss him."

"This doesn't look like an accident," Carter says, showing me the picture. "And Brigid says she's seen you and Sean together before."

Carter gives me a serious look. I look over to Brigid, who has a look of concern on her face. She's looking at me like *I'm* the crazy one. They both are.

"You're going to take her word over mine?" I ask him, even though I already know the answer. He's completely under her spell. Brigid has her hooks into him so deeply that he's lost all circulation to his brain.

"Why would she call a tabloid, Lily? I mean, it's bad publicity for the hospital. It just doesn't make sense," Carter says. "I think we both know what's going on here."

"And that is?"

"You're embarrassed. You're having an affair with Sean Gates, and you're embarrassed. It's okay. Just admit it."

"Carter, you're not hearing me. I wouldn't touch Sean Gates with a ten-foot pole." I'm crazy about you, not Sean Gates. It's you I want to kiss! Not him!

Carter just looks at me, doubtful. He doesn't believe me.

"I wish you could just be adult enough to admit you've made a mistake," Carter says, shaking his head. "This is going to cause the hospital a lot of problems. You really disappoint me, Lily. You really do."

Eighteen

REASON #18 TO DIVORCE A ROCK STAR:

Because the song you thought was about you isn't.

"Drowning," Ted's first hit single, was about falling in love so deeply with a woman that she "saved his life." I assumed the song was about me. After all, he did propose to me in the emergency room after his accidental overdose.

Turns out, the song was about a pothead named Gwen who used to follow the band around before they were legitimately famous. She was not particular about which member of the Dayton Five she slept with at any given time, just so long as it wasn't a roadie.

Gwen told me with some satisfaction after my separation from Ted became news that the song was about her.

A couple of weeks after Ted proposed to me, she said, she and Ted were fucking in the pool at a Motel 6. He passed out afterward in the Jacuzzi and nearly drowned. She's the one who dragged him to safety.

She's also the one who told me that if I were smart, I'd get a chlamydia test. It had made a few rounds with members of the band, she said.

"I want to sue this tabloid for libel," I tell my lawyer on the phone.

"The problem is that you're a quasi-celebrity, so that might be difficult," he says on the phone. "Do you have proof you didn't speak to them?"

"How would I have proof of that?"

"It would help, is all I'm saying," Larry says. "You know, evidence is always good in a court of law."

I think suddenly of the teddy bear cam. "Maybe I can get something that proves I never talked to the *Sun.*"

"If you can, I'll take back all the things I said about you driving me crazy," my lawyer says. He smells dollar signs, so I guess I am back in his good graces.

I've got no choice but to head to the hospital to get the proof I need to clear my name. I can't admit to Carter that I have feelings for him if he thinks I'm enough of an idiot to get into bed with Sean Gates.

Clearing my name, however, proves easier said than done.

Because of the tabloid stories, there are swarms of photographers in front of the hospital, some of them arguing with police officers who are trying to get them to leave the property. With them are about thirty scantily clad fans, wearing some tight spandex miniskirts and holding up signs that say MARRY ME, SEAN! and LOVE SEAN 4EVA!

I guess the very public advertisement for where Sean is currently staying works as an invitation to half of London.

I see Sal coming down the street, looking at the crowd with some puzzlement. I run up to her. She's wearing an ensemble of a baggy green wool sweater, loose leggings, and clogs. She also has on a trench coat and a floppy felt hat.

"Give me your coat, hat, and ID badge," I say. "I'll meet you around the corner in twenty minutes, okay?"

"That'll make me twenty minutes late, though," she points out.

"Please?"

I sneak in wearing Sal's disguise, past the guards, who don't look up when I scan Sal's badge past the magnetic strip and it beeps.

"Bloody hell!" cries Becca, seeing me in the hall. "What are you doing here? And where did you get that coat? It's bloody awful, it is."

"Long story, but I need that teddy bear tape."

"You've got to hide. *Now,*" she says, pushing me back toward the ladies' room.

"What's going on?"

"Tanya—Sean's fiancée is here. She's looking for you."

"Me?"

"Heads are rolling, yeah?" Becca says.

"But I should just talk to her. I didn't touch Sean Gates. She should know it's all a fake story."

"Trust me, luv, she doesn't want to hear it. She sees you and she's libel to put you in a condition where we'll have to wheel you out."

She shoves me into the handicapped access stall. Behind us, the ladies' room door opens. Becca throws herself into the stall and stands on the toilet.

"What are you doing?" I mouth to her.

She puts her finger to her lips.

I hear the *click-clack* of heels on tile.

"I'm bloody well in the loo now, aren't I?" says a voice I don't recognize. "They said I can't use my bloody phone in Sean's room because he's next door to some old tart with a pacemaker."

I glance through the crack in the door and see a spray of blond highlights and hair extensions covering a tiny-figured woman with a micro-miniskirt, fishnet stockings, and over-the-knee black patent boots. Her belly is round and unwieldy. She looks like a pregnant hooker.

"I don't care what Mum says about my clothing line. The skirts are supposed to be short enough to see your knickers. That's the whole bleedin' point."

She pauses again, listening. "No, I took care of it. I didn't give this hospital half a million quid last year to see this kind of abuse. I'm having anyone who even looked at Sean fired, and I'm taking Sean out of this place. What kind of rehabilitation is Sean going to get if he's got all these bloody distractions? How will he get back on the pitch with these tossers looking after him?"

She pauses.

"I'm going to move him to a hotel where I can keep an eye on him," she says. "That way, he'll stay out of trouble."

We hear the *click-clack* of heels again and the door slam as Tanya leaves the restroom.

Becca physically prevents me from leaving the stall and trying to follow her.

"What are you doing?" I hiss at her.

"I'm trying to prevent you from committing suicide, yeah?" Becca says.

"I'm not scared of her," I say.

"Well, fine. Then, do you want to get Sal and me sacked? Don't do this here, okay? Just wait."

"How would you two get sacked?"

"Just for knowing you. Trust me. Didn't you hear her? She wants to fire everybody. I heard Carter's sacked, and I might be next."

"Carter! That's crazy. What about the tape? The proof Brigid set all of this up?"

"Sal's trying to make it into a DVD so she can give it to the hospital board so the slag gets what she deserves. I'll tell her to make you a copy, yeah? In the meantime, Carter's suspended and there's nothing we can do."

"My hands are tied," Brigid says to Carter, who is sitting on the couch in his apartment with his head in both hands. He looks miserable. "The board asked me to fire you, but I convinced them to leave it as a suspension."

Carter looks at her with grateful eyes. I don't believe this. Carter's firing is *her* fault and yet she's somehow managed to convince him she's fighting for him.

"Do you want to move in with me?" Brigid asks. "I'll take care of you."

Carter hugs Brigid, and she hugs him back, giving me a triumphant look over his shoulder.

"Bloody hell," Ian grunts, rolling his eyes and shaking his head, as if he can't believe what he's hearing, either.

"I can't leave Ian to pay the rent alone," Carter says, looking over at Ian.

"Dead right," Ian agrees.

"Well, maybe Ian could find another roommate," Brigid suggests.

Carter is starting to look uncomfortable. Nothing scares Carter more than the idea of a co-lease. There have been many promising Mrs. Henry candidates who pushed hard for the cohabitation, and Carter just went screaming. His need to save every psychotic chick he meets is balanced by his deep-seated fear of sharing a toothbrush stand with someone.

"I mean, if I lived with my girlfriend, where would I put my porn stash?" he asked me once. I don't think he was kidding, either.

"Okay, sweetums," Brigid says, patting his knee. "Whatever you want to do."

Just like I could've predicted, Carter does not move in with Brigid. Instead, he sits on the couch for two days without showering, just playing video games with Ian and mowing down zombies with green plasma fire.

"I am so sorry," I tell him, rubbing his shoulders. He hasn't bothered to wash his hair or put styling product in it, so it's sticking out at odd angles. I haven't seen Carter, or his hair, in this bad shape since the ex-girlfriend who threw a brick through his window.

"It's only my life that's ruined," Carter says, shrugging. "I mean, the whole 'being a doctor as a career' thing was over-rated."

I want to wrap Carter up in my arms and make everything better.

"It's just a suspension. They'll probably reinstate you in no time."

"Because one of the hospital's biggest donors wants me fired. Oh yeah, I see that happening."

"She'll forget about it in a week, I bet," I say. "Do you want to yell at me? Scream? Punch me?" I offer up my hands for target practice.

"I would, but I've lost my will to live." Carter sighs. "How am I supposed to pick up women if I'm not a doctor anymore?"

"That's why you became a doctor?"

"Well, no, obviously. I became a doctor for good karma and to get my parents off my back about law school. The chicks stuff is just a nice perk."

"You are so shallow it's scary."

"I know."

"Carter . . ." I start. This is it. This is when I confess my feelings for him. I swallow, hard. "There's something I have to tell you."

He glances up at me. "What?"

I swallow again. Wow, this is much, much harder than I thought. "Well, it's about the other night, and . . ."

"And? Come on, spit it out. Why are you being so weird?" he asks me.

I wonder myself. Why *am* I being so weird? Can't I just say it? This is my best friend in the whole world. I never hesitated to tell him anything before. And now I'm just tongue-tied.

"Well, it's just that—"

Carter's buzzer rings. Dammit!

"Hang on a sec," he says, hopping up to get it.

A second later, Brigid walks through the door. I swear, she's got ESP. She's wearing a too-tight miniskirt, showing off her bony legs. "How's my poor baby doing?" she coos at Carter, wrapping him up in a hug. "Mummy's here and she's going to make it *all* better for you."

I know in an instant that Brigid is glad this has happened. Glad she's made Carter so vulnerable. She's practically celebrating.

This, I think, is war. I look at Carter and decide that I'm going to get his job back. One way or another, I'm going to do it.

Nineteen

REASON #19 TO DIVORCE A ROCK STAR:
His idea of good karma is singing at a benefit concert that also doubles as great exposure for his new single.

The first and only Thanksgiving Ted spent with my family, he managed to get everyone to play a game of charades.

This was close to a miracle, as my family is not the sort of family that plays board games or cards or anything like that. Once, when I was twelve, I tried to get everyone to play Trivial Pursuit. Mom ended up offended by the incorrect grammar in some of the questions, and Dad got frustrated that he couldn't answer any of the sports questions (like 1930s boxing trivia) and Lauren kept organizing the pie pieces in terms of their color shades, rather than in terms of what pie you actually won. And naturally, the whole game ended with some weird argument between Lauren and Mom about Lauren's hair (Mom didn't approve of the late-eighties hairsprayed look).

And yet, Ted convinced even my mom that we ought to play a game of charades. And everyone had a good time. We laughed. We felt like one of those TV families on the Parker Brothers commercials. It seemed to me that for the first time, everyone thought, Hey, we don't have to argue!

But Ted was like that. Just when you thought he was only about himself, he'd go and brighten up an entire room. It's what made him so irresistible to thousands of fans. And to me.

"What do you mean you're not going to be home for Thanksgiving?" Mom cries. I hear the sound of furious chopping in the background. She's probably making one of her casseroles. Mom is in the kitchen more than Martha Stewart. It's partly because Dad is a human vacuum cleaner.

"I'm sorry, Mom. Something has, uh, come up."

"But this will be the first year we're not all together," Mom wails.

It's true. I may be the irresponsible daughter, but I almost always manage to show up for Thanksgiving. I'm not one to turn down a free meal. I'm irresponsible, but not stupid.

"I'm sorry, Mom. It's important. Carter may have lost his job, and it might be my fault, sort of."

"You've lost *someone else's* job? Now that is a first. You usually just lose your own."

"Ha ha. Funny, Mom."

"Do you want me to send you some turkey and stuffing? I don't want you to go hungry."

"I'll be fine, Mom. They do have food in England."

"If you're sure," Mom says.

*   *   *

After hanging up the phone, I turn my attention to getting Carter's job back. I call Becca.

"You want to talk to Tanya Richards? Are you off your rocker?" Becca asks me on the phone.

"She can help Carter, and therefore, I've got to talk to her."

"You've bloody lost it," Becca says. "You don't have to do this. Sal's bringing a copy of the DVD today."

"Even better, I can show her the DVD," I say.

"Just how many pints have you had?" she asks me.

"I'm not drunk. I just want to go directly to the source. Straighten this whole thing out."

"What's really going on here? Are you trying to impress Carter? Admit it, you fancy him."

"I do not."

"You bloody do. It's obvious to everyone but you and Carter. But it doesn't mean you have to go and do something foolish."

"I think it does, actually."

Becca sighs. "Well, Sal only has one copy of the DVD, and the hospital board has to see it first," Becca says.

"I can't wait that long," I say. It seems urgent that I get Carter's job back. Maybe then I'll have redeemed myself. Maybe then we can have a serious relationship talk. "Is she at the hospital?"

"No, she's at the Dorchester. She dragged poor Gatesy out of here this morning. She thinks there are, erm, too many distractions in the hospital. You know, impeding his recovery and all that. She reckons she can do a better job with him at a five-star hotel. More like she just missed room service, yeah? Our café here ain't exactly cordon bleu, is it?"

"Do you know what name he's staying under?"

"Does the queen wear frilly knickers? 'Course I know," Becca says.

At the circular driveway of the Dorchester, things are remarkably quiet. I guess the press hasn't discovered Sean Gates is staying here yet. But then again, it's only been a few hours.

Arnold whines and pops his head out of my oversize tote bag. I'm guessing that it was a bad idea to bring him, but Carter and Ian were feeding him potato chips and laughing, and I felt I couldn't, in good conscience, leave him alone with those two. They would have probably poisoned him with chocolate chip cookies.

I walk through the front hotel doors, glad that I wore something that makes it look like I might remotely be able to afford a room. I go to the front desk. "Mr. Storry's room, please."

Dave Storry is a comic book soccer player whose cartoon runs every day in the *Daily Mirror* and is Sean Gates's pseudonym. Becca said the comic strip, which is more like a soap opera, follows the sexual exploits of a fictitious soccer player. Like all British entertainment, it contains a lot of nudity. I'm not surprised that Sean Gates chose him as his alter ego.

The hotel clerk frowns at me and at Arnold, but calls Sean Gates's room.

Sean picks up.

"It's Lily. From the hospital."

"Lily?" he echoes, clearly not remembering me. We were on the front page of a tabloid, and he still can't manage to remember my name. Unbelievable.

"The tarot cards?"

"Oh! Right! Lily!" he says, perking up. "Well, come on up then, I wouldn't mind some company. Put the bellboy fella back on the line, sweetheart."

I hand the receiver back to the hotel clerk. He listens for a moment, then nods. He's still frowning at Arnold, but he hands me a card key to operate the private elevator that will take me to Sean's suite.

The elevator opens into a small, private corridor, which leads straight into Sean's room. I try not to gawk openly at the sight of the six-room suite complete with a full kitchen, living room, and a bathroom that is larger than my bedroom at Carter's apartment. My eyes dart around the furnished room, taking inventory of the things I might theoretically steal. Not that I would. I'm just making a mental list of what isn't nailed down.

I glance over at the desk. Is that a Montblanc pen? It's just lying out there for anyone to pocket.

"Awight, luv!" cries Sean Gates, who is lying on the couch with his hurt foot propped up on pillows and wearing only a terrycloth robe, which is open to the waist. He's got a room service cart in front of him laden down with all the necessities: champagne, caviar, pâté, and olives. "So the Sean Gates taster portion finally brought you back for the seven-course meal. I hope you're hungry, darling."

Arnold barks.

"Jesus! Not that rat of a dog again," Sean shouts.

"He's not a rat," I cry, protectively cupping my hand over Arnold's ears in case he suddenly learned how to understand English.

"Right, yeah, sorry. He's a right plump little sausage, though, isn't he?" Sean says. "I s'pose he can stay. So, luv, let's get down to business, yeah?"

Sean stands and makes to undo his robe.

"Wait, wait, wait," I cry, throwing up my hands and turning my head away. "I'm not here to have sex with you. I'm here to see Tanya."

"Tanya? What d'you want to see *her* for?!" Sean's brow furrows. Like Ted, he can't quite understand the concept of a woman not wanting to have sex with him. I'm sure if he asked any woman on the street if she'd like to have sex, she would, even if he wanted to do it in a clear glass car of the London Eye on live television.

"I want to talk to her about Carter losing his job."

"Sorry, darlin', Tanya's out shopping. Spending my money is a full-time job; she won't be back for hours! So come over here and give Sean here a proper hello, yeah?"

"You realize we're all over the papers?"

"No use gettin' blamed for something we never even did, yeah? You know, if your arse is covered in bees, you'd better have a big gobfull of the good stuff for your trouble, right?"

Sean leers at me. There is really no moment he thinks inappropriate for sexual innuendo.

"Sean, focus. I'm here to help Carter get his job back. Remember him? Dr. Henry? The one your wife-to-be fired for no apparent reason."

"Tanya?" Sean says. "No idea what you're on about. I like Carter. He's a good doc."

"Well, Tanya got him fired. Can you ask her to get him re-hired?"

"Tanya didn't ask the board to fire Carter. She asked the board to fire you, but you don't get paid, do you? You can't bloody well be sacked, can you? Dr. Henry's all right, for a boring old Yank anyway."

"But . . ." This doesn't make any sense. If Tanya didn't want Carter fired, who did?

"Now, why don't you come over here and sit on me knee, yeah?" He pats his knee and grins.

"Sean, I am not going to have sex with you, right now or ever."

Sean's brow wrinkles. "What?" He's confused. I think he's not that bright. It's probably because he headed one too many soccer balls. "You bloody well aren't acting like a girl who's in love with me."

"Do you believe everything you read in the tabloids?"

Sean wrinkles his brow. "Oiy!" he shouts, not at all happy with the insults. "I'm Sean Bloody Gates! Let's leave off with the vicious personal attacks, all right? Now, if you must know, that skinny bird at the hospital, what's her name? She told me you had a bit of a thing for old Gatesy, so, you know, I thought I'd do a little favor, for a fan. . . ."

"Brigid told you I wanted to sleep with you?"

"Well, yeah, but who doesn't want to sleep with Sean Gates? Nah, she said you had a real thing for me. She said you were a right goer, real dirty girl! Seems like that was a load of bollocks. Never met such a fridge in all me life. I haven't even seen you in the buff yet! I've known you for weeks now!"

I can't believe this. Brigid not only called the tabloids, but she filled Sean Gates's head with ideas of a romance between us. She is evil. Next I'll discover she owns a white cat and has a plan for world domination.

There's a loud knock on the side door.

"Sean!" shouts Tanya. "Sean Gates, why have you put the lock on this door? Open this door right now!"

Sean turns a shade paler than white. "Hide," he hisses at me, as he pushes me toward the room service cart.

"But I want to talk to her," I say.

The next thing I know, Sean is pushing me into the room service cart. I crawl in, and he flings the tablecloth over me.

"Stay there," he warns me. "Or Dr. Henry will get more than sacked, all right, luv?"

I nod.

"One second, Tanya. One second!"

"Where is she?" Tanya shouts, as she storms into the room. "I'm gone a half hour and you bloody well invite one of your tarts up here."

"Tanya. There's no one here. Relax."

"I know there's someone. Ronny at the front desk rung me, Sean. You can't get away with it this time."

I hear what sounds like the room being torn apart. Glass shatters. A chair topples. I stop breathing. I realize that it is unlikely I'd win a face-to-face fight with Tanya. For one thing, she has real nails, and for another, I am a big sissy. Case in point: The closest I've ever been to an actual girl fight was when fifth-grade bully Kendra Pritchett challenged me to a fight after school. I hid in the bathroom until everyone went home.

I have another glimpse at my future: me being beaten to a pulp by Britain's Most Watched Top Model. Me in the hospital for six weeks recovering from serious internal damage. Me on the cover of the *National Enquirer* under the headline "Cat Fighter Gets Scratched Out." Me being the brunt of all late-night jokes (again).

It's hot, and I am starting to sweat.

Arnold, in my bag, which is sitting on my stomach, flattens his ears against his head and licks his lips.

I put my finger to my lips to tell him to be quiet, as if he knows sign language. He cocks his ear to one side, doing his best imitation of a patient listener.

I hear what sounds like a glass shattering against the door. Arnold jumps and whines. I put my hands around his snout. Arnold starts shaking. I'm sure the sound of broken glass reminds him of Ted. Tanya is wrecking the room like a genuine rock star. She missed her calling.

"Tan, be serious," Sean says. "There's no one here but us."

Sean sounds remarkably cool. I wonder if he finds himself in this situation often. Arnold wiggles in my grasp. He wants to be free, probably to run and hide under the bed. Either that, or to go and pee somewhere.

"I know she's here. The front desk has been watching for me. They would've called if she left."

Tanya sits down near the cart on the couch.

"Good God, is this caviar? You know I hate the stuff. The smell is bloody awful. You know I can't stand fish when I'm pregnant."

"I'll put it outside, yeah?" Sean says, giving the cart a hard and sudden push toward the door. The jolt sends me nearly careening off the cart and straight onto the floor. I manage to keep inside the cart, but I lose my grip on my bag, which flips over to the side and sends Arnold straight out from under the cart onto the carpeted hotel floor. The next thing I hear is the loud and unmistakable bark of Arnold.

I feel like shouting, "Man down! Man down!"

"What the bloody hell is that?" Tanya cries.

I am really not breathing now.

"Um, well, what does it look like?" Sean is not fast on his feet. He's definitely a bit thick.

"A bloody dog, Sean. It looks like a bloody dog."

"Well, right, of course it is."

"But what is it *doing* here?"

Sean can't think of an answer. He truly is a very, very handsome moron. But he is a man of action. He starts up pushing the cart again, recovering from the shock of having Arnold land at his feet. He keeps wheeling the cart straight out of the room. The last thing I hear before the door shuts behind me is Tanya's voice softening. "Is it for me, Sean? Did you buy this cute pup for me?"

I'm standing in the lobby of the hotel, trying to hide behind a ficus while I figure out what I'm supposed to do. I waited in the hallway for a while outside Sean's room, listening to him and Tanya argue. I kept hoping Sean would slide Arnold out of the door. But Tanya took to him right away. I guess she has a thing for overweight, lethargic lap dogs.

A maid came by, forcing me into the elevator and down to the lobby, where I'm standing, wondering what I ought to do next.

Should I run back up and try to get Arnold? How am I supposed to get Arnold back without alerting Tanya's stooge behind the front desk? How am I supposed to get him back at all?

I don't know what to do. I've got to save him, but how?

As I'm deciding what I should do, someone shouts my name.

"Hey! Lily Dayton! Over here!" It's a photographer. He came out of nowhere, like a roach. I wonder if the hotel stooge also called the paparazzi.

I throw the hood of my pink sweatshirt over my head and sprint toward the street. With my aviator sunglasses and pink hood, I must look like a Mary Kay version of the Unibomber, but I don't care. I just need to get free. The last thing I want is another tabloid story.

The photographer chases me, flashbulbs blazing.

I am not someone used to physical activity. A gym is a foreign place to me, like the men's department at Nordstrom. Despite the fact that my pursuer is carrying heavy equipment and by and large is overweight, he gains on me easily. I am sure this has something to do with the fact that I smoke half a pack a day and that even looking at a flight of stairs makes me winded.

Now I know why stars like Madonna work out so much. It's to evade paparazzi.

I look right and left, praying for a cab. I take a sharp turn down the alley between the two buildings and nearly collide into a limo that pulls out in front of me.

The back passenger door opens then, and a woman leans out. She's wearing a large-brim hat, sunglasses, an empire-waist dress, and matching heels.

"Get in. We need to talk," she says, taking off her sunglasses.

It's Melanie Slate.

Twenty

REASON #20 TO DIVORCE A ROCK STAR:
Being in the National Enquirer is overrated.

The night I caught Ted with Melanie at the Iron Cactus was the first and last time I'd seen Melanie Slate in person. What I remember, aside from the fact that her lipstick was smudged, because it was all over Ted's face, was that she was rail-thin and had boobs that seemed to defy gravity. She was also tiny—I think she only came up to my elbow. It was why she could easily sit in Ted's lap and still have room to put her hand down his pants.

There are many scenarios in which I imagine one day seeing Melanie Slate again. Being chased by paparazzi in a state of complete terror is not among them. I like to imagine that some day after the settlement, I'd marry an Onassis-like billionaire and be approached by a destitute and impoverished Melanie Slate, who would be reduced to doing *Showgirls 2* and would beg for a loan to finish financing the movie. And, of course, Melanie's famous breast implants would implode in a spectacularly embarrassing way, preferably on *The Tonight Show* or *Today* while I am a guest promoting my new book, *Ted Dayton Kicks Puppies: The Unauthorized Biography of a Real Asshole.*

"Well?" Melanie says to me now, her eyelashes perfectly separated. Her makeup is so flawless that I wonder if she had it professionally done before she came over. "It'll just take a few minutes. Please." She swallows the "please" as if it's a very difficult word to say. I'm sure she doesn't use it very often.

A quick glance behind me says that I have little choice. It's Melanie Slate or be devoured by a fat, slovenly photographer who seems to have more than the average amount of ear hair and a top running speed much greater than mine.

I slide gracefully (read: dive awkwardly) into the limo, slamming the door behind us. The photographer runs up against the limo, but he can't see anything through the tinted glass.

He snaps a few shots, but then gives up as we pull away. Looking at the buildings pass by my window, I suddenly think this is a very bad idea. I think I saw on *Oprah* once that you're never supposed to let an attacker take you from the scene. That the FBI says your survival rate drops by eighty percent.

Melanie doesn't look pregnant at all. The famous "bump" that all the tabloids seem to be talking about is about the size of a golf ball and is smaller than the flab I normally carry around with me. Otherwise, she's thin as usual, her biceps well-defined from the no doubt daily sessions with her personal trainer. Her ankles aren't swollen, and her skin is glowing with either the flush of pregnancy or with Bobbi Brown shimmering powder. I just know that she'll be one of those stars who gives birth and then a month later poses in *Playboy*.

"How did you know where to find me?" I ask her.

"Like, my assistant has *totally* been following you around." Melanie looks twenty, but sounds thirteen.

"Wendy?"

"She was supposed to call if you do anything that I might be able to blackmail you for."

"And did you find something?" I ask her.

"I don't know. You tell me."

"Why would I tell you a secret that you could use to blackmail me?"

"I don't know. Why would you?"

Melanie quirks an eyebrow as if she has the upper hand. It's nice to confirm in person she truly has the brainpower of a hamster.

There's a long pause as she just stares at me expectantly, blinking.

I sigh.

"Are you going to blackmail me, Melanie?"

"Oh my God. I totally spaced. One second." She clears her throat and closes her eyes as if to meditate. When she opens them again, her eyes flick down to my sweatshirt. "Hey, nice hoodie. Is that Juicy Couture?"

I'm beginning to think facing the paparazzi would be better than trying to have a conversation with Melanie Slate.

"Can we just get back to the blackmailing?"

"Oh, yeah. Like, I am such a space cadet." She giggles. "Okay, go ahead. I totally won't interrupt you. You were saying?" She stares at me some more, blinking her big, blank, cornflower blue eyes.

"No. You were going to blackmail me. Not the other way around."

Melanie giggles some more. "Oh my God. Right!" she says. She dips her head, as if trying to get into character. She raises it again with a stern expression.

"Sign the divorce papers and I won't tell anyone that you've snuck over to see Sean Gates again. If you don't sign them, I'm afraid you'll have to go to jail."

She pauses, lowers her head, and says "scene."

"I'm sorry? Did you say 'scene'? Did you memorize your lines for blackmail like it was a movie?"

"Did you like it? I can do it with more anger, too."

I officially have entered the Melanie Slate Zone. I am scared. I might be losing IQ points just by breathing the same air.

I'm beginning to wonder if Melanie Slate is so gorgeous that probably since she was a baby she never had to lift a finger to do anything. She never even had to bother to develop a personality. Or her brain.

Melanie looks at me and blinks.

"Do you even have the settlement papers?"

"Oh, right! I forgot," she says. She digs them out of her bag and hands them to me.

"Like, pretty, pretty please, sign the papers. I want to marry Ted, okay?"

"No," I say.

"But *why* not?" she whines.

"You're blackmailing me. That's not very nice."

Melanie considers this a moment.

"Okay, forget the blackmail. *Please* sign the papers. I'm dying to marry Ted. I'm pregnant, as if you couldn't tell. I mean, I look like a *total* cow, right?"

Melanie Slate is skinnier than I am. And I am nowhere near being pregnant, since you have to have sex first and I am going on a six-month drought. She continues. "And like, I *totally* respect your marriage, okay? I like, really want you to know that."

She didn't seem to respect the marriage when she was shoving her hands down Ted's pants at the Iron Cactus.

"Melanie, what I want from you and from Ted is an apology. Then I'll sign those papers."

I watch as Melanie's eyes, as if on cue, start to glisten with tears.

"I feel terribly about how things have happened," she says and sniffs. "I know I've made mistakes. If you let me make it up to you, I promise you won't regret it."

This sounds far too coherent and grammatically correct to be spontaneous. Is that a line from her movie *Beautiful?* I think this is the speech she gives her boyfriend/manager when he confronts her about her heroin use. Un-freakin'-believable.

"Is that a line from *Beautiful*?"

Melanie, taken aback, blinks fast. "You've seen that?"

I don't believe this. She's acting, right at this moment. I know it, because she's a terrible actress, and because she's biting her lip in the same way she did when she broke down in front of the forest ranger in *House of Screams*.

"I want you to apologize without quoting a script."

She blinks at me.

I look at her.

"Like, I am really, like, totally sorry," she says.

"Oh, I don't want you to just say it to me," I say. "I want you to issue it to *People* and *US Weekly*. I want everyone to read about it."

Her eyes narrow, and instantly her victim face from *Beautiful* disappears.

"Um, no way," she says. "That is *not* cool. I mean, pardon my French, but that is totally like, bitchy."

And here I thought pregnant Melanie would be somehow nicer than husband-stealing Melanie. I am just too optimistic about people.

"Okay, you need to step off, because you are like, so not better than me," she says. "And if you don't sign these papers you are like, *so* going to jail. That's what Ted says." She thrusts the divorce papers at me. "Sign!" she implores.

"No," I say, even though I know I'll live to regret this decision. Especially later on, in jail, when I'm braiding the hair of my "protector" Marcy and trading cigarettes for eyebrow wax and hair dye.

"Oh my God," Melanie says, shocked. "Like, why are you being so bitchy?"

I'm sure people don't say no to Melanie very often.

"Those are my terms. Take them or leave them."

The limo screeches to a halt.

"Like, you are so *not cool*. Get out!" she says, dumping me on the street. I dust myself off and glance up and find myself staring at Buckingham Palace.

I ask the tarot cards if I am going to go to jail and the answer is "probably yes." I suppose this is slightly better than "definitely yes." I know I should get on a plane and take my chances with being recognized, but I think I can't leave Arnold, and furthermore, I can't leave Carter, either. Not until I know if he feels the same way about me as I do about him. Every time I think about leaving, I just *can't*. Not until I know for sure.

My mobile rings. It's my lawyer, Larry.

"How's that true love thing working out? You and the Tooth Fairy going to live happily ever after?"

"Nice. Did I mention you are way too cynical about love?"

"I'm a divorce lawyer, Lily. It's part of the job description." Larry clears his throat. "So, tell me you really are in Austin."

"I'm afraid not," I say.

"Tell me you changed your mind about Melanie's offer."

"Strike two."

"Okay, then I've got strike three right here. I've held off the

DA as long as I can, but they've issued a warrant for your arrest, Lily. I suggest you turn yourself in."

"By the way, should I have gotten another attorney for that charge? Do you have any criminal court case experience?"

"More than you have, which is quite a lot, I might add."

"That fills me with confidence." I sigh. "You're sure there's nothing else I can do?"

"You could move to France. They love harboring American fugitives."

"Does that include the French Riviera?"

"After you pay me my fees, you won't have enough money left for the French Riviera."

"That's a comforting thought."

"Lily, I want you to go outside and ask someone where the nearest Scotland Yard offices are, and turn yourself in. Your trial is in one week."

"Will they really arrest me?"

"If they find you, yes."

"So you're saying I have a chance."

My call waiting beeps. It's my sister, Lauren.

I click over and hear a gurgled choking sound on the other end.

"Hello? Lauren? Is that you?"

More sniffling.

"Tyler? Have you got Mommy's phone? Ty?"

"No, it's me," Lauren says, drawing a deep breath.

"What is it? The baby?" I have a sudden horrible thought that Lauren—who's in her third trimester—lost the baby.

"No," she sniffs. "The baby's fine. Ty is fine. But can you come get us?"

Okay, she's officially gone off the deep end.

"Lauren, I know when you're pregnant you're forgetful, but you do realize I'm in London?"

"I know," says Lauren, sniffing again. "So are we."

Twenty-one

REASON #21 TO DIVORCE A ROCK STAR:

You can't be accused of breaking up the band.

After the Iron Cactus, when I confronted Ted about his infidelity, he gave me the five stages of caught-in-the-act cheating:

1. **Denial** (Ted claimed first the photo in *US* was fabricated, and that the light in the Iron Cactus bar was terrible.)
2. **Anger** (He blew up at me and said he's tired of my jealous rants and that he's going to leave me because I'm insecure.)
3. **Bargaining** (He blamed the drugs and drinking, and told me if I gave him a second chance, he'd change. He'd stop drinking. Stop drugs. And then, two days later when he calls, he's high again. Proof that he won't ever stop.)
4. **Depression** (When I realized that Ted wasn't really

intent on apologizing, not really. He actually wanted me to dump him. He wanted to run off with Melanie Slate.)

5. **Acceptance** (Me realizing that after a year Ted is an asshole and is never going to change).

Lauren says you can never trust a man who has cheated: "Once he's got a taste for it, he won't give it up," she always says, as if infidelity is like cannibalism.

A very pregnant Lauren and her toddler, Tyler, are standing outside of Heathrow looking jet-lagged and disoriented. I know it's serious because Lauren never shows up anywhere unannounced, and she doesn't usually take a trip unless she's got everything planned out a year in advance. Not to mention the fact that she's not supposed to be on an airplane in her third trimester, much less taking a cross-Atlantic flight.

She's crying, but she's also eating a king-size Snickers bar. There's nothing, I think, that gets in between a pregnant woman and food, not even marital trouble.

After calming her down, she manages to tell me that she wants to leave her husband.

Nick's crime? Receiving a love letter via e-mail from coworker Cori and failing to tell Lauren of it *the second* it arrived. Lauren, who was snooping, saw the letter in his in-box ten minutes after it arrived and assumed from this scant evidence that he was having an affair.

In typical nonconfrontational Lauren fashion, she didn't confront Nick about the e-mail, she just left it printed out on the kitchen counter and packed up Tyler and headed straight to London. She says she couldn't stay at Mom and Dad's because they're spending the week looking for a condo in Florida. This is just like Lauren. She spends her whole life planning out every detail and then she implodes when something unexpected happens and just runs off, abandoning everything without thinking. It's like she saves up all her spontaneity for one colossally bad improvised move, like jetting off to another country two weeks before her due date.

"What were you doing reading his e-mail?" I asked Lauren.

"I always read his e-mail," she says, as if this is something all wives do.

"And he knows this?"

"Of course."

"So why would he conduct a clandestine affair *right under your nose* then?"

"I don't know, but he is." Lauren sniffs. She looks like a wreck. Her eyes are puffy and red and her already swollen feet are even more swollen after eight hours in a pressurized cabin.

"How did you get here?" I ask her. "I took your passport."

"I borrowed Mom's."

"You pretended to be *Mom*?! Did the customs agent even look at your face?"

She's clearly suffering from severe pregnancy brain if she thought this was a good idea.

"No one looks at a pregnant woman. We're invisible."

"You know this is probably all some misunderstanding," I

say. "I think you ought to call Nick. He's going to be worried about you and Tyler."

"I am not calling him. He cheated on me. And I'm pregnant!"

"We don't know that he cheated on you. All we know is that this woman has a crush on him. Did you see his reply to the e-mail?"

Lauren sniffs. "No. He didn't have one in his sent box. But it's too late. We're going to have to get a divorce. I'm going to be divorced twice before I'm forty! It's like I'm cursed."

"Lauren. Calm down. We haven't heard Nick's side of things."

"Does that really matter? Did it matter with you and Ted?"

"Lauren, look, I know you don't want to hear this right now, but there is a difference here. Ted's affair was all over *People* magazine. All you know is that some woman has a crush on Nick. What woman doesn't have a crush on Nick?"

Lauren's bottom lip starts to quiver.

"Oh, no, no, no. I didn't mean to make you cry. Lauren. Please."

"Lily, I'm just a wreck. Can we stay with you and Carter for a few days?"

"Will-wee," cries Tyler. He gives my legs a hug and then he backs away from me and tugs on his pants, dropping his Pull-Ups to the floor and exposing himself. He claps his hands and giggles.

"That means he's glad to see you," Lauren says.

*   *   *

"Yes, of course they can stay," Carter says later. "But if the rest of your family is planning on coming, or maybe your high school gym coach, then I'm going to have to say no."

Carter gives Lauren a hug and then scoops Tyler up and immediately turns him upside down. Tyler shrieks with laughter.

"I'll go pack a bag," Carter says.

"Why?"

"I'll go to Brigid's and they can take my room," he says.

"Carter! That's really not necessary."

"Niceun," Ian says to me, and then he turns to Lauren. "Nastameetyew," he says.

"What did he say?" Lauren asks me.

"You'll pick it up eventually," I say.

Tyler is staring at Ian, transfixed. Then, after several moments, he points to Ian's bright red hair and cries, "Wonab McDonab!"

"Bloody hell," Ian sighs.

Lauren heads straight to the refrigerator. She opens it and starts eating a block of cheese, without bothering to get a knife.

Ian looks on, amazed. He's never seen anyone put away so much food so quickly. But then, he's never seen a pregnant woman eat, either.

"Ice cream!" Lauren bellows from the kitchen. "I need some freakin' ice cream!"

I turn around and Carter's already in his bedroom packing a bag. I follow him.

"Are you sure you want to do this?" I ask Carter, as he packs up his things.

"Brigid has been wanting me to move in, and it just makes sense. There aren't enough beds."

"But it's Brigid. And it's *living* with her."

"Just for as long as Lauren stays, okay?"

My mobile phone rings. It's Mom.

"Hello? Mom?" I say into my phone, as I walk back into the living room.

"Don't tell her I'm here," Lauren says.

"Nick called and said he and Lauren had some sort of fight and that she and Tyler left, but no one knows where they are, and we're all worried sick."

"Don't worry. She's here with me."

"Lily!" Lauren shouts at me, her mouth full of cheese.

"There? In London! But she's not supposed to fly. And what about Thanksgiving? You ask her about Thanksgiving!"

I look at Lauren, who is finishing the block of cheese.

"I don't know if she and Tyler will be back in time for Thanksgiving, but it sure looks like Lauren could put away the entire table this year."

"Lily! That's not very nice." Mom sighs. "Why is she there? This is not like her."

"To be spontaneous? I know. She thinks Nick cheated on her."

My mom lets out a long, sad sigh. "Not again."

"I know!"

I look at Lauren wiping Tyler's nose and wonder if I'm going to end up like her. Her first husband cheated, and even though she found a practically saintly replacement husband, she's still looking for disaster around every corner. Is that how I'm going to be? Doubting every man I ever meet?

"Okay, just keep her calm. We're going to have to figure out a way to get her back here as soon as possible. Her due date is in two weeks!"

"Does that mean what I think it means?"

"If she doesn't fly back in the next week, then she's going to end up having that baby in London."

"Pee-pee!" shouts Tyler, who breaks free of Lauren's grasp and runs straight to the potted plant near Carter's fireplace and takes a whiz on its leaves.

"Is that grandson of mine still using the world as his urinal?" My mom asks and sighs.

"I'm afraid so," I say.

I look over at Lauren, but she's too busy glaring at me to be paying attention to the fact that Tyler is out of control. She's upset about me telling Mom where she's hiding.

Ian, coming out of the kitchen, sees Tyler.

"Och, how about we do that in the toilet, aye?"

"No!" Tyler shouts, and runs, pants-free, away from Ian.

"All he needs is a good spanking," Mom says. "You know that I don't believe in spanking *all the time.* Just *some of the time.* That's what I try to tell Lauren, but she just doesn't listen. You just have to do it once or twice, and then you'll see an instant improvement."

"Mom, I really don't . . ."

I point out to Lauren that Ian is chasing Tyler around the

apartment. Seeing that he's not wearing pants, Lauren sighs and scoops him up on one of his rounds around the couch.

"Gotcha!" she says, and Tyler starts squealing. "You know that wee-wees stay in our pants," she adds, as she pulls his pants up without missing a beat.

My call waiting beeps.

"Mom, hang on a second, I'm getting another call."

"I'm sorry, Lily, but that is just rude, I'm not going to hang on a second—"

I click over. It's Nick.

"Lily, thank God, I've been trying all day."

I watch as Tyler wiggles away from Lauren's grasp and immediately pulls down his pants again. He runs away from Lauren and straight to Carter, who swoops him up in his arms.

"Nick! They're here in London. They're both fine."

Lauren marches over to me, hand out, asking for the phone. Carter, not quite sure what to do with a pantsless toddler, holds him out away from his shirt. Tyler, sensing right away Carter's uneasiness, goes straight for Carter's hair and manages to pull on a good chunk.

"Ow," Carter says.

"Thank God," Nick is saying, sounding relieved. "I was so worried. Honestly, you don't know what can happen to people sometimes, and Lily, Lauren has the wrong idea about Cori. The totally wrong idea."

"I figured," I say. Lauren nudges me. She has the cheese in one hand and is trying to use the other to grab the phone.

"I'm on my way to the airport," he says, a little breathless. He sounds like he's running there. "Try to keep Lauren calm."

"That's not going to be easy, Nick."

"Lily, you have to believe me. It's all a big misunderstanding. Cori sent the e-mail, but Lily, I don't have feelings for Cori. I never did. Nothing happened between us. I told her so. Cori took the news hard. She asked to be transferred out of the precinct. I don't even see her anymore."

Lauren is trying to bodycheck me for the phone. She's pretty aggressive, and she's not afraid to use her tummy, either.

"Give me the phone, *now.*"

"No, Lauren . . ."

"Lauren? Is she there? Let me talk to her."

"Nick, she's here, but I can't promise—"

Lauren whips the phone out of my hand. She clicks it off.

"Lauren, you said you were going to talk to him," I say.

"No, I said 'give me the phone.' I didn't make any promises to talk to him."

She sits down and tries to cross her arms across her chest, but her belly gets in the way. Frustrated, she throws her arms down by her sides.

"You're going to have to talk to him sooner or later."

My phone rings again in her hand. She spikes it like a football on the carpet and the plastic covering flies off. My sleek freebie Motorola phone now has a cracked screen and a cover that's chipped.

"Oops," Lauren says.

"If that phone wasn't free, I'd make you pay for it," I say, putting it back together. It works, but the screen is half gone.

"Thanks, *sis*. Argh! I can't believe you told them where I was! Now they'll all be coming here."

"The rest of your family is coming?" Carter asks, emerging from the bedroom with his packed bag, ready to go to Brigid's.

Tyler stops in front of Carter and promptly pulls down his pants.

"That means he likes you," I tell Carter.

Twenty-two

REASON #22 TO DIVORCE A ROCK STAR:
They're all just boys in men's leather pants.

I should have suspected Ted earlier of cheating. After all, you don't spend months on tour with an incredibly popular band and not have offers. But Ted called nearly every night, even if it was 2:00 A.M., and he'd want to talk about how the set went, and what the city was like, and how things were going.

I would find out that him calling me had nothing to do with being faithful. He took advantage of the groupies just like everyone else in the band. The really sad part is, I could've lived with that on some level, because it wasn't in front of me. I could pretend it wasn't happening, and because he always wanted to come home with me.

That is, until Melanie Slate.

The next morning I wake up staring face-to-face with Tyler, who is half naked and has got something that looks like chocolate smeared across his hands. At least, I hope it's chocolate.

He's holding my tarot cards.

"Weading!" he says, and hands them to me. For some reason, they're all sticky. It's got mystery toddler goo on it. Why are toddlers always sticky?

"Give me one second, Tyler, okay? And where are your pants? What's your mommy doing?"

I hear the sounds of pots and pans clanking in the kitchen. Uh-oh. This isn't good.

When my sister has emotional troubles, she doesn't sulk and watch VH-1 or E! like the rest of us. No, she cleans and organizes. It sounds like a good thing, but trust me, it's a problem. When her prom date broke things off with her a day before the prom, she practically melted Mom's linoleum with a gallon of bleach. And if any of your stuff happens to be in the way, you might as well kiss it good-bye because you're never going to see it again. After the prom date fiasco, she color coded my closet and lined up my shoes according to heel height. Honestly, she's practically obsessive-compulsive.

I pull myself out of bed and discover Lauren in mid-cleaning frenzy. Ian, amazed by the thoroughness of her cleaning, is standing by and watching, speechless.

She also has a burrito of some kind in her left hand, and in between cleaning swipes, she takes a big bite.

Being jet-lagged and foregoing sleep, she's managed to re-arrange everything in Carter's bedroom and kitchen, the two most sacred rooms in the house, as well as alphabetizing his LP and CD collections, ruining his filing-by-date system. Not to mention that Ian's Xbox games, normally strewn about the living room, have been placed in alphabetical order on the shelf next to Carter's CDs. Carter, who has spent the night at Brigid's, would be pissed if he saw this.

She must be stopped.

"Lauren, why don't we go sightseeing?" I ask her.

"Busy—later!" she mumbles.

"But Lauren, you've got to stop."

"Later!" she shouts.

The apartment buzzer rings. It's Becca and Sal.

"We've got it," Becca says, holding up a DVD, looking triumphant. The Brigid DVD.

"Is now a bad time?" Sal asks, watching as Lauren frantically scrubs between Carter's floor tiles with a toothbrush.

"That's my sister. She's suffering from pregnancy insanity."

"I heard that!" Lauren cries out from the kitchen.

"My cousin got pregnant last year and knocked down a supporting wall in her husband's living room, yeah?" Becca says, nodding. "Said the baby needed better fung shooey. It was a supporting wall. Lucky they weren't both buried alive."

Sal puts the DVD into Carter's player. Becca sits down on the couch and gets comfortable.

"I thought you guys already watched this," I say.

"It's good for multiple viewings," Sal explains.

"What is it, aye?" Ian asks, walking into the room.

"Brigid caught red-handed." I say.

Ian sits down and prepares to watch it with us. When I look at him, he says, "What? She stole my games, aye? I want to see what else she's been up to."

We hit Play on the DVD player. The DVD shows Brigid's office, the camera positioned so we see her from behind. We have a full view of her desk and computer.

"Fast-forward for a bit, yeah?" Becca says.

We fast-forward through Brigid surfing the Web (mostly wedding sites but the occasional horoscope page).

"Wait! Stop there," Sal says.

I press Play.

I watch as Brigid opens her desk drawer and pulls out Barbie and Ken dolls.

"What the hell?"

"Och, aye?" Ian asks, looking at the screen.

"Just watch. This is good."

Brigid puts on a puppet show. "Hi, Brigid!" she makes the Ken doll say.

"Hi, Carter," she makes the Barbie say.

Ian bursts out laughing. "Bloody nut," he says.

"I love you more than *anyone* else in the whole world!" She makes the dolls kiss.

"Will you marry me?" she makes the Ken doll say to the Barbie doll.

"Oh . . . my . . . God," I say, looking at Sal and Becca. The two of them dissolve into giggles. "I knew Brigid was crazy, but I think now she's certifiable."

"Well, we have at least answered the question: What *does* she do all day," Sal says, recovering.

We watch as Brigid makes Barbie jump up and down in a show of jubilee, and then kiss Ken again. Her puppet show is interrupted by the sudden appearance of a nurse. Quickly, Brigid hides the dolls.

"Fast-forward," Becca says.

"Okay, stop!" Sal commands.

I press Play, and we watch as Brigid conducts a whole phone conversation pretending to be me. She answers more than an hour of questions by a *Sun* reporter. She puts off the reporter's continued requests for an in-person interview, and when asked for proof of her identity, she gets out my wallet (which she stole from Carter's apartment, along with the five hundred dollars that was in my bag) and faxes him my Texas driver's license.

"Truly evil," I hiss.

"I know." Sal nods.

"Slag," Becca agrees.

"Wait—this is the best part," Sal says.

We watch as Becca opens a cabinet behind her desk. It's filled with what I can only imagine are stolen goods. There's lots of things from the gift shop—with tags still on them, along with my purse and Ian's Xbox games.

"Och, aye!" Ian shouts, pointing at Resident Evil, which is lying in the cabinet.

"Please tell me this is enough to get her fired," I ask them. They both nod.

"Wait, here's the good part. Pause it."

I freeze-frame.

"See her computer? Read that letter she's writing."

"I can't make it out."

"Here," Sal says, giving me a magnifying glass. "I just found this when I watched it again last night."

"How many times have you seen it?" I ask her.

"It really never gets old."

Just as I'm starting to read, Sal blurts out, "She's faking a letter from Tanya. Can you believe that? She's *faking* the letter that asks the board to suspend Carter. It wasn't Tanya's fault at all."

"Why would Brigid want Carter fired?"

"So she can lock him up in her flat, just like Kathy Bates in *Misery,* yeah?" Becca says.

"Has Carter seen this?"

Sal shakes her head. "We thought maybe you could give it to him."

"Will-wee!" cries Tyler, at his loudest possible setting, interrupting our conversation. "Where's Anowld? I want play with Anowld! Mommy said Anowld be here!"

Tyler's face crumples and he looks like he's about to have a fit.

"I'm sure Arnold's around here somewhere, Tyler," Lauren says. "Go ask your Aunt Lily where he is."

"Tanya took him," I say.

Tyler looks at me, biting his lower lip, about to erupt in tears.

"Who the hell is Tanya?" Lauren says, stopping mid-cleaning frenzy and putting her rubber-gloved hands on her hips.

"EEWLOSTDAWEEPUP!" Ian shouts, catching part of

the conversation on his way to the bathroom. His shock of red hair is messy and he's wearing a T-shirt that says MY OTHER SHIRT IS A BLOODY T-SHIRT AS WELL.

"You lost the dog?" Sal echoes. "How could you lose the dog?"

"Long story," I say.

"Aye, we have to get him back," Ian says.

"I know, but we can't exactly waltz back in there," I say. I feel bad about losing Arnold, but it is true that he's probably eating better than I am at the moment. And he *did* do a lot of peeing in my bags. Still, I do miss him, I admit.

But apparently I don't quite miss him as much as Ian or Tyler, who both look like they're about to cry. I guess I am a very bad doggie mom.

"Anooooooooowld!" Tyler wails, crying. He throws himself on the sofa and beats the cushions with his tiny fists as if he's lamenting the loss of his one true love.

"It'll be all right, lad," Ian says. "We'll get the wee pup back."

"We can't. Tanya has him. There's no getting him back."

"No man left behind!" Ian cries, standing on the couch. "We go to get the wee pup!"

Becca and Sal stare at Ian.

"What about Carter?" I ask Ian.

"Aye," Ian says. "We go break him out first from the clutches of evil Brigid. And then it's off to get the wee pup."

"Who's Tanya?" Lauren asks, still looking puzzled.

"For the wee pup!" Ian cries, putting the blanket from the

couch over his shoulder like a tartan. "I'm gonna go get dressed. Then we go."

"It's already daybreak," I point out.

"Well, we leave now then, aye?" he says.

"Who's Tanya? And what the hell is Ian saying?" Lauren asks me, starting to get upset. "What is going on around here? And why am I always the last to know?"

Sal, Becca, and I bring Lauren up to speed.

"Okay, so what you're telling me," Lauren says, "is that you've gotten on the cover of all the major tabloids for allegedly sleeping with a soon-to-be-married man with a pregnant fiancée. You lost Arnold, your sole responsibility on this earth, to that man's girlfriend. You got Carter fired and pushed him into the arms of his psychotic girlfriend, who acts just like Kathy Bates in *Misery* except she's younger and doesn't eat and is obsessed with framing you for crimes you didn't commit. There's also, as the cherry on top, a warrant issued for your arrest by the state of Texas."

"Yes, that's pretty much it."

"Wow," Lauren says, whistling. "You really have outdone yourself."

"Thanks."

"No, I mean it. Throw in some arson or murder and we might have a Lifetime movie on our hands."

"I appreciate the sisterly support."

"No problem. Anytime." Lauren sighs. "So we're just going to walk straight up to his hotel room and ask for Arnold back?"

"They're not there, yeah?" Becca says. "They're tying the

knot today. At their country estate. It's been in all the papers."

"Ye know where the matrimonials are do ye, aye?"

"'Course I do," Becca says.

"She could draw you a map, I'm sure," Sal says.

"But how would we get in?"

"Leave that to me," Lauren says.

Outside Brigid's apartment, Ian starts hurling chunks of asphalt at the window he thinks is Brigid's. He picks progressively bigger rocks until he actually succeeds in breaking a pane of the window.

"You are a complete psycho nutjob," Sal tells Ian, who frowns at him.

Becca and Sal have insisted on coming. Apparently, they take perverse joy in watching people view the Brigid DVD for the first time. They say they want to be in the room with Carter when he watches it. It's probably more likely that they didn't want to watch Tyler.

Ian throws another lump of cement, which sails straight through the broken window. The next thing we see is Carter's angry (and somewhat messy) head of hair poke up. He slides the window up.

"What the hell are you doing? We've got an apartment buzzer."

I shrug. "Ian thought the front door would be too obvious."

Ian is dressed in full Scottish regalia, including kilt and

matching sporran. It's the only time I've seen him wear something that isn't a T-shirt. He even brought bagpipes, why, I am not sure.

"Ian? What are you wearing? Oh, never mind. One second. I'll buzz you guys up."

Carter disappears for a minute and then the front door buzzes. We all head up the stairs.

Carter answers the door wearing a T-shirt with an imprint of a photo of Brigid and Carter smiling. It's clearly much worse than I thought. He really does need saving. And fast.

"What da bloody fook?" Ian says, pointing at the shirt.

I can't help it. I start laughing.

"What?" Carter asks, "Oh! The shirt. Well, I didn't have pajamas, and Brigid gave me this and she thought it would be a good idea . . ." Carter looks at our skeptical faces. "Never mind. Come in."

Brigid's apartment shows her softer side. Everything is pink, except for her sofa, which is white. There's no mistaking it for a guy's place. There's no television for one thing, except a tiny one in the bedroom. And there are stuffed animals on the couch and piled high on her bed. It looks like the apartment was decorated by my thirteen-year-old cousin. She even has a poster of kittens in the bathroom, and her toilet is covered with a pink furry seat.

"You have got to be kidding," I say, looking around. In the bathroom, she also actually has his and her towels. I think I'm going to vomit.

"Bloody hell," sighs Becca, looking around.

"Kitty! I want da kitty!" Tyler says grabbing one of Brigid's stuffed cats and promptly banging its head hard against the floor.

"Careful, Ty," Lauren chides, even as Tyler whacks the stuffed cat harder.

"I told you it was a mistake to bring him," I say to Lauren.

"Who was I going to leave him with?" Lauren reminds me. "Becca and Sal wanted to come, too."

"We can't take him to the wedding, though," I say.

"What wedding?" Carter asks us.

Ian fills him in on our plan to rescue Arnold.

"No, absolutely not," Carter says, "I won't go."

After a drawn-out discussion about the size of Carter's balls and whether or not he actually has any since moving in with Brigid, Ian gives up trying to convince him. By this time, Tyler has worn himself out beating up on all the stuffed animals, and he's fallen asleep on the couch.

"Maybe you could watch Tyler?" Lauren asks Carter, who sighs.

"Fine," he says. "I'll watch Tyler. But I still think you three ought to rethink this. You're going to get arrested."

"No one's going to arrest a pregnant woman," Lauren snaps. "Besides, I know a thing or two about weddings."

"Lily . . ." Carter calls as I'm about to leave. I pause and turn. My heart skips a beat. Is he going to change his mind and come with us? Or better yet, declare that he loves me?

"Uh . . ." he falters. "Be careful, okay?"

I sigh, disappointed. "Yeah, I'll be fine," I say.

Sal jumps in. "Dr. Henry, we've got something you need to see."

"Yeah, you stay put, Dr. Henry," Becca tells Carter. "We've got a diagnosis we need to break to you, and I'm afraid it's terminal."

We leave Carter with Becca, Sal, and the DVD, as well as Lauren's instructions on how to care for Tyler, which includes a schedule so detailed it actually has "potty times" on it. She also left him food in small sealed containers, with measured portions of Cheerios and organic, hormone-free cheese.

"I think we'll be okay," Carter says. "I have nephews, you know."

"Just stick to the schedule or Tyler gets all loopy," Lauren says.

"So what is your plan?" I ask Lauren once we're back inside the car and Ian's driving.

"Don't have one yet," Lauren mumbles, her mouth full of chips. She carries more snacks than a vending machine.

"Do you ever stop eating?" I ask her.

"Not for the last trimester, no," Lauren says, spraying chip crumbs on Carter's dashboard. "Wait! Stop here!" Lauren cries, pointing to a flower shop. She comes out of the store five minutes later carrying an orchid plant and a cooler.

"What's that?" I ask her.

"Our ticket in," she says.

A half hour later, we pull up to an enormous wrought-iron

gate supported by two giant stone pillars. We drive by a mob of fans of Sean Gates, and even more photographers, hoping to get pictures of the wedding party. Overhead, a helicopter hovers. Through the gates, I can almost see a glimpse of a small city of white tents on the enormous green lawn.

We pull up to the gate, where a guard motions for us to roll down the window.

"Let me do the talking," Lauren says.

"I could run it," Ian says, his hands tighten around the steering wheel.

"No, just let me talk, okay?" Lauren says. Ian rolls down the window and smiles at the guard.

"We're delivering the Tyleranian orchid," Lauren tells the guard, who gives us all a dubious look.

"What's that?" the guard asks.

"You don't know about the Tyleranian orchid? It's only the rarest flower in the world, growing in only one place, a remote waterfall in Phu Ty Ran Ka province in Thailand. Locals say that lovers who swear their love before it will be protected by the ancient Thailand gods of love for this life and the next."

"But . . ." the guard starts.

"This orchid is so rare that I have two of the world's premiere botanists here"—Lauren motions to Ian and then to me—"to make sure that these flower treasures, which, by the way, are known to bloom only once every decade, make it to this ceremony in one piece. We have exactly"—Lauren looks at her watch—"five minutes to get these into the climate-control chamber inside that house before they will start to deteriorate."

"I think I should call ahead. . . ."

"That's it. Give him the cooler," Lauren tells me. "I'm not going to be the one who tells Tanya that the orchids she's spent fifty-thousand pounds on are ruined because we couldn't get to a refrigerator in time."

Lauren snaps her fingers. Ian lifts the cooler and offers it to the guard through the open window.

He lifts the lid and shows him the white orchids inside (the orchids Lauren bought).

"Don't breathe on it, you fool!" Lauren cries. "The carbon dioxide will turn them yellow."

Lauren throws down her hands in disgust. "Give him the case. I'm washing my hands of this right now. You can tell Tanya how you're going to repay her twenty-five-thousand-pound deposit."

The guard, looking uncertain, and more than a little scared, hands the case back to Ian.

"Take it," he says.

"Don't take it, we're leaving," Lauren says. Ian revs the engine, as if preparing to run through the barricade.

"Please! No—take it. Go on in."

"I can't work under these conditions," Lauren says.

"Please!" the guard begs, practically tossing the container inside. "Wedding help goes up and to the left."

"You better hope you haven't ruined these flowers," Lauren says to him, giving him her sternest look.

Ian, in awe, drives forward. "You're good, aye?" he says.

"Yeah, but Tyleranian orchid? I can't believe he bought that," I say.

"It's all in the delivery."

"I assume there's no Phu Ty Ran Ka province, either," I say.

"Not that I know of," Lauren says, burping. "God, pregnancy heartburn," she says. "It's the worst."

The wedding is the largest party I've ever seen. There are a small town of white tents and an army of caterers, florists, designers, and more guards with headsets than you usually see with the president's motorcade.

Ian whistles. He brings out his handheld camcorder.

"Do you think that's wise?" I ask him, as he shoots the enormous white stone manor in front of us. It's a house straight out of a Jane Austen novel.

Ian does some filming, and then clicks the camcorder off.

"The trick is, act like you belong and you will," Lauren says. This coming from a woman who's so pregnant, it takes her three tries to get out of the front seat.

"Oh, right, we're not going to stick out or anything," I say, looking at Ian and his bright green tartan, matching kilt, and bagpipes.

"Mmphrt," Lauren disagrees, with her mouth full of chips.

Two guys dressed in waiters' uniforms struggle to move an ice statue that looks suspiciously like Sean Gates. I'd recognize that smirk anywhere. One of them looks up and sees Ian.

Uh-oh. We're done for.

"Oiy, mate, they've been looking for you," one of them says to Ian.

Ian looks right, then left, and then points a finger at his own chest. "Me?"

"Yes, you, you bloody ox. You're one of the bagpipe players, yeah? They're looking for you. Over there."

The waiter motions toward the house.

Ian looks at us. "Let's go then," Lauren commands, in her wedding-planner voice.

On the way to the house, Lauren is distracted by the buffet.

"Oh, food!" Lauren cries.

"Lauren, wait. Wait!"

She moves fast for a pregnant woman. Before I know it, she's in front of some of the warming platters, inhaling chicken kabobs.

"What are you doing? We have to stay focused here."

Lauren, I swear, growls at me.

"Do not come between a pregnant woman and food," she says, devouring a stuffed cherry tomato.

"You!" cries someone else.

We all turn.

"Bagpipe players over here," says a man who takes Ian by the arm and leads him off to another tent by the house. He ignores Lauren and me.

Ian looks at us, eyes wide, as he's led off in the direction of the band.

"What do we do now?" I ask Lauren.

She hands me an empty tray. "Take this, follow them," she says, pointing to the line of waitstaff headed into the side room of the house.

"You are coming with me," I say, taking Lauren by the arm. She grabs a small plate and loads up on food before following me.

"Do I have to do everything myself?" she says, sighing and licking her fingers.

We make it into the kitchen, an enormous room larger than the Dorchester Hotel suite, and it's full of people all wearing white. Most of them ignore us, but when Lauren's condition and her snacking become too obvious, one of them—I assume a head chef of some sort—stops us.

"*Excusez,*" says a man with a French accent, who appears to be the head chef, "you do not belong here, no? I have to call secu—" Before he finishes his sentence, Lauren pounces.

"This appetizer is unacceptable," she says, throwing down her plate in disgust. "Didn't the organizer tell you she has a severe pine nut allergy? Dammit, this food could kill her."

"What? Who are you?"

"Who are you, is the question. You call yourself a chef? What is this!" Lauren shrieks, looking down at the floor. She picks up what I can only imagine is a piece of lint, or nothing at all. "Is this a dog hair? *A dog hair in Tanya and Sean's kitchen.*"

Lauren is using a pitch usually reserved for bat sonar.

"Dog hair?" The chef is completely confounded by this point.

"Do you realize that we have five hundred guests out there expecting the finest we have to offer, and you can't keep your kitchen clean? Have you let Tanya's Chihuahua in here? What kind of kitchen are you running?"

"No d-d-dog," he stutters.

"How do you explain this?" Lauren says, waving the imaginary dog hair in his face.

Lauren gets out her mobile and flips it open.

"Hello? Sean? We've got a problem here. There are pine nuts in two of the appetizers, and God only knows what's in the entrees. . . ." Lauren pauses. "And Tanya's Chihuahua is loose."

The chef blanches.

"We can fix, yes? We'll fix," he says.

"The dog is upstairs," says another waiter. "It's not here."

"I'll take care of it. I promise, Sean." Lauren flips the phone closed.

"It's obviously gotten out. You—take me and show me where you think the dog is," Lauren commands. "And you," she tells the chef. "You'd better do something about these pine nuts or Sean and half of the British press are going to hear about it from me."

The waiter stands staring. "What are you waiting for? Move!" Lauren commands.

The waiter jumps. The chef seconds her command with a wave of his arm. The waiter is already halfway to the servant staircase when Lauren stalks after him, belly first.

You have to hand it to my sister. She sure knows how to boss people around, like almost all firstborns. It's what makes her a great wedding planner. But it was only after her divorce that she really found her talent for it—other, of course, than bossing me around, which she's been doing since we used to play "wedding" and she'd make me play the groom (Lauren, naturally, was always the bride).

The jittery and somewhat sullen waiter leads us to a room, where we find Arnold sitting on a gold-embossed footstool and wearing a minituxedo. Complete with tails.

He barks when he sees us and wags his tail, which causes the back of his tuxedo to flip back and forth.

The waiter smirks at us. Lauren frowns at him. "What are you still doing here? You're needed downstairs!" she snipes. He looks at the ground and shuffles off, probably imagining our untimely deaths.

"Arnold!" I say, getting down on my knees. Arnold jumps off the stool and waddles over to me, hopping up on his hind legs and licking my face. He is actually glad to see me.

"Grab him and let's go," Lauren says.

We make it out to the hallway before we're accosted by what can only be the bridal party. It's Tanya, wearing a white empire-waist gown that still doesn't quite hide her pregnancy, and several bridesmaids, along with a woman wearing a headset, who must be the wedding planner.

To hide, I step behind Lauren and hold up Arnold so he covers my face.

"What are you doing to my Chi-Chi?"

Chi-Chi?

I look at Arnold, and he sniffs.

"You realize that having a dog about when you're in your third trimester can affect the baby's birth weight?"

"Excuse me," Tanya says, frowning at Lauren.

"And who are you?" the wedding planner asks.

"Esther sent me," Lauren says, smiling bright. "I was her pregnancy specialist." Lauren pats her own stomach. "As you can see, I know what I'm doing."

"Esther?"

"Ritchie," Lauren says.

Tanya still looks blank. "Madonna?" she ventures at last.

Lauren nods and rolls her eyes, as if she can't believe Tanya didn't pick up on "Esther."

"I'm your wedding/baby shower present," Lauren says. "Now tell me about the swelling in your feet. We can relieve that with some sea salts. I assume you're drinking only fresh Kabbalah-blessed water."

"No, but . . . I didn't know Madonna liked me."

"Esther," Lauren corrects. "And she loves you! She can't stop talking about how excited she is you and Sean are going to be parents. Believe me, she must like you because I'm not cheap."

Lauren laughs, and Tanya, still a bit off balance, gives a weak laugh.

"What's a pregnancy specialist?"

"I can't believe you've made it this far without one, dear," Lauren says.

"This isn't the best time," Tanya says.

"Oh, no, it's the perfect time," Lauren says. "You see, I can show you some relaxation techniques that will help you get through the ceremony. And we can't have those swollen feet get in the way of you standing up during your own wedding."

"You look familiar," one of the bridesmaids says as she walks around me.

I mumble something into Arnold's fur.

"We'd better get started," Lauren says, distracting Tanya. She takes her by the arm and leads her out of the room. The bridesmaids and wedding planner reluctantly follow.

Alone, I grab Arnold and head for the door. I make it down the stairs and out of the house. Out on the lawn, I get to the car with Arnold, but I don't have the keys. Ian does, naturally. And I have no idea where he is.

I'm not sure what to do. Do I hide? Mingle with the guests? What do I do with Arnold in the meantime? He looks up at me with pleading eyes. I put him in my bag and go looking for Ian. I walk by the rows of golden flocked chairs, lined by giant ice sculptures of Sean Gates on the groom's side, and Tanya on the bride's. Given the unnaturally warm November day, the sculptures are melting faster than I would've thought, and they're forming a mud trench on the outer aisles.

Guests begin to arrive for the wedding, and it dawns on me that this is a celebrity event. The guest list reads like a Who's Who of British celebs. Sienna Miller, Kate Winslet, Hugh Grant, and, of course, Sting and Trudy. I doubt Sting remembers me. When we met at Elton John's Oscar party, Ted had been throwing up in the bathroom for an hour, and our conversation lasted two-point-one minutes and involved something about the contents of a spring roll and whether or not there was meat inside it or not. I decide against waving. And then I see the coup de grâce: Justin and Cameron, taking their seats.

I guess the rumor about Sean Gates having a cameo in her new movie is true, after all. Ted would be pissed. Justin is his idol, next to Tommy Lee.

There are more cameras than I've ever seen at a regular person's wedding, and they're all trained on the celebs. It's like a red-carpet event. There's even a video camera and a reporter interviewing guests. I assume it's for a wedding scrapbook, but then again, they could be working for *Access Hollywood*.

Selling an exclusive means Sean and Tanya wouldn't have to pay for their wedding at all.

I look over and see my sister, her belly straining against her otherwise neat black dress, being seated by an usher in a row next to Stella McCartney.

You've got to be kidding me.

She glances over at me and waves. Unbelievable. Only my sister would manage to get a front-row view of Sean Gates's wedding.

And then I see Ian. He's standing with a bunch of other bagpipe players, only they're all wearing blue plaid. He's the only one in green and red. Ian is fumbling with his bagpipes. When he sees me, he points to the left and waves his hand, like I should move.

I don't understand what he's trying to tell me, not to mention the bagpipes are getting in the way of his signaling. And then I look over and see what he's been trying to tell me.

There, standing by the bar tent, is Ted Dayton. And hanging on his arm is Melanie Slate.

Twenty-three

REASON #23 TO DIVORCE A ROCK STAR:
Because a wife is just one more devoted fan.

After the Iron Cactus, Ted told me that I didn't understand what fame did to a person. How Melanie "understood" him in a way I couldn't. "You don't know what it's like to be hounded all day. To be famous," he'd said, as if having thousands of fans throwing themselves at his feet was somehow a burden, and not a perk, of fame.

But I knew what it was like to be famous by association, to be the person people look through to try to see the famous person. I knew what it was like to have to explain myself to overzealous new roadies protecting the backstage, or to *Rolling Stone* reporters who weren't interested in anything but having greater access to Ted. And I knew what it was like to be scrutinized by the groupies, the ones who thought I wasn't good enough for Ted. I knew what it was like when Ted's manager and the record producers were nice, but not too nice, all betting on the fact that I wouldn't be around for very long. That was almost worse than the betrayal—knowing that all the people who were betting against you were right.

Ted and Melanie look just like their wax figures at Madame Tussaud's, except that Melanie's hem of her dress is even shorter in real life. Ted's eyes are bloodshot and he's swaying a bit because he's already had too much to drink. His eyes are starting to look puffy. I take some solace in the fact that when he's forty, he's probably going to look completely puffy and bloated, like all heavy drinkers do.

Melanie is wearing a spandex dress, with the stomach cut out so that everyone can see her rounded belly. It's nice to know that impending motherhood hasn't made her rethink the tastefulness of her wardrobe.

At the sight of them, I feel my blood pressure rise.

I watch as Ted and Melanie argue over Ted's drink (probably because it's his seventh or eighth of the day) and then they make their way to their seats. I imagine that Ted has been shotgunning drinks to work up the courage to say hello to his hero, Justin. I imagine at some point in the evening Ted will make a complete fool of himself in front of Justin and Cameron, which may or may not end in an actual fistfight. Then later, when he sobers up, he'll make it someone else's fault. If I were there, it would be mine. Like the time he got too nervous at the after Grammys party thrown by Sony Records. In his enthusiasm, Ted accidentally spilled his drink down the back of Tommy Lee's shirt. The next day, somehow I'd been the one who'd nudged him, even though I'd been waiting in line for the bathroom at the time.

This should make me glad that we're no longer together. But it doesn't. For some strange reason, it just makes me sad.

Ted and Melanie sit on the groom's side. I wonder if he's hoping Sean Gates will make a cameo in his next music video. I wouldn't put it past Ted to think in terms of international sales. Becca says that Sean Gates is the most famous athlete in the world, next to David Beckham. I hear he's huge in Japan.

Ted, who has, like I thought, already had too much to drink, belches loudly.

Everyone in the near vicinity, including Justin and Cameron, turn to look at him. At that moment, I am so glad I'm not with Ted anymore, I could cry. And then, as if he can feel my eyes on him, Ted looks up and sees me.

For a second, I don't move. He looks surprised. Then he smiles.

I'm frozen to the spot. It's like I'm caught in the tractor beam of his rock star mojo (which, despite his drunkenness, is still going strong). He nods at me. Instead of nodding back, I turn around and start walking quickly back toward the car. I make it halfway there before the wedding planner grabs me and turns me around.

"Where are you going with the ring bearer?" she says. "He's got to be ready to go down the aisle in ten minutes!"

"Ring bearer?" I echo, and then I look down at the tuxedo-clad Arnold in my bag and it occurs to me that he's actually in the ceremony. Before I can protest, the planner with the headset has plucked Arnold out of my arms. I watch helplessly as she gives him over to a waiting bridesmaid.

"What are yee doing?" Ian hisses at me, breaking away from the band long enough to get close to me. "You had the wee pup and you gave him up! This is a rescue mission."

"What was I supposed to do? He's in the wedding and you have the car keys. I couldn't exactly make a run for it."

Ian sighs. "Okay, plan B then. I'll grab the pup and run. Just wait fer my signal."

Great. There is no way now to avoid a certain arrest. With all the people around and the guards at the gates, I doubt a smash-and-grab plan is going to work.

The wedding planner is signaling me to move away from the band, and I assume away from the wedding. Ian hands me his keys.

"Go and start the car," he says. "I'll be there in a minute. And grab your sister now, aye?"

I try to catch Lauren's eye, but she's preoccupied with talking to Cameron Diaz. I suspect she's selling her wedding-planning expertise.

Failing to get my sister's attention, I'm stuck watching the ceremony behind a giant shrub that's been sheared into the shape of a cupid.

The band starts up, and I notice Ian struggling with his bagpipes. There's clearly someone off in the trio of bagpipe players, and I know it has to be Ian. Some of the guests turn and look at him. The other bagpipe players are looking at one another and then at him.

Other than Ian's atrocious bagpipe playing, the ceremony goes off without a hitch, aside from the steady melting of the ice sculptures. By the end of the ceremony, the ice Sean looks more like a turtle than a famous soccer player.

During the ceremony, the real Sean manages to look appropriately serious, and I'm surprised that the vows don't include a sexual innuendo. It's the longest I've ever heard him speak without using one. Tanya is model perfect, in a flowing Vera Wang silk dress, her arms tanned and toned and bone thin, her belly a perfectly rounded basketball. Like Melanie Slate, she'll probably be back to modeling six weeks after birth.

The only odd part about the ceremony is that both Sean and Tanya look like they're in pain. Tanya, in fact, can't keep from wincing. It's probably because she knows she's in for a lifetime of tabloid headlines.

It occurs to me if incredibly beautiful women like Tanya and Sienna Miller can't manage to keep their men faithful, then it could very well be hopeless for me. I definitely understand the root of my sister's paranoia.

After the ceremony ends, the guests start to meander toward the tents for food and drink. Lauren finally looks in my direction and sees me signaling her frantically. She seems to understand. She gets up slowly and makes her way out of the aisle and toward me.

"I don't think those chicken skewers are agreeing with me," Lauren says, holding her stomach. "I've got some serious cramping."

"I realize the miracle of pregnancy is an amazing thing, but can you manage not to share every update with me?" I ask her. "I don't need to know when you have gas."

"Oww," Lauren says, and holds her stomach. "Don't look now, but we've been spotted."

I look up to see Ted walking toward us. Staggering, actually. He has had quite a lot to drink.

But Ted isn't the only one who's spotted us, the wedding party is also making their way toward us, and Tanya is staring right at me.

Uh-oh.

I see the recognition start to dawn on her face.

We need to get to the car—and quickly. Just at that moment, Ian comes rushing in, green plaid skirts flapping, with Arnold tucked under his arm like a football.

"FREEDOM!" he shouts, and leaps into the driver's seat. He starts up the engine, and then promptly floods it. "Bollocks," he says.

"Lily? That *is* you," Ted says, stumbling into us. He's followed in short order by Tanya and Sean.

"I knew I recognized you," Tanya says, tapping her finger on the window. "And what the bloody hell do you think you're doing with my dog?"

Before I can answer, Lauren, next to me, gives out a low-pitched moan.

Then, as if it's contagious, Tanya doubles over, clutching her stomach.

"Are you having contractions?" Sean asks her.

"Of course I am, you bloody twit," Tanya says. "Why else would I be doubled over?"

Immediately Sean panics. "We have to get you to a bloody hospital," he says, all thumbs, as he throws open the driver's side door and pushes Ian over so he can drive. The ignition turns over after another try, and Sean nearly drives off without Tanya.

She gives me a wary look. "He really is a wanker," she says, sighing.

Sean drives five feet before he realizes his mistake. He throws the car in reverse and then throws open the passenger door. "Get in," he says.

"I'm not going anywhere. I've paid a million quid for this bloody reception." Tanya doubles over again.

"Get *in* the car, Tanya."

"We have a bloody limo, or have you forgotten?" Tanya says.

"No time!" Sean cries, panicked. "You're about to have the baby!"

"Arrrggghhhh," Lauren says, digging her fingernails into my arm. "She's not the only one," Lauren spits out through gritted teeth.

Twenty-four

REASON #24 TO DIVORCE A ROCK STAR:
So you don't have to worry if "baby" is a term of endearment he uses to avoid calling you by another woman's name.

After news of Melanie Slate and Ted broke, my neighbor Fran told me that I needed to let go of my negative energy.

"You've got a lot of anger issues," she told me, as if diagnosing me with a disease.

"Did *US Weekly* clue you into that?" I asked her.

"It's true. I can see it in your aura. You've got a red overlay."

"Is that good?"

"Nope," she said.

Tanya gets her way and takes the limo to the hospital, but she's not alone. All five of us (Lauren, Tanya, Ian, Sean, and me) end up in the white limo, racing down the stretch of highway that will lead us to London and to hospitals that, as Tanya says, "are more than glorified vets."

I call Carter on my mobile, to try to get some sort of via-phone medical help.

"Lily! Listen, I saw the DVD. Why didn't you *tell* me about Brigid? She's a complete psychopath. She got me fired!"

"I tried to tell you but you wouldn't listen to me," I say. "Anyway, we'll talk about it later. I've got a medical emergency. I'm in a car with my sister and Tanya and they're both in labor."

"They're *both* in labor?" Carter echoes. I hear the sound of metal banging against tile in the background.

"What is going on there?"

"Tyler is learning how to play percussion on Brigid's pots."

"Oh. Great. Now can you focus here a second? What do I do?"

"Ask them when the contractions started. And ask them how far apart they are."

I relay the questions.

"Last night," Tanya says. "But I wasn't going to postpone the wedding. It's cost us a million quid. And besides, I have a C-section scheduled for tomorrow morning."

I just stare at Tanya. For someone with excellent beauty genes, she clearly didn't get much in the brains department.

"How far apart are your contractions?"

"Every few minutes or so."

"Is that bad?" I ask, relaying the information to Carter.

"I don't know for sure," Carter says.

"But you asked me to ask them!"

"Right. Well, I'd say you should probably get to a hospital as quickly as you can."

"Uh, duh, Dr. Henry. That's what we're doing. You need a medical degree to tell me that?"

"I'm a bone doctor, not an obstetrician, remember?"

"Great."

"Just keep them calm. The closest hospital to you is probably my hospital, since you're coming from the south, okay? Save your phone battery and call me back in five minutes."

Tanya objects immediately to going back to the hospital where she says "blindfolded clowns" made a mess of Sean's recovery. Sean, for his part, just keeps murmuring "John Hurt" over and over again and looking in the rearview mirror at Tanya as if she might combust.

Sean explains that he watched *Coupling* recently and said the characters on it referred to birth as the "John Hurt moment" because John Hurt is the actor who appeared in *Alien* and has the notorious achievement of being the first actor to have an alien burst from his stomach.

"Of course you'd say that, you're a man," Tanya snaps at Sean. "The scariest thing men can think of is having to give birth. That's why a man wrote *Alien.*"

Lauren, sitting next to Ian, seems to be in some kind of daze. She keeps murmuring "I'm eleven days early!" over and over again.

Tanya eyes me. "So? You're Lily, yeah? You're the one that all the fuss is about?"

"Me?" I ask. I glance around to see if she has any sharp objects within her reach. "Yes, that's me, but believe me, *nothing* happened. You have absolutely *nothing* to be jealous about. I mean, I wouldn't touch Sean with a ten-foot pole. I mean, he's such a self-centered ass, you know? I would never in a million years go for someone like—"

"Oiy! Leave it out," Sean says. "I'm Sean Bloody Gates, yeah, no one says—"

"Shut up," Tanya shouts.

"I mean, if you want to know the truth," I tell Tanya, "I think he's totally and absolutely revolting. I mean, the way everything is about sex, and let's face it, he isn't all that bright, either. I think he's been heading one too many soccer balls, if you know what I mean. I like guys who can spell, you know?"

I trail off, seeing the expression on Tanya's face. She's frowning at me. I realize this is making her now-husband out to be a total loser. I've gone from potentially sleeping with him to now trashing him in the worst possible way. "I mean, not that he's not attractive in his own right, but you know, I mean, not that *I* find him attractive. I mean, I definitely don't."

I make a puking sound. I actually simulate gagging. It's like my body has been taken over by an alien life force determined to completely humiliate me.

"Uh . . . right," I finish. "I am going to shut up now."

Tanya just stares at me. After a moment, she speaks.

"What I was going to say was that I know all about it," she

says. "One of the hospital board members called me and told me about that administrator, or what's her name, setting up the whole thing. They wanted to make sure to tell me that they've taken care of the problem and apologize to me and Sean for our suffering."

Lauren makes a strangled sound as she deals with another contraction. As it passes, I swear, my sister is possessed by the devil, because a booming voice comes out of her that I've never heard before. "THIS ISN'T PART OF MY BIRTH PLAN!" she shouts in a voice several octaves deeper than normal.

Amazed by the James Earl Jones quality of the voice that comes out of my sister's small mouth, we all stare.

My highly organized, wedding-planner sister had everything about the birth of her second child planned down to the minute. By the end of her first trimester, she had her hospital bag packed and a color-coded, tabbed notebook she'd given to Nick outlining when, where, and how everything was to proceed, from the route he should take to the hospital (avoiding the highest amount of traffic) to her hospital forms (two identical sets already filled out—typed, double-spaced—and ready to be handed to the admitting nurse).

My sister has only now realized that her plan does not apply here, in a foreign country. I think she might have a nervous breakdown. This is vintage Lauren. She overplans everything and then completely negates the whole plan because she gets too emotional about something (in this case, jealous) and does her one spontaneous act of the century (jetting off to London before her due date).

"Lauren, calm down," I say. "Everything is going to be okay."

"IT IS NOT OKAY," Lauren shouts. "I DON'T HAVE A PLAN!"

She is definitely losing it. Even Tanya, who normally doesn't consider other people's feelings, takes notice. Lauren is a woman on the edge. Her eyes are wild and she looks capable of violence.

"It'll be okay," Tanya says. "Look, we won't argue anymore, yeah? No more fighting."

"BIRTH PLAN!" Lauren growls like an animal through gritted teeth. "No birth plan! Birth plan! Birth plan! Birth plan!" Lauren puts her hand over her forehead. "I was supposed to be at the women's hospital with lilies around me and my labor coach," Lauren wails. "I'm in a foreign country! I don't even know if I'm covered by health insurance here. Oh. My. God."

Lauren is babbling like a patient in a psych ward.

"Why don't we all just calm down and take a deep breath," I say, trying to imitate Carter's professional doctor's voice, the one he uses on patients who typically have very serious problems, like a broken bone sticking out of their leg.

"My birth plan was in the perfect, pink three-ring binder," Lauren is saying. "All the pages were laminated."

"Laminated? Really?" Tanya asks, a bit in awe.

"It was the perfect birth plan. It had no flaws. I'd thought of everything. I even picked out Nick's clothes."

"You can't be serious. The birth plan told Nick which clothes he should wear?"

"I was thinking of the pictures," Lauren snaps. "We'd have to be color coordinated, okay?"

"Wow, I'm impressed," Tanya says. "But then, I wouldn't expect less from Madonna's pregnancy guru. Nick's the father, yeah? Where is he then?"

"He's busy cheating on me with some two-bit firefighter who calls herself a civil servant, but from what I can tell the only service she provides is stealing other women's husbands. That's why I'm here and not at home."

Tanya's eyes widen.

"Oh, luv, I've been there. Men are all bastards, ain't that right, Sean darlin'?"

"Hey," Sean cries.

"Aren't they, though? Why can't they keep their little firemen in their pants is what I want to know," Lauren says.

"Oh, tell me about it, luv. This one"—Tanya nudges Sean hard with her elbow—"I was on holiday, visiting me mum for only three days before he was on the front page of the *Sun* with two strippers in my bloody living room, and I was barely three months pregnant!"

"No!" cries Lauren. "That sounds like my first husband. He screwed my neighbor on our brand-new leather couch."

"What is it about men?" Tanya cries. "Why do they have to play away and ruin perfectly good furniture, as well?"

The two women share a conspiratorial laugh.

They talk for the next twenty minutes straight about men and pregnancy, leaving no detail too personal or grueling out of the mix. They broach topics ranging from ankle swelling to hemorrhoids. Even bawdy Sean is a little taken aback, but he dares not interrupt.

My phone rings. It's Nick.

"I'm in London," he says. "Where should I go?"

I give him convoluted directions to the hospital, but before I can finish, Tanya whips the phone out of my hand.

She gives Nick a bawling out that I doubt he's ever heard before. She tells him he ought not to cheat on his wife, and that she's better than he deserves, and on and on. By the end of it, Lauren's eyes are glistening.

"That's how us girls stick together, luv," Tanya says, hanging up.

"My sister is insane. Her husband is not cheating on her. You've just berated an innocent man," I say.

"No such thing as an innocent man. All men cheat, luv. It's just a matter of catching them," Tanya says. "So are you going to tell me why you're trying to knick my bloody dog?"

Sean clears his throat.

"It's actually my dog," I admit. "Sean just, uh, *borrowed* it. Said it would help him heal."

"Your dog? My Chi-Chi is your dog?"

I nod.

Tanya sighs. "Sean Bloody Gates, you've messed up again, haven't you? Why didn't you just tell me it wasn't your dog to give me?"

Sean shrugs.

I have Carter back on the phone, and I give him an update on the state of everyone's condition. "No time to lose. Make sure you don't take any detours. Get to the hospital as soon as you can. I'll meet you there, okay? I already called it in. They'll be ready for you." With that, he hangs up.

"I'm not going to London Central Hospital," Tanya says, sounding resolute. "I want my C-section at St. Mary's Hospital."

"There's not time," Carter tells me on the phone. "Tanya is going to have that baby in the car unless you get her to the nearest hospital."

"I'm not bloody going to London bloody Central!" shouts Tanya in a red-faced rage. "That's a public hospital! I'm going to have a C-section. With a tummy tuck!"

We all look at her.

"That's what Posh did, and that's what I'm doing, too."

"You have two choices at this point," I say, getting very close to her face. "You can have your baby at London Central, or you can have your baby right here in this car. Your choice."

"I could film it," Ian says, waving his handheld camera around.

"Shut up!" Lauren and Tanya say at once.

"And put that thing away," Lauren says, grimacing.

Tanya considers her options.

"London Central," she says.

*　　　*　　　*

In the public hospital where Carter used to work, the maternity ward isn't like the ones you find in the United States, hospitals with a line of pastel-colored individual rooms, with room enough for families and for lots of epidurals. At London Central, the maternity ward is one big room, with a few privacy curtains. Overall, the effect is like the communal dressing rooms at Loehmann's.

Neither my sister, nor Tanya, are pleased.

"I am not going to broadcast my privates to everyone in London," Tanya declares. "They'll end up on some bloody tabloid!"

"Not part of the birth plan! Not part of the birth plan at all!" Lauren says when she sees the room.

There are women in various stages of labor, many taking epidurals or some form of pain relief, but others are not. You can tell the difference. The ones without are groaning, sweating, crying, or shrieking. The ones with epidurals are calm, collected, and asking for tea.

"This is not happening," Lauren says. "This is not happening! She's *early.*"

"Well, we know where the baby gets that, don't we?" I ask Lauren. She doesn't think this is funny.

Carter, who has called in our arrival, walks into the room then.

"Where's Tyler?" I ask him.

"Becca and Sal are watching the little devil," Carter says. "But you and I need to talk," he tells me.

"Talk on someone else's time!" Lauren says, lashing out and

grabbing his hand. Her grip is steely. "I don't have my birth plan, but I'm going to have at least one doctor in the room that I know."

"But I'm an orthopedic surgeon. I fix bones." Carter looks a little pale.

"Birth scares you?" I ask him.

"You know I have a low threshold for pain," Carter says.

"But it's not your pain," Lauren points out.

"I empathize, okay? I'm sensitive."

"You just don't like looking at a woman in that state," I say.

"The John Hurt moment," Sean offers, and then makes a motion like an alien is jumping out of his chest, complete with sound effects.

We all stare at him. "Well, that's what it looks like," he says lamely.

"Anyway," Carter says, looking at me, "Becca told me about you trying to help me and everything. . . ."

Carter is interrupted by Tanya shouting.

"Where is the bloody doctor? I am not staying here!"

The doctor on duty comes in, looking quite a bit like Paul McCartney, with the same easygoing manner and soft brown eyes.

"I'm Dr. Oliver, and I'll be—"

"No, you won't be anything," Tanya says, sweat popping out on her brow. "I am having a C-section and a tummy tuck!"

"I'm sorry?" Dr. Oliver looks over at Carter, who shrugs and puts his hands up.

"I'm Tanya Bloody Richards, and I've been on the cover of the Victoria's Secret catalog five times!"

"I'm sorry, Ms., uh, Richards, but we're not equipped to do a tummy tuck here. I'm afraid you'll have to schedule the surgery some other—"

Tanya grabs Dr. Oliver's collar and pulls him so that they're nose to nose. "C-section! Tummy tuck! I want Dr. Anderson. Call him!"

Dr. Oliver examines Tanya as she's shouting, like a union worker for better pay. He pops his head back up, looking slightly nervous.

"I'm afraid we can't do a C-section. Too far along for that, but don't worry, we'll have things tidied up here in a moment."

Lauren watches, wide-eyed.

"I want an epidural. Gas. Something!" Tanya cries.

"Too far along, I'm afraid," Dr. Oliver says, putting on his mask and getting situated on a stool by Tanya's feet.

"This is all your fault," Tanya says, poking her finger into Sean's chest. "All your bloody fault."

"You're going to need to push now," Dr. Oliver tells Tanya. "You might want to hold your husband's hand."

"It's not his bloody hand I'm going to hold," Tanya spits, and then before Sean can step away, she reaches down and grabs his groin in a viselike grip. Sean goes white as a sheet, then red-faced and sweating, tears pouring down the sides of his cheeks. Both Sean and Tanya shriek. She doesn't let go until the end, when I'm pretty sure that Sean has experienced close to the pain of actual childbirth. Afterward, it's Sean who looks pale and shaky and can't stop crying. Tanya is calm, collected, and holding her baby boy in her arms.

Lauren's husband, Nick, arrives then, with perfect timing.

He's looking jet-lagged, unshaven, and harried, triumphantly holding Lauren's birth plan notebook above his head.

"I've got it," he cries, out of breath, "I've got the birth plan."

For the first time since her arrival in London, Lauren smiles.

Twenty-five

REASON #25 TO DIVORCE A ROCK STAR:

Their idea of family is to have one in every state.

The irony is that before the Melanie Slate incident, I thought about leaving Ted. Whenever Ted and I would fight, like after one of his really bad benders, I'd threaten to leave and he'd tell me he couldn't live without me. He'd blame the drugs. The drugs made him flirt with other girls. The drugs made him abandon me in bars. The drugs made him an asshole.

And then, if I didn't forgive him, he'd threaten to kill himself without me.

Once, after he'd left me sitting in a bar for hours waiting for him, while he was off doing coke with some of his friends, I packed a bag and threatened to move out.

He took out a knife and cut his arm—a shallow cut that barely bled. He told me he'd kill himself without me, and so I stayed.

At the time, I thought it meant he *really* loved me. Now

I realize there's a fine line between obsessive love and psychosis.

It turns out to be a long labor, and Lauren and Nick have plenty of time to talk over their issues. By the time the baby comes, Nick has convinced her (again) that he has no interest in any woman but her, which I'd told her in the beginning, if she'd only listen to me. But what do I know? I'm the irresponsible sister.

"I can't believe I missed the birth of my second grandchild," my mom cries on the phone. "Will there be pictures in *People*? That's where I seem to get the news about my daughters these days."

"Mom, calm down. Lauren's fine. Everybody is fine." I'm standing outside the hospital. The wind whips through my thin leather jacket. I stamp my feet and finish off my cigarette.

"Does this mean she's a limey Brit?" my dad asks on the phone. His first concern is his granddaughter's citizenship.

"I don't think it works that way here, Dad," I say.

"And I can't believe you've left me with just *your father* on Thanksgiving. You know how much he's eaten? It's sickening. Really."

"I'm sorry, Mom."

"Between you two girls, I am surprised I haven't had bypass surgery. Honestly. The stress you two put me under. Are you going to tell me the baby's name? Or is that something I should just look for in *US Weekly*?"

"Emily Rose," I tell her.

"Good. At least I get something before the press does."

"I'm sorry, Mom."

"And when were you going to tell me that you and Ted are getting back together?"

"What? We're not getting back together. Where did you hear that?"

"*Extra* says you are. Mark McGrath had an interview with Ted, and he says you two are getting back together."

"Mom, you must've been imagining things. I've never even talked to Ted since the separation." This is true. I saw him at Tanya and Sean's wedding, but technically didn't speak to him.

"I know what I saw on TV. Ted says you two are making up. Isn't that right, Frank?"

Silence.

"Frank!"

"Mmmmpf," says my Dad.

"Frank! Put those cookies down. I was going to mail them to Lauren and little Emily! Put those down right now."

There's a clatter and a shuffle, and then I just hear a dial tone. My parents. Honestly.

I join Carter in the baby nursery. He gives my shoulders a squeeze. "How did the parents take it?"

"Put it this way, I don't think we're invited to Christmas this year."

"Ouch."

Carter and I stare at the babies in the nursery. I know I should probably tell him about the Ted rumors and my attorney's advice, but it feels like the wrong moment. Emily is sleeping, her fist is curled up by her head like Rodin's *Thinker* statue.

"I've never seen anyone take sleep so seriously," I say. "Now I know she's a Crandell."

"Why didn't you tell me about Brigid?" he asks me.

"I did, if you remember. You were so infatuated with her uninhibited, ahem, performances that you completely ignored me."

Carter thinks about this. "I guess you're right. You know, Brigid was jealous of you."

"Why?"

"Because you're smart and funny and gorgeous."

"Are you actually giving me a compliment? I can't believe it."

"And because she thinks I still have a thing for you."

I turn to look at Carter. "And do you? Have 'a thing' for me?" My heart is thumping hard in my chest. This is it. What I've been waiting to hear.

Carter clears his throat and takes a step closer. "Depends on what you mean by 'thing.'"

I smile, taking a step toward him. "Well, what do *you* mean by 'thing'?"

I'm so close to him now that I can see the pores on his nose. I'm starting to feel a little dopey.

Carter puts his hands on the outside of my arms and rubs up and down. I can smell his hair wax. It smells good.

"This is what I mean," Carter says, and then he's kissing me, hands roaming up and down my back, his mouth covering mine. After a few breathtaking moments, he pulls himself away from me, panting, and leans his forehead against mine. Our eyelashes are practically touching. My whole abdomen is on fire, and I'm breathing hard.

"Wow, that is some 'thing' all right," I say.

"I thought so," Carter says.

"Is there anyone in your apartment right now?" I ask him.

Twenty-six

REASON #26 TO DIVORCE A ROCK STAR:
You don't have to be married to one to have rock star sex.

Ted never apologized for falling in love with Melanie Slate.

In the fights that followed the Iron Cactus, and there were many, Ted told me that Melanie Slate "had just happened," as if she were a meteorite or a comet that fell from space. He said neither one of them had planned it. Still, it seemed pretty premeditated to me. A penis doesn't just collide by accident into a vagina, which is how he made it sound. As if he tripped and fell between her legs, and then did that over and over and over and over again until he fell in love.

And the worst part about it was that he didn't beg me to stay. When I packed a bag, he let me walk out the door. It's as if he wanted me to go.

Suddenly he could live without me. He just couldn't live without Melanie Slate.

*   *   *

I doubt anyone has ever driven as fast as Carter drives to get us back to his apartment. We tumble through his front door, Carter whipping off my clothes as we go. My sweater lands on his couch, my jeans on the floor by his bed.

His touch is both familiar and strange, like something I remember from a dream. He takes his time, exploring my body and getting reacquainted with every inch, from my toes to the top of my head. I've forgotten how strong Carter is, how his muscles are taut and hard beneath my touch. I've forgotten what it's like to be with someone who's in shape. Unlike Ted, whose belly had the resistance of a bowl of Jell-O.

Carter remembers more than just the ticklish spots, he remembers my most sensitive spots, too, and just how I like to be touched.

But he's learned a few tricks, too, and as Carter sends me over the big O, not just once, or twice, but I swear to you three times, I remember something else about him. He never put himself first in bed. Never. It's no wonder girls go crazy for him and stalk him. It's his gentle but steadfast determination to send you over the edge again and again. For that sort of service, I can imagine easily turning into a stalker. I've had so many comes, I have a come headache, and by the time it's Carter's turn, I'm practically all jelly. Carter doesn't seem to mind.

All I can think is: Why did we break up again?

"Wow," Carter says afterward, cuddling me up into a ball and putting my chin on his chest. "Why did we break up again?"

"Exactly," I say. "I have no idea. I think it was something you did."

"Well, you dumped me, as I remember," Carter says.

"You nearly jumped for joy when I broke up with you," I say.

"That's not true! I was heartbroken for weeks."

"You started dating someone the very next week," I nearly shout.

"That wasn't dating, that was rebound sex," Carter says. "There weren't even any dates involved."

I give Carter a nudge in his ribs.

"Ow," he says.

"So when did you know you first wanted to sleep with me?"

"The first day I met you," Carter says.

"No, recently! When?"

"I've been wanting to boink you for years, but figured I would just fuck it all up," Carter says.

"You probably still will," I say.

"I know, but God, it was worth it," he says. He sighs and nuzzles the back of my neck. "You know, I'd almost gotten you into a place in my head that was reserved for sisters and friends of my mother. You know, asexual."

"What changed?"

"Have you seen yourself in those rock star wife clothes? God. When I saw you in the airport, I needed a cold shower."

"That's so romantic," I say.

"It's the most romantic guys get," Carter says, giving me a hard squeeze. I reach over and grab the tarot cards from my purse. "Okay, pick a card," I say. "It'll tell me if I should date you or not."

Carter makes a face. "I don't believe in this stuff," he says. "And neither should you."

"Just pick a card," I say.

He picks the Ten of Cups. It shows a man and woman looking up together and a golden rainbow. Kids are dancing at their feet. This is one of the best cards in the deck. It means happiness, fulfillment, and love.

"I was hoping for Death," Carter jokes.

"Funny," I say.

He nudges me from behind, clearly ready for round two.

"Fortune-telling time is over," Carter says, rolling me over to face him. "Time to tackle the second half of the *Kama Sutra.*"

The next morning, I wake up to the sounds of the shower going and to Carter humming a BeeGees song.

This is not a good sign.

I go into the bathroom and push back the shower curtain.

"Morning, sexy," he says, and grabs me, pulling me into the shower and giving me a wet kiss. It makes me weak in the knees, and Carter something else entirely.

He nuzzles my neck with wet kisses and then pulls back from me, gazing at me with his most serious expression.

"Lily, I think I lo—"

I cut him off by putting my hand over his mouth.

"No," I say, shaking my head.

Carter mumbles against my hand. He quirks an eyebrow and looks confused.

"You are not to say the L word, and you aren't going to start humming seventies music."

He mumbles some more.

"I'll take my hand away, but you have to promise not to go all love-sick Carter on me. Because if you do, I will pinch you. Because I don't want you freaking yourself out like you do every time you sleep with someone. Agreed?"

Reluctantly, Carter nods. I remove my hand.

I look carefully at his face for any signs of love-sick Carter. I don't see any. I don't know if this is a bad or a good thing. I'm still not sure whether I'm Mrs. Henry material, or if we're just friends with benefits. I'm trying to think too much about it. The good thing is that all the sex hormones in my brain seem to cloud my ability to think at all, so it's not too much of a problem.

"But what if I really do think I'm in . . ." Carter pauses, and watches me simulate a very harsh pinching motion with my fingers. "Um, the L word."

"You've got to wait at least six weeks to tell me, like all the other guys I know."

Carter grins, and pulls me closer. "Lily, where have you been all my life?"

"Right in front of your face, you dumb-ass."

"Only you can make 'dumb-ass' sound like a term of endearment," Carter says, pulling me closer and kissing me.

"Will-wee! Wook! I have Anowld!" cries Tyler, running

into the bathroom. He's got Arnold on a leash and no pants on.

Arnold, for his part, looks terrified. I would, too, if I weighed only twenty pounds and was being lead around by a pantless toddler. Tyler tries to open Carter's shower door, but I hold it closed.

"Give us a second, Ty," I say. "Is your daddy here?"

"Wonab McDonab is watching me," he says. I think he means Ian.

Carter and I finish showering and get dressed. In the kitchen, Ian catches us holding hands.

"Bollocks!" he exclaims. "You two shagged!"

Ian shakes his head at me and looks disappointed. "I thought you of all people would know better. Now he's going to be singing Abba for the rest of the week, aye?"

"I told him no seventies tunes," I say.

"And *you*," Ian adds, thrusting a finger into Carter's chest. "You had better not fook this one up, aye? This is the only non-crazy bird you ever slept with, aye?"

"I L word you," Carter says, hugging me. I pinch him.

"Ow!" he cries.

We head to the hospital to visit my sister and Emily.

Becca stops us in the hall. "You are not going to bloody believe this," she cries, taking me by the arm. "Brigid's been sacked!"

"Is she here?" Carter asks. He sounds a bit nervous. I give him a curious look.

"We all just found out this morning. She's packing up her office now."

Carter's mobile phone rings.

"Aren't you going to answer that?" I ask him.

"No," he says, sounding resolute. He glances over his shoulder. He's looking suspiciously like the Carter who hasn't actually broken up with his girlfriend, but who is hoping, through some sort of dating telepathy, that she knows they're through.

"Carter, you *did* break up with Brigid, right?"

Carter gives me a nervous look. "Right. About that."

"Carter Henry. You didn't break up with her, did you?" This is what I was afraid of: Carter hasn't evolved.

Becca looks at me, then at Carter. "Did you two shag? You did! You two shagged! Sal is going to piss her sides laughing when I tell her, yeah?"

"Carter. Answer me." All I can think is that I've made a mistake. A big one. I've run straight into his bed without even checking to see if there's any oncoming traffic.

"Wow, *look* at the time," he says, glancing at his watch. "I am really very late for rounds. I should be going."

At that moment, Brigid comes around the corner carrying a box with some files, a potted plant, and her Barbies.

"Carter!" she cries, seeing us all standing together. "Carter, I've been calling you all morning! Where have you been?"

Carter makes a move to bolt, but I grab the corner of his doctor's coat. And then, while Becca and I watch, Brigid throws herself into Carter's arms, giving him a hug and sobbing, "They've fired me! Can you believe it?"

"Carter," I say, hands on my hips. "I think you have some explaining to do."

He looks at me, and then down at Brigid.

"What's going on, Carter?" Brigid asks him. "Why aren't you hugging me back?" Brigid steps back. "What's wrong?"

"Well . . ." Carter falters.

"You have exactly two seconds to tell her the truth," I say. "Or I'm leaving."

"Tell me what?" Brigid blinks at him.

Carter takes a step back and clears his throat.

"One," I say.

Carter looks at his shoes. I can tell he's trying to figure a way out of this that doesn't actually involve him having to tell Brigid to her face that he doesn't want to date her anymore.

"I'm gay," he says, grasping at the first thing he thinks of.

"What?" she cries.

"Two," I say, and then I turn around and walk out the door.

Twenty-seven

REASON #27 TO DIVORCE A ROCK STAR:
No more herpes scares.

The thing about making mature decisions is that they aren't any fun. You don't thoughtfully skip ice cream and think how much fun you had eating spinach instead. You don't get to work early and think what a blast you're having. You don't pay your bills on time and get a coke high.

Because part of what makes fun *fun* is taking a risk. You eat chocolate, you're risking getting fat. You get on a roller coaster; you're risking whiplash. You get into a bad relationship with someone who makes your heart race, and you're risking heartbreak.

Fun is betting against the odds of fate that you'll come out all right in the end. That the thrill ride will be worth it.

I'm done taking those kinds of risks.

I decide I've learned my lesson. I'm not going to make the same mistakes twice. I'm not going to wait around to be left—again.

*   *   *

I head to Carter's apartment and carefully pack up all of my belongings.

Carter tries calling me, but I ignore the calls.

I'm not ready for another risk-versus-reward scenario in a dishonest relationship. I don't want to find myself in a relationship with Carter where six months from now he's not returning my calls. I don't want to wake up one day soon and wonder if Carter's lying to me. If he's actually already broken up with me and I just don't know it. I don't need to walk into another relationship with an emotional cripple.

I think this means I'm actually becoming responsible. Next thing you know, I'll be wearing tweed.

"You're sure this is what you want to do?" Lauren asks me.

"You're the one who's always saying I need to face up to my responsibilities," I say. "So I'm going home. I can't avoid Ted and that stupid trial forever. It starts in a few days, and, anyway, I should be there."

"Do you want us to come?" Lauren asks.

"You just had a baby! You need to rest. And so does Nick. I'll be fine. Really. My lawyer says we'll probably settle. It's no big deal." I hope I'm right. I sound more confident than I feel.

Before I go, Tyler gives me a sticky-fingered hug and then hands me Arnold's leash.

"You don't want to keep him?" I ask Tyler, who's been nearly inseparable from Arnold since we brought him back from the wedding.

"You need him maw," Tyler says, being very serious. "He'll turn your fwown upside down."

I pack my things and head to the airport to fly standby on the next flight out. Part of me is hoping for one of those romantic, last-minute saves by Carter, like you always see in the movies. I keep glancing up, hoping to see him jogging down the hallway, a bouquet of roses in his hand.

My phone rings.

It's Carter, and I decide to pick it up.

"Don't hang up," Carter says.

"I'm listening."

"I'm sorry about Brigid, okay?"

A guy sits down in the chair next to me and he has his headphones blaring "Drowning."

"Fuck," I cry. Can I never have a moment's peace?

"What?" Carter yells.

"Nothing, it's just 'Drowning' again."

"What?"

"Ted's song. Someone is playing it."

"I can't believe this."

"Can't believe what?" I ask.

"You. You're angry at me because of Brigid, but it's *you* who is still holding on to another relationship. You're still in love with Ted."

"What!? I am not."

"So that's why you haven't signed the divorce papers yet? So that's why you seem to like being reminded of Ted, talking about Ted, all the time?"

This conversation isn't going how I thought it would at all.

"Maybe you're attracted to me because you think you can't have me," he says. "Maybe I'm safe to like, because you're really still in love with Ted."

I'm so confused. Is Carter right? I just don't know anymore.

"Maybe you're the one with the problem," he says suddenly.

I can't think of anything to say.

"Maybe I am," I say.

"Lily . . . wait . . . I didn't mean to say that . . . don't—"

I hang up.

I celebrate my twenty-seventh birthday in coach over the Atlantic, eating salty peanuts and trying to avoid the dog breath of the overweight, sweaty guy sitting in 26B. He's using my shoulder as his own personal pillow, but, on the plus side, he's not reading *US Weekly*. He's got a rumpled copy of *Sports Illustrated* shoved into the pocket of the seat in front of him. I'm fairly certain that's at least one magazine I haven't been in, yet.

In astrology, on your birthday all the stars align with the way they were the day you were born. Some people feel this is a time to reflect, but my neighbor Fran used to always say that it's a subtle reminder that no matter how much progress you make, you always end up back where you started from.

I look up and see that the in-flight movie is *Beautiful,* starring Melanie Slate.

I know it by the flash of credits at the beginning. The ones that start off with a long shot of her cellulite-free legs and then her bare bottom. It's one step above a soft-porn movie masquerading as a serious drama about drug abuse among supermodels, which is why all the supermodels do drugs while sitting around in skimpy lingerie.

This is the PG-rated version, so we never see any actual nudity. I'm surprisingly unaffected by the movie or by Melanie Slate's atrocious acting. I think this means I'm getting over it all. It's only taken me a trip halfway across the globe, being on the cover of every English tabloid, and getting my heart stomped on again. It's nice to know I'm low maintenance.

I guess I never really needed to clear my chakras in the first place. All I really needed was some time for self-reflection as provided by one ex-boyfriend.

I look at my tarot cards. I'm irrationally mad at them for telling me I'd have a happy ending with Carter when I wouldn't. I *know* that they can't tell me the future, and yet, I guess I sort of hoped they could. I put them in the back of the pocket of the seat in front of me and decide that I'm done with them. They've been a crutch to me. Something I've depended on for advice when I really should've just been looking in my own heart. Life is hard, and the decisions we have to make just aren't easy. Tarot cards don't make them any easier; they just make us feel better sometimes about what we know we have to do. And sometimes, even worse, they give us false hope.

I shove the cards deeper into the pocket. I feel like a fool for depending on them for so long. What was I looking for? The future? Something to make me feel better about the bad decisions I knew I'd make anyway?

From the airport I take a cab to my parents' house. Mom is baking one of her casseroles when I get there, and I've never been so happy before to smell American cheese.

My parents show surprise at seeing me, but they aren't too shocked. I guess I've been home again enough times since college that it's never quite a total surprise when I show up on their doorstep. That's a perk of being the irresponsible daughter. Your parents always have a bed made up for you.

"Well, you can stay here as long as you need to," Mom says, patting my arm.

"As long as she needs to! Why don't we just put a Hilton sign out front," Dad grumbles.

"I'm not going to be here long, I promise. I'll get things all sorted out."

Mom pats my hand. "That's great, dear," she says, as if I've just declared that I'm going to be president of the United States. As a mother, it's her job to be encouraging, but I can tell she doesn't actually have faith in me.

"Now this is what's going to happen," my lawyer tells me in his office the next day, "we're going to trial, but you aren't going to have to do anything but sit there, all right?"

"I'm not going to take the stand in my own defense?"

My lawyer lets out a loud gaffaw.

"My mama didn't raise no fool," Larry says.

"What about settling?"

"The prosecutors say that their witnesses are solid, and that means Ted hasn't changed his mind about the charges."

"So what should I do?"

"Just wear a suit, look responsible, and show up on time. Let me take care of the rest."

"What's the worst-case scenario?"

"I lose what's left of my respectability."

"No. I mean for *me.*"

"Oh, right. Well, ten months in jail."

"That's nearly a year," I cry.

"Yes, but not quite."

My assault case is heard at the Travis County Courthouse, in a small courtroom filled with reporters and cameras, because after all, I've become a local celebrity, bigger even than Lance Armstrong. The jury is picked out for my case in less than an hour. There are eight women and four men. I take this as a good sign. Surely most of the women would understand wanting to kick a cheating husband in the groin.

The prosecutor for my case is a short man with a mustache and round glasses named Fred Barnes.

Both Mom and Dad come for the trial. They take their seats behind me, waving like I'm in a school play. It's only mildly embarrassing. Even my neighbor Fran manages to come to court. She smiles at me and gives me a thumbs-up sign. I assume this means that the stars are aligned for acquittal.

Fred Barnes's opening statement paints me as a person with

severe anger-management problems and a potential alcohol problem. My mom frowns. Dad looks like he's going to jump the court partition and tackle the prosecutor to the ground.

"Do you want me to go over and talk to those prosecutors?" Dad whispers to me, leaning forward. "I will, you know. I think he's picking on you, and I don't like it."

The prosecutor calls his first witness: Ted Dayton.

Everyone, including the reporters, turns to look at the courtroom doors. They're all anticipating the star's dramatic entrance.

Nothing happens.

Ted doesn't walk through the door. The prosecutor talks to his assistant prosecutor. My lawyer looks at them and then at the judge.

And then, the court door opens. Ted's manager, Ed Reiner, walks through. I know it's him without having to turn around because I can smell him from a distance of fifty feet. He bathes in Obsession cologne. He walks up to the prosecutor's table and whispers something to him.

A miniargument breaks out. The prosecutor isn't glad to be getting whatever news Ed is telling him. I hope this means that Ted is on another one of his benders. Maybe it means he's too high to make a court appearance today. Maybe the judge will see the obvious: Ted should be in jail, not me.

"We need a recess, Your Honor," the prosecutor says, standing up.

"Counsels, approach," the judge demands, signaling the lawyers to come forward. Larry walks up to the bench, as does the prosecutor. Words are exchanged, but I can't read their expressions well enough to see if it's good or bad news. They could be talking about the sandwiches they want to order for lunch for all I know. After a few minutes, Larry returns and sits next to me.

"Don't worry, sugar, I think we finally got a break," he says.

"What break?" I ask him, but by then the judge has banged the gavel and sent court into a fifteen-minute recess.

"Just go into the witness waiting room," Larry says. "That way," he points to a door at the far side of the courtroom.

I swing open the door, and there, standing on the other side with his mojo rising, is Ted in torn jeans, a tight-fitting, faded T-shirt, and a leather jacket.

"Hey, babe," he says, slouching against the doorjamb and giving me a slow, devilish grin. "Surprised to see me?"

Twenty-eight

REASON #28 TO DIVORCE A ROCK STAR:

So they will come begging to have you back.

Everyone thinks that I left Ted. That after Melanie Slate and the Iron Cactus, I boldly left with my head high. The sad truth is that I didn't leave Ted. Ted left me.

I packed the bag and left, but for months after, I would've taken him back. I wanted him to call. I wanted him to beg for forgiveness. I wanted him to beg to have me back.

I imagined letting him sweat it out. I imagined torturing him with uncertainty. I imagined how I would make him pay but eventually forgive him and take him back. But he never called. Not once. Not once after I left him standing in our driveway.

He never called.

I was the one sobbing into his voicemail. I was the one sending him long e-mails he ignored. I was the one who wanted him back.

The truth is, Ted is the one who didn't want *me*.

*   *   *

"Hey, sexpot," Ted says to me now, as if we're still married and he'd just stepped out for a quart of milk. He gives me his rock god smile, the one he used on his first album cover, the one that landed him on *People*'s list of sexiest people.

My body has the same reaction it always does to Ted. My heart speeds up. I'm either excited to see him, or my body is releasing the same level of adrenaline it would if I were about to face off with a brain-eating zombie.

Ted, I notice, has both hands behind his back.

"Before you say anything," he tells me, "take this."

He hands me a single gerbera daisy, my favorite flower. While I'm looking at it, I consider my options: 1) slam the door in his face; 2) throw the flower at him and then slam the door in his face; or 3) kick him, throw the flower at him, and then slam the door in his face. I congratulate myself for not impulsively acting one of them out without considering all three options in depth. This must be the work of the new, more responsible Lily.

Ted is showing me what's in his other hand. It's a jockstrap reinforced with a cup. He sticks it down the front of his pants.

"If you want to kick Daddy, Daddy's ready," he says. He's smiling at me. It's his Gap jeans commercial smile.

This would be charming and funny if I didn't actually hate Ted's guts. I try very hard to focus on something that doesn't make me want to assault Ted. I settle on his shoelace. It seems innocent enough, even if it is attached to one of Ted's black Converse sneakers.

"What are all these rumors about?" I ask him. "Us getting back together?"

"You don't want to get the band back together?"

"It's not funny."

"Why are you smiling then?" he asks.

"I'm not smiling."

"You are. On the inside. Daddy can tell."

The five brain cells not affected by Ted's evil charm want to know why I haven't slammed the door and why I'm talking to the man who returned my love with lies, betrayal, and ultimately complete public humiliation. The shock from seeing Ted back on this side of the Atlantic is beginning to wear off, and in its place is the same kind of curiosity that I'm sure got Pandora in trouble.

I'm dying to know why he wants to talk to me, and why he isn't on the stand making sure that I go to jail.

Those five logical brain cells, the ones that can do math, tell me to shut the door. The rest of my brain shouts that the longer he stays, the more chance I have to crush his will to live. I don't know how I'm going to accomplish this exactly, but I'm pretty sure I can do it, either with some razor-sharp witticism or by kicking him again.

I feel my heart thumping. It feels like I'm getting ready for a fight. I haven't had one for more than five months with Ted, and I realize I'm not done with him yet. He's like a scab I thought had long since healed, only to find that with a little scratching it bleeds.

"What do you want?" I ask him.

He smiles at me. "That's my Lily. Always to the point," he says.

"And that point is?"

"God, babe, you look good," Ted says.

"Get to the point."

"Still mad, huh?"

That is the understatement of the millennium.

"I'm facing *criminal charges,*" I say, trying to keep my voice calm. "That *you* brought against me. Um, yeah, I think I'm 'still mad.'"

"You've got every right to be mad at me, Lily. I fucked up. Big time. I know that, okay? But I came here to say I'm sorry."

This throws me for a moment. Ted never apologizes. Even when he's clearly in the wrong, he never says he's sorry. He'll get around it by saying "I wish it hadn't happened that way" or "I won't do that again," but he never actually says he's sorry because that would be like admitting he's wrong. And he's never wrong. Being wrong isn't cool, and he's the epitome of cool.

"Lily, God, I am such an ass."

I'm not sure what to do since Ted is beating himself up, which I thought was my job. He's sucking the air right out of my fire, since my only alternative is to agree with him. And being on the same side as Ted is the very last place on earth I want to be.

"I've been going over it in my head, and all I can think is that the whole fame thing hit me so fast that I didn't know what happened, you know?" Ted puts his hands behind his head and looks at the ceiling. He exhales a large breath of air. "Now I think I've fucked everything up."

Signs of introspection? Who is this person? He's certainly not Ted. Ted could barely tell you whether or not he was angry or elated, so little is he in tune with what's happening inside his own head.

"Fame is like a drug, I don't know, it is, and well, it's been making me act like a total dickweed."

Okay, blame shifting. This is starting to feel familiar. Only usually I'm the one he would shift blame to when something went wrong for him. A recording session didn't go well because I woke him up too early or had had the last beer. Or he played a concert poorly because we'd been in a fight. I'm starting to suspect that this is all an act so Ted can convince me to sign the divorce papers. Maybe this is Melanie's backup tactic.

"So you're here to ask me to sign the divorce papers, so you and Melanie can make things official?"

Ted looks stricken. "God, no, are you kidding? We're not getting married."

For a second, I'm shocked. "That's not what she thinks," I say. I can feel my anger start to drain away. I'm not sure what I'll do without it.

"What do you mean?"

I fill Ted in on Melanie's botched blackmail attempt in the limo and her assistant's trying to buy me off.

"Fuck." Ted breathes hard, getting up and pacing the room. "Fuck. Fuck. *Fuck.*"

"Yes, that's what you two do, and that's how she got pregnant."

"Lily, you have to help me," Ted says. He takes hold of my hands.

"Me?" I pull my hands away from his, and he sits down and puts his head in his hands. When he comes up for air, he looks like a man who's cornered, like he's got no way out. I've seen that look of panic in his eyes before. It's the same look he gave me when he thought I might be pregnant.

I feel strangely reassured by this. And, I must admit, a bit smug, too. I'm suddenly dying to know how Melanie broke the news, and if Ted knocked over a chair like when we were married.

"Melanie doesn't speak for me, okay? Whatever she told you, it's a total lie."

"She told me that you're going to get married and have a big family," I lie. I can't help it. It's just too easy.

"Fuck, Lily, what am I going to do?"

"I would suggest not fucking for the time being," I say, giving his hand a pat.

"I know this is all my fault, and it's what I deserve, but, Lil, I'm miserable. Melanie is . . ."

I lean forward. I wish I had a tape recorder for this.

"She's such a . . . a . . . bitch. I mean, you should see her. The way she talks to people."

"I have an idea," I say.

"And this pregnancy. I don't think it's an accident." What a surprise. Ted being paranoid about entrapment. It's nice that in a world where so much changes, some things stay the same.

Ted looks so sad and dejected. I want to take a picture, frame it, and put it on the wall.

"This is what happens when you don't take care of me, Lil. I make stupid decisions."

"I know. Like right now. You're prosecuting me for something you know you deserved."

"I know," Ted sighs. "Come back to me, Lil. I'll drop the charges, okay? And then everything will be like it was."

I think back to me sitting alone in an empty house, wondering why Verizon works everywhere except where Ted happens to be. I think about Ted passed out on the toilet seat. I think about Ted shouting at me for touching his guitar.

"You know we're good together," he says. "You are, and I mean this, the best thing that ever happened to me."

Bingo.

I think I can die now, because I've heard it all. Ted couldn't have said anything better if I'd given him a script. Has he changed? Really changed? Is it possible?

And then I realize that I don't care if he has or not. I'm completely, absolutely over Ted.

It feels like I've just dropped a giant dumbbell. And maybe I have.

Maybe I've been carrying Ted on my back for the last eight months. It feels good to put him down.

I almost feel giddy. I'm over Ted. The fact that he wants me back means absolutely nothing to me! I don't want *him* back. It feels like such a relief. I almost want to kiss Ted.

And that's when I see that Ted is mistaking the look of relief on my face for approval of his overtures. And even worse, he seems to be planning to kiss me.

I put my hand to his chest and do my best to stop his forward momentum.

"Wait. Whoa. What the hell do you think you're doing?" Clearly, Ted has been around groupies far too long.

Ted's face falls. He looks contrite. "I'm sorry. It's just that you're so beautiful, and seeing you again, well, I just wanted to touch you. Man, we are just *right*."

"Don't touch me." I'm feeling panicky and sweaty, as if my resolve might falter, just like the president of the Abstinence Club on prom night.

"Lily, don't be stubborn. You know you want back with me. Come on. What have you got without me?"

"I've got my self-respect, for one thing," I say.

Ted frowns. "It won't keep you warm at night."

"I'm not having any trouble with that," I say.

"So I'm too late? You're in love with him?"

"With Sean Gates?" I ask.

"Who the hell is Sean Gates? I'm talking about Carter. I knew you'd go running to him, and that he'd be all too happy to take you in. Did you wait until you got home from the airport or did you just fuck in the backseat?"

Okay, I've officially had enough of this freak show.

"I think you'd better go now."

Ted stands. "I knew you had a thing for him. You've always had a thing for him."

"You're jealous of Carter? You have no right to be jealous."

"Dammit, Lily. I love you!" Ted shouts the words, as if they're some sort of curse.

"You should've thought about that before you got Melanie Slate pregnant."

"You think this is my fault?" Ted says. "You think I ran off to Melanie because you were the doting wife? Look, the fact is you *never* got over Carter. You think I'm an idiot? You've always been obsessed with him. You never felt that way about me. Never. How do you think that made me feel? To be loved by whatever part of you didn't still want to be with Carter? It felt rotten, that's what."

"You're saying I made you cheat? You're saying that I forced you to fuck those groupies? To run off with Melanie Slate?"

"I didn't care about any of them. They meant nothing to me. I loved you. But you didn't really love me."

"So you admit it? You admit you slept with them?"

"Your heart belongs to Carter. It always has. You pushed me away every chance you got. You're the one who opened the door, Lil."

And it's at this moment that I realize Ted is right. He's hit upon the truth, which is surprising enough in itself. It's true. I don't just "have feelings" for Carter. I am in love with him. Capital L love. That's why it hurts so much to imagine that he'll leave me. That's why I've been so eager to push him away, because I've been trying to protect myself. Protect myself from falling in big L love again.

"Anyway, I dropped the charges, so you're free to go, you

know," Ted says. "I'm not going to testify and the prosecutors don't have a case."

Ted tosses an envelope at me. "I was going to rip these up to show you I was serious, but now I think that's not what you want. I'll do whatever you want me to do, okay?"

I open the envelope. Inside, peeking out from the envelope, are our divorce papers.

Twenty-nine

REASON #29 TO DIVORCE A ROCK STAR:

If he destroys hotel rooms, imagine what he'll do to your house.

I sign the divorce papers and am left with Arnold and $10,000 in debt. But I'm not angry or even sad. I'm just relieved. It's over. It's really over.

And on the upside, I'm not in jail and so I do actually consider myself lucky. Given all that's happened, things could be much worse. For instance, Ted could've given me herpes. But he didn't. That's a decided plus. Also, since it's after Thanksgiving, all the stores are playing annoying Christmas music instead of annoying Dayton Five songs, so there's hope that I might be able to keep my sanity.

I'm living at home with my parents, but at least I have parents to live with. As the New Responsible Lily, I've enrolled in some local college classes and will hopefully finish my degree by the summer. Until then, I'm working a temp job at an insurance company where the youngest person is forty-eight, and no one has ever heard of the Dayton Five, or me or Sean Gates, or anybody else that regularly graces the pages of *US Weekly.*

I sell all my free designer clothes, including all the freebies I ever got while I was with Ted. I sell them to help pay my lawyer. For the first time in a year and a half, I'm completely without tarot cards, horoscopes, or designer clothes. It feels surprisingly good.

Fran, who comes to see me regularly, tells me that my aura is fixed. I take this as a good sign. Carter tries to call repeatedly, but I ignore his calls. I don't want to get sucked into Ted the sequel. I think I more than learned my lesson there. Guys don't change.

Weeks go by.

A few days before Christmas, I get a letter and a DVD in the mail from Ian.

I pop in the DVD and see Becca and Sal.

"Is it on?" Sal asks.

"Of course it's bloody on, you silly cow," Becca says. "That's why Ian's waving to us, yeah?"

"Right, well, okay, should I start?" Sal says.

Becca rolls her eyes and sighs. "Duh," she says.

"Okay. So. This is a video we made," Sal says.

"And if I were you, I'd watch it till the very end, yeah?" Becca says. "And if you don't, we're going to bloody well find you and beat you to a bloody pulp. D'you understand, do you, yeah?"

"She's kidding," Sal says.

"I'm not either, am I. Don't mess, all right? We've slogged all week on this," Becca says.

"Okay, so don't turn it off till the very end, all right?" Sal says.

The picture cuts to a sign that says CARTER MAKES AMENDS.

The next scene shows Carter holding the nanny-cam bear.

"I realize that I'm a big, stupid idiot," Carter says. "But I also know that there's a way to fix being a big, stupid idiot, and that's by apologizing to all my old girlfriends and giving them closure. I'm going to carry this bear with me, as proof that I'm doing it." He clears his throat. "And I'm not just going to visit the nice ones, either."

The next scene, Carter is standing at someone's front door. A brunette woman answers, looking wary.

"I know we haven't spoken for a long while, but I've come here to apologize. . . ." Carter says.

The woman slams the door in his face.

The next woman shouts at him. "You told me you would call. You never called! You're a bleedin' liar!" And so forth.

The third woman listens to him apologize and then says, "Who are you again?"

There are a few televised phone conversations with women from America. Carter makes these while holding up a picture of the ex he's talking to. One hangs up on him. One calls him "the worst scum on the face of the earth" and another one says, "Your mother can't be proud of you" before she hangs up on him. The final one accepts his apology and asks him if he wants to get a drink.

"Yikes," Carter mouths to the camera.

The picture fades to another sign that reads THE BIG KAHUNA.

The next thing I see is the door to Brigid's apartment.

Ian is holding a separate camera and is filming Carter. The door swings open and Brigid is standing there.

"I'm here to apologize for not properly breaking up with you," he tells Brigid. "I am here to say that I should've broken up with you rather than stopped calling. I owe you an apology. So here I am."

Brigid stares at him. Her face turns red. And then she winds up and punches Carter in the face, laying him out on the carpet. He lets out a squeak, and then the next thing we see is Brigid slamming the door on the camera.

Carter is holding his nose, which is bleeding profusely.

"That went well," Carter says after he's recovered enough to speak. Ian hands Carter an old T-shirt to stop the flow of blood from his nose. "Did I cry like a girl? Or did I just imagine that?"

"Aye, like a wee lassie," says Ian, who's still holding the camera.

"I have a low threshold for pain, it's nothing to be ashamed about," Carter says to the camera.

Ian snorts. "She dunna weigh seven stone in the pourin' rain, and she knocked you arse over tatties, lad."

"That doesn't help me, Ian," Carter says.

"Och, I'm just sayin' whot I saw. She comes up to your elbow, man. Never seen a lass banjo anyone like that before."

"Enough!" Carter says, waving off Ian, who's following him with the camera.

"Should we go to a school playground next, aye? See if there are any nursery kids who want to take you on, man? That might be more your speed, aye?"

"Shut up, Ian."

"We'll make it a fair fight, aye? We'll tie back one arm o' the wee ones, that way they canna hurt ye too bad."

"I'm seriously not listening anymore."

"Och, my li'l sister can give you fightin' tips if you like, lad."

"Thanks. Really." Carter tilts his head back. "I think I may need to go to the hospital."

"For a doctor, you're bloody squeamish," Ian says.

The picture fades. The next scene is Carter holding a sign that says PLEASE FORGIVE ME. MY NOSE HURTS.

My heart is filled with so much love, it feels like it might burst. For the first time in eight months, I want to cry for the right reasons.

I call Carter.

"Nice movie you sent me," I say.

"I thought you might like it," he says. "But it's not finished. I have one more apology to make."

"Yes?"

"But I have to do it in person."

My parents' doorbell rings. My mom answers it, and the next thing I hear is her calling up the stairs. "Lily! It's for you."

I come downstairs to find Carter standing with the nanny

cam bear. Carter is sporting a shiner and a swollen nose. I can't help it. I smile when I see him.

"I'm ready if you want to kick me," Carter says. "Go ahead."

"Carter!" yells my dad. "You here to play poker?"

"I can only take one beating at a time," he says.

"Frank!" Mom calls. "I need help in the kitchen."

"But we're talking poker."

"Frank! Now!" Mom shouts.

"Okay, so here's the thing," Carter says after Dad's disappeared. "I don't really want to give you closure."

"You don't?" I step closer to him.

"No, I want to do the opposite of closure." He steps closer to me. "You see, I realized something."

"Yes?"

"I really, really, *really* . . ."

"Yes?"

"L word you."

"I think I L word you, too."

I throw my arms around Carter, and he kisses me, long and deep.

VH-1's Where Are They Now?

IAN

Won the Halo Champion of the United Kingdom in 2006. Got his own Chihuahua and named him Colonel Combat.

SEAN GATES

Scored the winning goal for England in the 2006 World Cup semifinals. Still refers to himself as "Sean Bloody Gates" and continues to find the use of sexual innuendos appropriate for all occasions, even funerals.

TANYA GATES

Bought her own Chihuahua, which she named Chi-Chi.

TED

The Dayton Five abandoned their namesake, Ted, in favor of a lead singer who could actually play guitar. Ted Dayton is currently under contract negotiations to become the next host of the reality show *Cheaters*.

MELANIE SLATE

Melanie Slate had her baby (a girl), named her Palestine because she heard it on the news during labor. Does not realize the name might be construed as controversial. Still does not know if Chicken of the Sea is chicken or tuna.

TYLER
His hands are still sticky.

LAUREN
Despite all her best efforts, Tyler's hands are still sticky.

NICK
Continues to run into burning buildings to save people. Is still madly in love with his wife and no longer uses e-mail as a safety precaution.

BRIGID
Is currently stalking an attorney named Clarkson who asked for her number at a bar but did not return her calls. Is planning marriage to Clarkson, even though the two have not yet been on a proper date.

ARNOLD
Arnold is fatter than ever, and spends his time begging for table treats and lying on the couch.

CARTER
Has a successful medical practice in the United States. Believes Lily is the best thing that's ever happened to him and has not fallen into any of his old ways. Still uses copious

amounts of styling gel and makes no apologies for his low pain threshold.

LILY

Can now hear Dayton Five songs and not feel an urgent need to vomit. Won a substantial lawsuit against the *Sun* for falsely quoting her. Donated the settlement to charity. Graduated in 2007 with her bachelor's degree, and currently holds a job working as a volunteer coordinator for a hospital. She has been tarot-free for a year, and her chakras are currently clear.

Up Close and Personal
with the Author

I DID (BUT I WOULDN'T NOW) IS A SPIN-OFF NOVEL FROM YOUR FIRST, I DO (BUT I DON'T). HOW DID YOU DECIDE TO WRITE THIS BOOK, AND WHY NOW?

I've always had a fondness for the characters in my first book, and I had intended to write a sequel or spin-off of sorts for some time. Many people had been writing and asking me to revisit the lives of Lauren and Nick (the main characters from *I Do*). I put it off because I wasn't sure of the best way to revisit their relationship, since their story ended so nicely in the first book. After venturing into new territory with *Pink Slip Party* and *Dixieland Sushi*, I decided to come back to the characters in *I Do*. I got the idea of writing a book from Lily's perspective (Lauren's little sister) and thought that would be the best way of exploring the characters with a fresh perspective.

WHAT ABOUT LILY'S CHARACTER MADE YOU WANT TO GIVE HER A BOOK OF HER OWN?

I was interested in exploring the life of Lauren's little sister, Lily, because I wanted to have a different take on Lauren and Nick. I also liked Lily a lot. She was the little sister who was always in trouble, and she was also one of the most candid and fearless characters in *I Do*. Lily is a great character because she's incredibly spontaneous, and she's the sort of person who would do the kinds of things that you and I wouldn't dream of doing, like jetting off to London on a whim or prank calling her ex. She doesn't think about consequences, and while this gets her into trouble, it also gives her a freedom that I think I envy.

DO YOU THINK YOU ARE MORE LIKE LILY OR MORE LIKE LAUREN?

I'm definitely more like Lauren than Lily. I have Lauren's sense of responsibility and her older-sister-knows-best personality. I don't think I could do the kinds of things Lily does without feeling too guilty. I would love to sign my ex up for spam, but I doubt I'd actually go through with it. I would be too scared of being caught.

LAUREN AND LILY ARE SISTERS, AND YET THEY'RE VERY DIFFERENT PERSONALITY-WISE. DO THEY HAVE ANYTHING IN COMMON?

I think Lauren and Lily are very different in terms of their approaches to life, but in some ways they are the same. Both Lauren and Lily have a "running away" philosophy for dealing with trouble. Their mechanism for coping with some of life's more difficult problems is to leave, and usually in a hurry. Lauren runs away when she thinks Nick might be cheating on her, and, of course, Lily flees the country when her ex-husband's single starts racing up the charts. So, in that way, I think they do have some common ground.

LILY'S EX-HUSBAND IS A ROCK STAR. HAVE YOU EVER DATED A MUSICIAN?

I dated a drummer and a bass guitarist. Neither one became famous (thank goodness), and luckily I outgrew my attraction to musicians and married a very practical actuary instead. I'd say they're much more reliable than rock stars.

WHY DO YOU THINK MUSICIANS ARE SO ATTRACTIVE?

I think they're creative and fearless—you can't get up in front of a live audience and sing or play unless you're really willing to put yourself out there. The successful ones also have more than their share of charisma. But the same traits we love about them can be the same things that eventually become too much to handle. Musicians crave excitement and change and, of course, being adored by fans.

THE BOOK IS SET IN LONDON. WHY THERE?

I love London. Like my mom, I'm a complete anglophile. I watch BBC America more than any other network and am a big fan of shows like *Footballers Wives* and *Coupling*. I thought it would be fun to set a book in London, especially because of the tabloid culture there. Celebrities in London have far less privacy than even celebrities here.

CELEBRITY PLAYS A LARGE ROLE IN THIS NOVEL. WHY DO YOU THINK WE'RE ALL SO FASCINATED WITH THE LIVES OF FAMOUS PEOPLE?

I think we live in a culture that really obsesses over fame and wealth. I'm certainly no different. I love *People* magazine. I think we're all curious, on some level, with how celebrities live and work, and in large part, many celebrities do invite us into their lives by seeking fame.

HAVE YOU CONSIDERED WRITING SPIN-OFFS OR SEQUELS TO OTHER BOOKS?

I would love to write a sequel to *Dixieland Sushi*. I think it would be great for Jen to meet Riley's parents and for Jen's family to meet Riley's family. I think there would be a lot of great comic material there.

WHAT ARE YOU WORKING ON NOW?

My next book is going in a different direction. It's going to be aimed primarily at teens, although all age groups will enjoy reading it (I hope!). It's called *Bard Academy: Wuthering High,* and it's about a boarding school for teenage delinquents that also happens to be haunted. It's a new direction, but I had a lot of fun writing it. It's a little like *Harry Potter* meets *Buffy the Vampire Slayer.* There's humor there and action, too.

Never buy off the rack again—buy off the shelf... *the book shelf!*

Don't miss any of these fashionable reads from Downtown Press!

Imaginary Men
Anjali Banerjee
If you can't find Mr. Right,
you can always make him up.

2cool2btrue
Simon Brooke
If something's too cool to
be true, it usually is...

Vamped
David Sosnowski
SINGLE MALE VAMPIRE ISO
more than just another
one night stand...

Loaded
Shari Shattuck
She's got it all: Beauty.
Brains. Money.
And a really big gun...

Turning Thirty
Mike Gayle
27...28...29...29...29...
Let the countdown begin.

Just Between Us
Cathy Kelly
The fabulous Miller
girls have it all.
Or do they?

Lust for Life
Adele Parks
Love for sale.
Strings sold separately.

Fashionably Late
Beth Kendrick
Being on time is so
five minutes ago.

Great storytelling just got a new address.

DOWNTOWN PRESS
A Division of Simon & Schuster
A VIACOM COMPANY

Available wherever books are sold or at www.downtownpress.com

13459